Return to the Crooked Sea

Return to the Crooked Sea

TREVOR RAISTRICK

First published in the United Kingdom in 2010 by
Bank House Books
PO Box 3
NEW ROMNEY
TN29 9WJ UK
www.bankhousebooks.com

British Library Cataloguing in Publication Data
A catalogue record for this book is available from the British Library

ISBN 9781904408802

Cover artwork by Colin Beats

Typesetting and origination by Bank House Books

To those dear friends who gave me encouragement and support in my writing, and have now passed away

Acknowledgements

Many thanks to:

Brian and Anne Lewis, Ray and Margaret Baddeley, Jacki Jackson, Sandra Whitehurst, Mick and Chris Winkle, Susan Raistrick and Ann Grainger for their help in the research for and writing of this novel;

Mr Colin Beats for the cover design;

My wife Pauline for her forbearance and encouragement in the writing and editing of this book;

My son Matthew for his work on the website www.thecrookedsea.com.

I also extend thanks to my many friends and fellow writers for their support and encouragement.

Introduction

At the end of *The Crooked Sea* Walter Clough, having trekked across the wild and lethal sands of Morecambe Bay, is desperately trying to reach the shore – in an attempt to effect his disappearance and begin his life anew.

Now read on . . .

Chapter One

A re you sure this is your missing husband's jacket, madam?'
Annie was enraged by the sergeant's persistent questioning, but too upset to give her usual biting reply. Instead she nodded, and turned to cry in the arms of her brother James. Her daughter joined them in a tearful embrace.

'I can confirm that this was washed up on the shore at Bare. It was found on the shingle by a couple of fishermen as they were beaching their boat.'

'And have you any more information or reports?' Annie's brother butted in. 'Surely he's left some other trace or sighting. You can't just vanish like that, even in Morecambe Bay.'

'No, sir. We asked around, fishermen and cocklers mainly, but with no success. I wouldn't always believe 'em: they're an unreliable, immoral bunch. A lot of hard drinking and all kinds of goings on happen out on those sands.' The policeman folded his arms, satisfied with his little sermon. 'But things like this do happen from time to time. Visitors don't know how dangerous the sands are. We had one incident only two summers ago, in 1897. Young holidaymaker from Oldham, he was. He went for a walk one afternoon across the bay. Either got stuck in some quicksands or stayed out too late 'fore the incoming tide. Faster than a train it can be. Folks don't realise it. They found his body washed up by the Battery. He had a wife and four kids. Terrible tragedy it was. People do the daftest, most reckless things out there.'

Hannah, who had been silent throughout the proceedings, could stand it no longer. Though the convention was that children should be seen and

1

not heard during adult conversation, she let fly at the startled policeman. 'That's not fair,' she shouted. 'Daddy wasn't like that. He always thought about things. Besides, he knew the sands. We lived at Arnside for months and he took me out with one of those fishermen. Reuben was a lovely man, and he taught Daddy all about the bay and how to avoid the dangerous places.' She burst into tears.

The sergeant was too shocked to reprimand her, and Annie was too embarrassed to say a word. Hannah dissolved into the arms of her uncle, burying her strawberry blonde tresses in his chest as he silently comforted her.

'I suppose the young lady is a bit overcome,' the policeman muttered. 'I think it's time we finished with all this for the moment. Let her get a bit of sea air. And there's no more information you can give us?' Annie and her brother shook their heads. 'Then we'll make further enquiries, but it might take a little time.'

'That's all right,' said Annie, regaining her composure. 'We'll call in a couple of days. We're booked in at the Queen's Hotel along the promenade. If anything happens in the meantime you can reach us there.'

'Good afternoon then, sir, madam, miss. Don't worry. We'll let you know if there are any more developments.'

They wandered back towards the front. The streets were thronged with gay and chattering holidaymakers, but the sad trio ignored them all. They turned left at the clock tower, which showed half past two, and after five minutes' walk they found an empty bench further along the promenade. While her mother and uncle sat chatting, Hannah wandered across to the railings and stared out across the water. The high tide had brought in a stiff onshore breeze, which had deterred many walkers from taking their habitual stroll along the front. The water lapped against the sea wall, breaking into small patches of foam which settled on the pebbles and shingle below. If there were any droplets on Hannah's freckled face, it was from the invisible specks of spray that were borne over the sea wall by the breeze. She was too heartbroken to cry. The sea and sky were a blank canvas on which she painted her own memories of the tall, handsome, comical man, who had played with her and her brother and sister on those very sands. He talked to her not as other stern, dominant fathers, but like a gentle, understanding friend and guide, who knew her better than anyone else in the whole world, had encouraged her in her drawing and writing and had shared the same ridiculous sense of humour. Hannah finally succumbed. Her tears mixed with the fine spray and trickled down her cheeks. Yet along with the sadness there was an unease she couldn't understand. It was as if she didn't see the whole picture. Something was missing in that vision, among those memories, and despite all the tears and tribulations she had to find out what it was.

'Hannah, come away from there! If the wind picks up any more it'll throw spray over and you'll get soaked.'

Her mother's words burst the bubble of her thoughts. She returned to the bench. Now was not the time for the defiance and rebelliousness that were often her hallmark.

'I think we'll go over to the Summer Gardens,' James suggested. 'An afternoon concert might sooth us.' He put his arm around his sister to comfort her.

By the time they had finished the short walk along the promenade the tide was slowly ebbing, the sharp breeze had dropped and the sun had come out. The enormous glass and brick pavilion, Morecambe's largest centre for amusement and entertainment, was busy – with visitors walking around its grounds and gardens, groups playing croquet, young women and men, for once abandoning their bonnets and straw boaters, playing tennis. Families wandered about or sat in the shelters, parents watching noisy children running on the grassy expanse, playing ball or chasing each other in games of tag. It all seemed so strange to Hannah – as if she wasn't part of it, but an observer looking in from the outside.

They paid their sixpences and took some seats half-way back. The light and airy hall was scarcely a quarter full: under its glass dome there was space for over a thousand. Quiet and polite applause rippled among the palms and ferns and echoed up to the vaulted roof as the orchestra entered. Their sedate overture seemed to catch the sad mood of the three who listened unconsciously to the calming music that floated over them. For a short while it took them back to a better time, to happy memories past. A programme of lively pieces from operettas and several rousing marches woke them for a moment from their sad reverie, but these were followed by languid, dreamy airs that brought them back to sad contemplation. During one flute solo Annie broke down. Tears flowed relentlessly down her cheeks. Was she remembering that holiday two years before, the concert on the end of the pier and the same flautist who had wielded his magic over her, her husband and the family? Or maybe she recalled the chaotic afternoons on the beach when Walter had dug, paddled and chased around with his children. Or perhaps it was times long past, when as a pretty young bride she had shared the Pavilion's delights with her tall, handsome husband in the first flush of love; they had been so engrossed in each other as scarcely to notice the hundreds who listened with them.

The next day was spent in a busy determination to do something; anything. Just waiting around was not an option. They went to the early morning fish market and spent half an hour talking to the fishermen and cocklers about a man who, fifteen days earlier, might have taken a walk far out on to the sandy wastes. They were met with suspicion, indifference and only occasional politeness.

Hannah chatted to the few children who were helping their parents with the catch. Her friendly manner and casual approach was more successful.

'My, you're a fine, posh lass to be talkin' to the likes of us,' a thin, dirty-faced girl teased.

'I've been out on the sands myself,' was Hannah's studied reply. 'I've helped with a fishing bawk, done fluke padding and caught a big un.'

'Oooh, you're not as prissy as you look then,' laughed a cheeky-faced youth with a mop of blond tousled hair.

Hannah turned to him. 'No I'm not. But we've come here to try to find out about my father, and I want to know if any of you has seen him. We think he might have gone walking across the sands more than a fortnight ago.'

'You best forget 'im then,' commented an older girl, who had been eyeing Hannah jealously. 'Townies who go out on the bay don't come back. Can't read the sands. Don't see the melgraves and the other muddy traps that lie in wait fer them. They wander back onto the quicksands and marshes above Hest Bank 'n' die a slow an' terrible death. They's lost – *forever*,' she added cruelly.

'No, no, he knew the sands,' Hannah protested. 'He went out with the fishermen from Arnside when we stayed there. He knew the bay's dangers.'

'Sounds like that bloke who passed us by Priest Skear,' the blond lad interrupted. 'Mind you, he were heading out right across Warton Sands on the old coach route. Very bad that can be. They don't always make it that way.'

Fascinated by the tall, well-dressed girl, who was more interesting than he had first thought, he was about to add some more when a large red-faced man pushed him away.

'Eh Jim, what's thee doin' wastin' thy time talkin' to town girls. Thee won't get far with them,' he added with a leer. 'Thee's got work to do, and we've got to be out on the ebbin' tide in half an hour.' He stood between them, eyeing Hannah suspiciously. 'Next thing we know is these questions will bring police round, and we don't want coppers stickin' their noses in our business.' He turned to Hannah. 'Now bugger off.'

Hannah was affronted but not shocked. It was useless to continue: the man had dragged the lad away and was barring her path. She turned back to her mother and uncle, who had met even less co-operation and more hostility.

Their visit to the police station that afternoon met with more success. Annie was immediately greeted by the sergeant with the words, 'I'm glad you called, madam. We've a bit more information for you now, but it ain't any more hopeful. We've also got something in our possession, a kind of clue, you might say.'

'At least you've made some progress. We tried talking to the fishing folk down at the jetty, but it wasn't any good. They shut up as soon as we started asking questions.'

'That's no surprise. The fishermen aren't too bad, but the cockling gangs are a rum lot, as I told you. They don't trust anyone, keep themselves to themselves. They drink a lot, don't go to church or to school like respectable folk . . . and they don't observe the Sabbath either. There's fights some nights, and what the lads and lasses gets up to far out on the sands – well, it's nobody's business. Almost as bad as the Irish gangs they've brought over to dig the new harbour out at Heysham.' He stopped dead in his tracks. Annie's withering stare could be almost as powerful as her acid tongue. 'Sorry, madam, sir, miss. Got carried away there. It's just that we have a lot to put up with 'cos of these folks. It's worse in the high season with thousands of holidaymakers as well. I suppose you want to know about our enquiries.'

'That's the reason we're here,' snapped Annie. 'If we wanted a sermon we would have gone to a church, not a police station.'

Humbled, the sergeant cleared his throat and continued. 'Young Constable Fawcett made enquiries round the town. Difficult it is with so many people here for the summer. Anyway, on an impulse he tried the railway station, and spoke to a few of the staff. Bright young lad he is. Ambitious. Got a good instinct, but still has a lot to learn, mind you.'

Even the phlegmatic James was starting to get impatient. 'Please will you come to the point, Sergeant?' he said, drumming his fingers on the desk.

'Well, sir, he spoke to the luggage clerk, and we think we might have a sighting and a clue.'

'Can we speak to your constable?' asked Annie.

'Certainly, madam,' beamed the sergeant, keen to pass on the enquiry in the face of her growing impatience and hostility. 'He's just on his break. I can fetch him now.'

He disappeared through a pair of doors, to return a minute later with a fresh-faced constable with bright ginger hair, keen, sparkling eyes and an abundance of freckles.

'Fawcett. This lady and gentleman would like to speak to you regarding the missing gentleman. We understand your enquiries may have turned up a few clues.'

The young policeman searched through his notebook, then turned to face Annie. 'We have reports of a gentleman of the description given being at the railway station, the left luggage office to be precise. The clerk remembered him immediately. He thought he was acting rather strange.'

'How do you mean?' Annie asked.

'The clerk said he seemed agitated, a bit nervous like, even, how can I say it . . . disturbed.' He looked away from the piercing blue eyes. 'Is that like your husband?'

'Certainly not!' interrupted Annie's brother. 'Walter was a confident kind of chap. Are you sure you've got the right person?'

'I don't know,' the constable replied, 'but this is what he left behind.' He lifted the brown leather case onto the desk.

'That's Daddy's case!' interrupted Hannah. 'It's what he kept his samples in.'

'Very smart it is,' observed the sergeant. 'The clerk noticed that, didn't he, Fawcett?'

'Yes, and he said it complemented the gentleman's appearance, but not his manner.'

'Be that as it may,' the sergeant interrupted, 'I think the first thing we need to do is look inside. You never know, there might be a clue, a note – even a letter to you, Madam.'

Annie froze and Hannah clung to her with fear in her eyes, realising they might be near a resolution to the whole fearful business.

'I don't suppose you've got a key to this, madam?' the sergeant asked. Annie shook her head. He took a penknife out and tried to force the locks. They didn't budge. 'It looks as if we need something stronger. Fawcett, pop into the ironmonger's and see if they've got a big screwdriver. Unless you don't mind us cutting it open.' Annie nodded, and the policeman immediately slit the case along the hinge. Two further short strokes down the corners released the lid, so that it hung limply away from the still undamaged locks. 'Perhaps madam would look in and confirm it belonged to her husband.'

Slowly Annie eased back the lid and looked at the contents of the case. It was over half full. Among the tightly packed sample boxes were small squares of cloth, bars of soap, small bottles and brushes and, in a compartment in the lid, a wad of unused order forms. An aroma of soap, chemicals and a sweet cloying scent rose from the case and filled the small office. 'That is certainly my husband's sample case,' she affirmed.

'Perhaps you'd like to see if there are any other items among the samples,' the sergeant suggested.

Annie carefully lifted some of the small cardboard boxes on to the counter and pushed the soap bars and bottles to the side, hardly daring to look below. A small brown envelope lay in the corner, peeping out from underneath a pile of small cloth squares. She lifted it up gingerly between her finger and thumb, and put it down in front of the sergeant. Silence had fallen across the whole room. Hannah had turned away and was hiding her face in her uncle's jacket.

'There's no name or address,' commented the constable. He lifted the envelope up and felt it carefully. 'It's not just a single note. There's too much paper inside. Shall we see?'

Annie nodded, and he pulled back the flap. Three five pound notes fluttered down on to the sample boxes scattered on the desk. The young policeman held the envelope between his thumb and forefinger and looked inside. 'There's nothing else in here.'

The colour returned to Annie's face and Hannah loosened her grip on her uncle.

'What does it mean?' Annie asked.

'I don't know,' answered the sergeant. 'I suppose he hid it there to keep it safe, so he certainly meant to come back to it.'

'Was there any money in the jacket?' asked James.

'No, sir, not a thing. Mind you, if them cocklers or shrimpers had found it they would have taken anything of worth, the scoundrels. Law unto themselves they are. They'll even take the shoes and clothes off bodies they find out there, never mind rings, watches, wallets or money.'

A brief silence was broken by James. 'In the circumstances I think that's all any of us can do for the present.' He held his sister and niece for a moment, while the policemen stood in respectful silence. 'Thank you very much. I can see you've done all you can in the circumstances.'

'Just a minute. I'll make a note of the amount in the envelope,' muttered the sergeant quietly, 'and then you can have it. I'm sure it'll come in useful. We'll keep the case and samples for the present. The constable here will write a short report and ask you to make your own brief statement. It'll be ready for five o'clock, if you want to pop back later.'

'Thank you,' replied Annie.

'Oh, by the way,' the sergeant called, as she moved towards the door, 'I'm afraid you won't be able to register it as a death, not for the present, anyway. The coroner will let you know if and when, so make sure you leave your address for us.' Annie nodded, and she and her companions trudged out into the street.

'Sarge?'

'Yes, young Fawcett?'

'Did you notice that though the case was full of samples and order forms, there were no completed forms, no calling cards or the like?'

'He could have kept them in his jacket, couldn't he?'

'Another thing. I interviewed a few shopkeepers around the town. A few remembered him. But they called him Mr Adams, not Mr Clough or even Mr Adams-Clough.'

'Could have got the name wrong. It does happen.'

'In three or four cases, Sarge?'

'He probably thought it sounded better than Clough. More distinguished, like. You know these commercial travellers: they're all airs and graces. Fancy suits, lots of fancy chat, to impress the women. You know what they're like. They've got a woman in every port, like a sailor. I'll tell you now, you hear some right jokes about them in the music halls . . . Now clear up this stuff. Folk will think this is a branch of the Home and Colonial, not a police station.'

The constable began to put the packets and bottles back into the dismembered case. After a while he stopped and looked up. 'Sarge, you know you said that he meant to collect the case 'cos he'd still got his wages in it?'

'Yes?'

'Well, if his wages weren't in it, it might be obvious he'd done a runner, whereas if he kept some money in the case it might fool people into thinking that . . .'

'Look, Fawcett, the trouble with you is that you've been reading too many of these new-fangled detective novels. What's that bloke called, Shylock something or other?'

'Sherlock, Sarge. Sherlock Holmes.'

'Just take my word for it. Fancy crimes and mysterious disappearances may happen in London, but not round here. Not in Morecambe!'

Chapter Two

Walter had never felt so alone, not even when he was out in the middle of that barren wilderness with only the ever-arching sky, the acres of muddy sand and the seagulls for company. At least out there he had been in charge of his own destiny, but safe on a rocky outcrop between Kent's Bank and Humphrey Head he was much nearer to civilisation. That meant people, people who were going about their work or holidaying along that busy shore between the mountains and the sea, and he knew they could betray him. One chance meeting, one vague remembrance of the strange figure of a fair, tall man with no jacket or hat and mud-encrusted clothes, might reveal his plan – if questions were asked in the right places of the right people.

He turned to view the scene behind him, and in his mind briefly retraced his steps. There was little time now to contemplate. Dusk was falling and there was no chance of catching a late train to Carnforth, where he had left a suitcase containing a change of clothes and a few carefully chosen essentials for his new life. The silence was broken by the occasional bleating of the sheep that were grazing peacefully on the narrow margins of the sea meadow. It grew on the mud flats for a few seasons, then vanished at the whim of storm and tide, slowly re-appearing in other spots where conditions allowed. The farmers took advantage of this bounty, for not only did it mean more pasture but it also gave the meat a rare salt taste, which was highly prized. Farmers, cocklers, shrimpers, fishermen: Morecambe Bay looked after its own, providing they gave it the respect it deserved. Walter had shown scant respect for the dangers and the waters had nearly claimed him for their own. He had been very lucky.

At first Walter had taken care as he crossed one of England's most dangerous stretches of sand. He knew the safer parts: the hard, flat, finer sand, the ribbed silt and the many acres where the water lay on top – where you felt as if you were walking over a soft, shimmering sheet. He had avoided the areas of quicksands, the deep, muddy marshland along the eastern edge and the sly, soft melgraves, which could appear anywhere. But he had become over confident towards the end, and his arrogance had nearly cost him dearly. Walter had struggled to make landfall when caught by the incoming tide. Channels and gulleys that might be easy to traverse when visible were deadly when covered by the calm, innocent water, and it had been a close-run thing. Had it not been for the spit of sand that reached out from the shore he would not have made it. The waves had surged above his waist as he desperately struggled to reach safety. When he felt his feet go from under him he had to swim to survive. Thank God he had taught himself to swim at Bradford Public Baths many years before.

But what of the old life, the one he had left behind? Just as his oldest daughter would look out over that same bay some two weeks later, so Walter too gazed out with tears in his eyes. As with Hannah, there was a sadness that was too intense for crying. He watched his footprints at the margin of the crimson sea as they gradually became fainter. It was like looking at his past life, a life to which he could never return. He would never again see the wife he had once loved, the mother who had cherished him and the family he had held so dear. That was the hardest wrench of all. He had left enough clues: his case at Morecambe station, his jacket to float in on the incoming tide and odd sightings out on the bay. It was enough to make them think he had died on those dangerous sands, probably by accident. There might be a suspicion of suicide, but there was no proof or even a hint of his motives. He had left no note, no hard evidence of his state of mind.

The insurances he had taken out would pay up. Life would be hard for Annie and his family, but not impossible. She was a tough, resourceful woman, and with help from his mother, her sister Nancy, her brothers Victor and James, who ran the Ackroyd family business, they would survive and might even prosper. His children would not suffer; that he could not bear. If he had thought they would, his plan would have been abandoned long ago.

'Hey, Rex, come to, come to!' The farmer's voice echoed from the low cliffs around the headland as his sheepdog raced around the small flock, hurrying them off the sea grass and up the gentle slope to safety. Its task done, it returned to its master's heel and scampered with him along a well-worn path. Catching sight of the lone walker in the distance, it started to bark. Walter turned towards them and gave a brief wave, which the farmer acknowledged and his companion confirmed with more barking.

'Hush, Rex.' The dog instantly obeyed, and turned away to follow his master through a gate and out of sight.

Walter resumed his gaze out over the sea. He knew he had covered his tracks almost perfectly. There would probably be no enquiries to his employers. Even if there were, Walter Clough had never existed to them. Field Brothers had a Walter Adams, of course, but he was their sales representative for the Cheshire area, having moved there to live with his wife in the comfortable suburbs of Wallasey. The death of a salesman named Walter Clough would mean nothing to them. It was all so perfect!

And yet Walter had doubts, a niggling feeling of insecurity and a sense of shame concerning his identity and the real circumstances of his birth. Who was his father? It was a secret his mother had held from him, and would never reveal. It was as if his mother had transferred the guilt of her secret to him, and yet she held the answer to it all in her comfortable little house in Bradford. It was the one nagging question that would never be answered now.

Out at sea fishermen lit their lanterns, and the few faint specks of bobbing light reminded Walter that the bay was never empty. Now was the time to move. He knew where he could spend the night, sheltered and far away from any living soul. But he had to get there before darkness fell. He carefully picked his way over the rocks, waded through a shallow gulley and scrambled up the bank to a gap in the hedge. Beyond it a field sloped upward, and at the end he came across a rough track that led inland away from the town. Walter walked on past farms and fields, the only sounds those of cattle and whispering leaves. A sheepdog barked a warning as the stranger ground stones beneath his sodden boots. 'Bess, Bess, shut up you daft dog,' came a cry from a farmhouse that fronted the lane.

There was just enough light for Walter to skirt the farm and make his way over the fields. The farm dog was still aware of his presence, but his soft tread on the grass was inaudible to human ear. He regained the track half a mile on. A little further on a signpost indicated the path over Hampsfield Fell. Walter climbed a stile, then followed a steep track on a steady upward climb. It was almost dark now but a full moon showed the way ahead. At a triangle of paths his instinct told him to bear right, as it was the steeper gradient. The grass was sparse and massive limestone outcrops gleamed in the pale, silvery light. The track flattened. He had reached the top of the fell, over eight hundred feet above the shoreline far below. A square tower at last came into sight.

Walter had learnt of Hampsfell Hospice from a hiker who stayed at The Crown at Arnside when he had been publican there three years before. He had never had the time to visit, but he knew its location; indeed, he had seen it when he was out on the sands with Reuben, netting for fish.

The hiker had told him how the stone shelter was built by a vicar from Cartmel for travellers across the fell. An oddity it was – built like a small castle, with magnificent views from its roof in all directions, and the imprint of its eccentric builder clear for all to see.

Walter staggered the last few yards, climbed the chain fence and pulled open the heavy wooden door. There was a scampering noise. He was not the only creature seeking shelter that night. He took off his sodden boots and socks and hung them over a beam, then stretched himself out on the rough wooden bench. Walter was fast asleep before he knew it.

He did not know what woke him up, whether it was the thin shaft of bright sunlight that pierced the rough wooden shutters and moved into his eye-line, the fresh breeze that rustled the short bent trees, or even the shock of dreaming that he was kissing Eliza's full red lips, then finding when he moved to put his arms round her that she was not there. Walter sat up slowly, reached for his socks and boots, then bent down to put them on. They were still damp. He was stiff and aching and there was a nagging pain of hunger in his belly.

The narrow shafts of light made patterns as they bounced off the rough stone walls. Walter stretched and rubbed his eyes, and gradually became aware of something around him that he had not noticed in his exhaustion the night before. The walls were not bare but had dark metal panels affixed. Messages were inscribed on them, indecipherable in the gloom. He got up, pushed back the door and let the light flood in. Intrigued, he carefully examined each notice in turn. Like the building itself, they proclaimed the idiosyncratic mind of its builder. This simple tower was no rough, anonymous shelter but a memorial to its scholarly, if eccentric, designer.

All four notices were written in couplets. To some it might have been poetry, but to Walter, who was well read and rated Wordsworth as the most enlightened poet of those parts, it was rhyming doggerel, though somewhat amusing. The largest panel was fixed above the window of the west wall. It held a mish-mash of discordant ideas, from instructions to close the shutters when departing to eloquent descriptions of the views around, finishing with a short stanza:

> For no man would think it pleasure
> To climb the fell to spoil your treasure,
> Your offer made in kindly spirit
> I hope You'll find our conduct merit.

Walter smiled but was puzzled, not by the thoughts and sentiments of the meandering verse but by its title: 'The Answer'. What did it mean? Was it an answer to God from the strange, whimsical architect? Still deep in thought he climbed the steps out on to the flat roof. The view in every direction was certainly magnificent, taking in the bay to the south and the Lakeland mountains to the north.

What was his answer, Walter wondered. Would it be his new life with Eliza and their child to be? Might it be a journey to a new land?

'Hello there. Fine day to see this bit of coast.' The newcomer was a young man dressed in plus fours, a tweed jacket and walking boots. Slung on his back was a small knapsack. He had approached from the Cartmel path, and with the sound of the wind and the rustling trees Walter had not heard his man's footfalls.

'Yes, marvellous isn't it?' Walter shouted back in a feigned enthusiasm. 'I climbed up from Grange this morning to catch the views before the clouds roll in and cover it all.'

'Do you want to share a bite? Bet you missed breakfast like me. I brought some bread and fruit along in my knapsack.'

Walter was in a dilemma. The pangs of hunger were churning inside and here was the devil come to tempt him. His first thought was that he was still asleep and this was all a dream, but no, the wind was biting his cheek and the wall was rough under his touch. Dare he risk the stranger's offer? He would notice his companion's muddy clothes and unkempt appearance, his missing jacket. Walter hesitated for a few moments. The temptation was too strong. 'Yes, I'd love to. That's very kind of you.' He climbed down the steps.

'I'm Algernon Bennett,' the stranger announced, 'How do you do? I'm up from Frodsham in Cheshire for a week, to do some walking and exploring.' The young man had sleek black hair combed back close to his head. His face was round, and he had a thin moustache. He offered Walter his thin bony hand.

'Ralph Ackroyd from Buxton in Derbyshire,' Walter replied. 'My wife and I are staying with her Aunt Maud in Grange. She always invites us up for the summer.' His mind was racing as he tried to anticipate questions.

The young man stared at Walter, obviously puzzled.

'Had a bit of an accident coming here,' Walter remarked. 'I took the route along the foreshore, missed my footing and fell into a muddy hole. I was carrying my jacket, and now it's gone. I decided to go on just the same. God knows what my wife will say when I get back.'

His companion said nothing, but sat down on a limestone slab and proceeded to open his knapsack. Walter's first instinct was to grab anything on offer and wolf it down, but he knew this would arouse the young man's suspicions even more. Instead he slowly ate the two slices of buttered bread that were offered, then declined to eat the apple, putting it into his pocket. 'I hope you don't mind if I keep this for later.'

'Not at all,' replied his companion. He was now less effusive, and the more he stared at Walter the more puzzled he was becoming. 'I say, old chap,' he said warily, 'I hope you don't mind me asking, but you haven't been sleeping rough, have you? Did you spend the night up here?'

'Certainly not!' insisted Walter, but there was a tremor in his voice that he could not hide. 'I'll have to be on my way now. Must get back to Aunt Maud's to tidy myself up. It's been nice to meet you, Mr Bennett. Thank you for the snack.'

With that Walter was off. A hundred yards along the path he glanced back. The young man had stood up and was watching him. Would he report his meeting to anyone? To his family, to locals or even the police? Walter followed the path briskly down the hill as if going back to Grange, then when he was out of sight he veered off to the right away from the town. Resting briefly in a gateway, he lifted out his watch to check the time. It had stopped, so he wound it up. It ticked for a few moments, then stopped again, no doubt fed up with the treatment meted out to it: it had been knocked, jarred and finally filled with seawater. Walter sighed and put it back in his waistcoat pocket. Despite his meeting with the suspicious stranger, he felt better. His hunger had abated, and he knew that in a few minutes he would be at Kent's Bank station. After a short ride to Carnforth he could pick up his case. Once changed, washed and shaved, he would be on the train south to Birkenhead: to his new home, his new wife and a new life.

His spirits dropped almost as quickly as they had risen when he suddenly realised he had lost all his money. The coins that had been in his trouser pocket had gone. He frantically searched all his pockets again. No coins. Damn! Had he left them in his jacket? No, he had checked it before throwing it on to the sands. They must have fallen out when he was scrambling to reach safety from the inrushing tide. A final frantic search confirmed his fears, and added to his despair. The left luggage ticket had gone too. How was he to retrieve his old case without a ticket?

Walter's first task was to get to Carnforth. It would be a long, weary walk and he knew he would be very noticeable. Everything that could go wrong suddenly seemed to be going wrong. He leaned against the gate and stared over a field of winter barley towards a figure in the distance. The figure didn't move. Walter stared at it for two minutes. Still it did not move. He had an idea. Climbing over the gate,, he made his way cautiously to the still silent guard. The scarecrow's tweed coat was well worn but had only recently been discarded. The black trousers were ragged and of no use at all: he would be better off with his own dirty but still substantial pair. It was the hat that interested him most, though. Brown and tattered, it was none the less substantial. Most importantly, its wide brim would shield his face from any prying gaze. Walter donned his new disguise, tying the coat tightly round him with a piece of rope that had served as a belt for the tattered trousers. He would look the part of a tramp, and he knew he could act it.

At a junction Walter turned left, away from Kent's Bank and back into town. Secure in his disguise, he knew he could pass through almost unnoticed. It would be a long walk round the estuary. It was less than nine miles over the sands to Carnforth, but the marshes on that part of the coast were hazardous at the best of times. It was better to stick to roads and tracks, sleep in a barn, beg a bit of food and remain almost invisible. But how could he collect his case from the left luggage office? It was his passport to freedom. He would work that out when he got there.

Chapter Three

I t was Thursday afternoon when Walter arrived, tired and hungry, on the outskirts of Carnforth. The railway station dominated the small town. Apart from the scattered farms and a few cottages that formed the original hamlet, its whole existence depended upon the railway. Its location on the flat valley of the Keer next to the sea meant that it was a natural junction, where the west coast mainline from London to Glasgow could meet the line running up from Yorkshire and the newer Furness line. What fifty years before had been a small halt, only used on market days, had quickly become a major junction station.

As Walter trudged past the endless limestone terraced houses, gleaming smart and bright under a summer sun, he was hatching a plan. He had to get his hands on the battered brown suitcase. It contained the essentials he needed: clothes, shoes and money, a few notes carefully secreted in the lining. But how was he to get it without a ticket? The staff certainly wouldn't let him into the station dressed as a tramp, as they would probably think he was trying to find a place to sleep. Walter's first thought was that he had to ditch his coat and hat, explaining his bedraggled appearance with the same excuse that he had given to the young man on the fell. Here, down on the edge of the bay, the story might be more plausible.

He stopped on a street corner, his head down, and stared into the gutter deep in thought. A couple of yards further along something glistening caught his eye. Walter stepped forward and saw that it was a silver threepenny bit. He picked it up and heaved a sigh of relief. An idea had occurred to him. Further into town he found what he was looking for.

Half-way down a street a red and white striped pole leaned out over the pavement. Walter hovered round the doorway and peeked in. The barber's shop was empty. He shuffled in, wheezing and coughing as he went.

'Hey, what do you think you're doing? We don't serve the likes of you in here!' The barber was a small thin-faced man with a bald shiny pate. He reminded Walter of old Jack, the demon barber of West Bowling, the one whom he and his schoolfriends had tried to avoid all those years ago.

Walter held the coin between his thumb and forefinger. 'What's the matter, guv? Ain't my money good enough for you? Can't a gentleman of the road get himself tidied up once in a while?' He put the bright coin down on the counter.

The barber relented. 'All right. But I don't want that flea-ridden coat and hat near me, or where my customers might sit. You can leave them on the floor in the corner.'

Untidy and dishevelled Walter might have been, with a few days' growth of beard on his chin, but he had made sure that he had washed during his journey round the bay, in streams or in horse troughs. His trousers had dried out, and with the help of a stiff brush he had borrowed from a friendly road sweeper he had managed to remove a great deal of the caked mud. He now looked nearer his thirty-four years. The barber was surprised by the young man who stood before him without his coat and hat. More intrigued than disgusted, he engaged his customer in conversation. 'What's a fit young man like you doin' wandering the roads round here?'

'I've been doin' bits of work here and there, guv. Farm work, mainly – pickin' 'taties and other vegetables. It earns a crust and a roof over your head. No good come winter, though. You've got to head for the towns 'n' cities then. More shelter, and some hand-outs. And a nice Salvation Army miss to tuck you up in bed at night.' He gave a sly wink in the mirror. The barber ignored his suggestive comment.

'Smart trousers and waistcoat you got there. Pity you got so muddy.'

Walter had to think quickly. This was becoming too much like an interrogation. 'A lady gave them to me in Ulverston. No jacket, mind. Said her 'usband 'ad grown out of them but could still squeeze the jacket on. I begged a broken spade she had as well. I tried my 'and out on the bay, to get some cockles or crabs to sell. But them cocklers didn't take kindly to it. Dumped me in some quicksand they did, and threw my spade away. Right bastards they are.'

'You're right there,' the barber answered. 'Wild immoral lot as well. We try to keep 'em out of Carnforth, especially Friday night when they've got paid. Always drinking, fighting and shouting they are. This is a respectable town, full of hard-working folk. Not savages like them.' He railed on for a few minutes as his razor deftly slid over Walter's skin, then his tirade slowly subsided.

Walter leaned back and closed his eyes as the hot towels enveloped his face and neck. It was the first bit of luxury he had experienced in four days. He thought of Eliza waiting for him in that neat new house in Wallasey, her welcoming arms, her sweet kisses, the feel of her warm body. The door banged – and his dream was shattered.

'Hello, Joe. How's business these days?' A tall blue-uniformed figure stood in the doorway, silhouetted against the light. 'Just on patrol. Thought I'd give you a few minutes as it's quiet.' The policeman took no notice of the figure in the chair, swathed in towels, and didn't even glance when he got up and paid the barber. It was only when the young man reached the door and picked up his tattered bundle that the penny dropped. Here was a stranger, and a vagrant to boot; someone who might mean trouble. 'What are you doin' giving shaves to the likes of him, Joe? Are you that short of business?'

'Oh, he's all right, Seth. Pleasant young fellow he is, very polite. He's fallen on hard times but he's still trying to make an honest crust. He got attacked by some cocklers out on the sands. If there's anyone you want to sort out it's them lot. Cause no end of trouble they do. Remember last year when my window was broken? I'll bet you a pound to a penny it was them.'

Any thought the policeman might have had of pursuing and questioning the incongruous figure had gone. He joined in the conversation. Joe had already put the kettle on, and he was not going to miss an afternoon's brew and chat.

Walter's first instinct was to run but he fought against it. He did not even look back. Instead he walked confidently down the street as if going back out of town, and at the first corner turned sharp left and out of sight to anyone who might want to follow him. After turning left again at the next junction, back in the general direction of the town, he took an oblique right into Warton Road. His instincts were right: he could see the station ahead of him. Plumes of smoke and steam rose above the Royal Station Hotel and the other main buildings of the town. To his right, beyond a wire fence, were engine sheds and railway sidings.

It was no use pretending to be a tramp, so he ditched his coat and hat a hundred yards from the station, throwing it over some railings and into some long grass that covered a railway embankment. Walter still had his last problem to overcome. How was he to get his case back without a ticket? The key was confidence and a plausible story. He thought hard about what to say, how to approach a railway employee.

It was quiet in the station forecourt. A couple of horse cabs waited outside, and an old lady and little boy stood under the portico, watching him walk confidently towards the long station frontage. It didn't seem to fit into the place. It was too grand, too impressive for what was no more than a small township. As Walter walked on to the station concourse, it was as if he had entered another world, a loud, bustling world. It surprised him how such a large, busy, noisy area could be almost invisible from the outside. He could see five platforms, each a mass of pillars, ironwork, cantilevered glass roofs, waiting rooms, ticket offices, refreshment rooms and timetable boards. Most impressive was the long elegant curve of the Furness platform. It seemed to go on for ever, its slim iron pillars ramrod straight, standing to attention to greet alighting passengers. Porters in blue serge uniforms hurried about, carrying luggage and wheeling trolleys full of mail sacks and parcels. The platforms bustled with all kinds of passengers: workmen, chattering families, silent businessmen reading newspapers. Walter was glad he had picked Carnforth, not Lancaster. It would give him the anonymity he craved.

He walked over to the left luggage office. An old lady was collecting a travelling valise from a sour-faced employee. His blue cap was slightly askew and two bright eyes glowered out from beneath dark, bushy eyebrows. The unwelcoming mask was completed by a luxuriant drooping moustache.

'Good afternoon,' Walter began.

His greeting was wasted on the sombre figure facing him, who just nodded.

'I've come to collect a brown suitcase I left here four days ago.'

'If you give me your ticket I'll find it, sir.'

Walter smiled. 'I'm afraid I've lost it. I'm sorry. I can describe the case in detail, and everything that's in it.'

The clerk was unmoved. 'That's as may be, sir, but if you haven't got a ticket you can't have the case. Rules is rules.'

'As you can see, my good man, I've no jacket. I lost it out on the sea marshes when I fell into quicksand this morning. I was out there observing. I'm an ornithologist.'

The face in front of him remained unimpressed. 'A what? An *orthinologist*? Can't say I've ever heard of one of them. It don't alter the rules, though, no matter how important you may be.'

'It means I watch and study birds, and write books about them. I went out on the mud flats to observe sandpipers and oystercatchers, even the occasional guillemot. Now I've lost my jacket, wallet, binoculars, notebook, left luggage ticket, everything. My change of clothes is in that case: brown tweed suit, shoes, shirts, collars, everything I need. You've got to help me.'

The expressionless face remained unmoved. Even if the clerk believed the story there was no compassion in his voice, and no hint of any desire to help. 'That's as may be, but I can't let you have that case, not without a ticket.'

The voice was gruff and without emotion, but behind the monotone Walter could sense the man was mocking him.

'You must have procedures if someone loses their ticket. I can't be the first person this has happened to.'

'Oh we certainly do, sir. But Mr Farnworth the stationmaster is very strict. We get all sorts in this station, and we can't have them walking off with other folk's luggage, can we? Costs a pound it does, and you have to prove your identity beyond doubt. You *can* prove your identity, sir?'

'I've no money, and with my wallet gone no proof of my identity. Surely you can see that?'

'Can't help you, then. Rules is rules. Can't bend them, can I? Might lose my job giving a case to someone with no ticket, no money, no identity.'

'But I can describe the case and everything in it,' Walter pleaded. He was about to say there was money in the case and he could pay the fine when he stopped. There was not just cruelty in the face across the counter but evil, almost imperceptible. With that would come dishonesty. If he admitted there was money in the case he was sure he would never get it back. But it gave him an idea, a last chance.

'I may not have any money,' he said calmly, 'but I have this.' He unhooked his pocket watch and swung it tantalisingly above the counter. Its gold colour glinted in the shafts of light that pierced through the glass canopy above. 'I know under normal circumstances you may not be allowed to take such things in lieu of cash. But in the present circumstances I'm sure your stationmaster Mr Farnworth wouldn't mind, particularly if he didn't know.' He awaited the clerk's protest, an honest declaration that he could never do such a thing. None came. A hand reached out from below the counter and snatched the watch from him.

The look of cunning greed turned to disappointment. 'Who are you trying to trick? It's not working.' The clerk handed it back, cruelly grinning.

In his desperation Walter felt a sickly burning sensation rising in his throat. It was mixed with anger too. It was everything he could do to keep control of himself and not smash the grinning face with his fist. 'It just needs winding up,' he said, with a slight tremor in his voice. As he held the watch below the counter he gave a few turns on its winder and gave it a careful, imperceptible shake. Small beads of sweat appeared on his brow, and the colour slowly drained from his face. It returned as he heard the relentless tick, tick, tick, tick. 'There, I told you so,' he said quietly.

'All right then.' A hand reached out across the counter.

Walter stepped back. 'Case first,' he said calmly, looking his enemy straight in the eye. 'Small, brown, battered, with a black taped handle.' His tormentor had shown his hand, but Walter was now in control. The clerk hurried back into the office and emerged with the case. While he was out of sight Walter gave the watch another short wind and an even more vigorous shake. On the clerk's return, Walter took the case from the counter without a hint of a smile, and slid the watch across into a grasping hand, which thrust it deep into a blue serge trouser pocket. Walter lifted the case off the counter, turned and was gone, marching across to the gentlemen's toilet on platform one. He slipped into a cubicle, latched the door, sat down and roared with laughter. He guessed that the pocket watch would run for only a minute or so, and if the fool couldn't tell cheap gilt from solid gold so much the better. His solid gold repeater he had left with his darling Eliza.

A confident young man in a smart brown tweed suit and brown shoes marched across to platform two. He carried a battered suitcase and wore no hat. He had a jaunty air about him and almost a smile on his lips. Stopping at a kiosk in the middle of the platform, which had the name W.H. Smith painted on a board above, he bought two newspapers, the *Manchester Guardian* and the *Morecambe Visitor*. The stall-holder complained because the young man tendered a sovereign, and he was short of change. The young man did not care. He settled himself down on a bench next to a woman in a large white hat who carried a blue flowery parasol. The little girl at her side played with a cup and ball. The man gave her a sideways glance, and smiled at her efforts to get the elusive object into its receptacle. She caught his glance and gave a secret giggle in return. He read one of his papers until the train steamed in half an hour later. The engine was a giant ten-wheeler with a tall chimney, a bulbous housing for the escape valve and a rather fat engine driver, who leaned out from his cab to observe the twenty or so passengers to pick up for his run down to Crewe.

Walter settled himself on the seat by the far window, so he could catch a last glance of the bay as the train sped by Hest Bank. It would be a final goodbye. The train pulled out and slowly gathered speed. For the last time the crooked sea flashed momentarily past his window. He opened the *Morecambe Visitor*, and settled down comfortably in the corner.

Chapter Four

BRADFORD MAN VANISHES OUT ON THE BAY.' Nancy stared in disbelief at the headline as the *Morecambe Visitor* was thrust into her hands. She resembled Annie but was slightly taller, with dark hair and eyes. Her features were a little sharper as her hair was drawn back into a tight bun.

'It's that police sergeant,' said Annie. 'I'm sure it's him. He likes the sound of his own voice far too much. A few drinks down his throat and I bet our business will be known far and wide, especially round Morecambe's public houses.'

'It's more likely that the local press contacted them for stories. They'd buy him a couple of drinks or some other small bribe. It goes on a lot, you know.'

'How do you know such things, Nancy?' interrupted James. He had spent the last few minutes slumped in the armchair, tired after the long train journey back to Bradford.

'We get a lot of reporters round the Mission. There's always something happening down Silsbridge Lane – fights, riots, attacks. And the local press are soon on to it. They have their contacts with the police, magistrates, publicans and informants all over the city, and with other newspapers all over the country.'

'You don't mean to say it'll make its way into the local papers as well?' groaned Annie. Her composure seemed to have broken at last. 'I couldn't bear the shame of it. All the sad business laid out for neighbours and tradesmen and anybody to see.' She burst into tears. James put a consoling arm around her, and for a few moments the silence was punctuated only

22

occasionally by sobs from the grief-stricken figure slumped over the arm of the couch.

'Hannah, I think you and I will go over to your grandma's house to fetch your brother and sisters,' suggested Nancy. She's been so good looking after them when I've been busy, especially when Mama hasn't been well with her nerves.'

Annie got up. 'Thank you so much,' she said, giving her sister a tearful embrace. After a couple of minutes she wiped her eyes. 'You've been wonderful these past few days. I don't know how you've coped, what with my children and those poor girls you look after at the Mission.'

'Oh, we've managed. Rosie and Tom have been charming, if a little noisy, and Agnes . . . well, she seems to have calmed down a little. And then Grandma Harriet's taken a turn, though how she manages in that tiny house of hers I'll never know.'

Hannah had been silent and sullen since her arrival, but brightened up at her aunt's suggestion of a walk out. She had been relieved to get back home but disquieted at the thought of living there without her father. The house held too many happy memories, stretching back as far as she could remember. She had never known it without his cheerful presence. She put on her coat and held the door open for her aunt.

'Thank you,' said Nancy, giving her a smile. Once out in the street, Hannah linked arms with her aunt. She had never done this before: Nancy had always seemed so aloof, but now it seemed the natural thing to do. They wandered through the park in the direction of her grandma's house.

'You're a brave young girl and a very sensible one,' Nancy said. 'I'm sure your mother's found you a tower of strength.'

'Thank you. I suppose you mean I'm not as noisy, rude or selfish as I used to be. This horrible thing's taught me to think of others a bit more, to help Mama and to be a bit more grown up.'

Nancy gave a sad smile and squeezed Hannah's arm. 'I'm sure things like this bring us a bit closer together, and make us think of each other more.'

'Aunt Nancy?'

'Yes?'

Hannah pulled her aunt gently down onto a nearby bench, which looked out across the path and on to beds of early summer tulips and primulas. 'Auntie, there's something not right about all this.'

'How do you mean?'

'It's as if I can't see everything. Something's missing, and I don't know what it is.'

Her aunt's dark and intense eyes stared at the mass of bright yellow viola across the gravel, then cast a sideways glance at her niece. For a few minutes she was lost in thought.

'Daddy knew the bay. We went with Reuben right to the middle of the sands. You remember me telling you?'

'Yes, I do. I read that lovely, funny story you wrote. You caught a fish with your hands and fell in the stream. Your mother was furious with you, and with your father!' For the first time in weeks Hannah laughed, and her aunt joined her, at the same time fighting back her tears. 'How I would have loved a daughter like you,' she whispered, 'or a son. So full of life; someone who would mean so much to me.' Her eyes clouded and she looked towards her niece, but past her, far beyond to another time.

'Don't you see, Aunt Nancy? He *was* careful. He loved the bay but he knew it was dangerous. And I'm sure what that boy said . . .'

'What boy?'

'He was with some other children, cleaning and sorting the catch on Morecambe pier. He talked to me, but not to Mother and Uncle. He'd seen someone out there, but this older man stopped him, wouldn't let him talk.'

'You don't think they might have robbed him or killed him?' Nancy gasped.

'No, no, they're not like that. Anyway, this boy said a man was heading out right across the bay. There's something more to all this. It's like a jigsaw. There are pieces missing, and I can't find them.'

Nancy pulled her up from the bench, and they resumed their walk across the park. She walked briskly and avoided Hannah's gaze, staring intently ahead. It was as if she had suddenly turned back to the old Nancy, the stern and distant maiden aunt who was always in full control of her emotions.

'You know there's something not right, don't you, Auntie? What is it? What won't you tell me? It's a secret, isn't it? Not even Mother knows, but you do.'

'Nonsense, child!' Nancy snapped. 'You've got too vivid an imagination. You read and write too many fanciful stories for your own good. One day that imagination of yours will get you into real trouble.'

They were both silent for the remainder of the walk. As they approached her grandmother's house, Hannah ran on ahead down the short, wide street. Each small cottage was identical, with gleaming sandstone walls, arched windows and doors and new grey slate roofs, shining in the afternoon sunshine. Hannah wondered why they were called tradesmen's homes when there were no tradesmen in them, just elderly folk. Some of them sat on chairs; others tended the small but colourful gardens that stretched out a few yards from the green painted doors. Small yellow and red floribunda roses were the order of the day. Nearly every garden had some.

Hannah had once tried to sketch her grandmother's street, but had found it too difficult and was dissatisfied with her final result. It was

Harriet herself who had shown her how to lay down lines of perspective and keep the doorways and drainpipes vertical. Once she had mastered this, Hannah's sketch of the terrace had drawn delight from her grandmother and praise from her father. She had managed to capture the angle and proportions of the arched doorways and imposing chimney-stacks, only finding the bedroom windows set in the roof almost impossible. It was her father who had carefully drawn one, showing her how to get the angle and curve of the slates exactly right.

The normally peaceful street was noisier than usual. At the end three children were playing. This did not seem to bother the older residents, who chatted and watched them with pleasure. Harriet sat on a kitchen chair by the front door, while Tom and Rosie played ball and Agnes tottered unsteadily around, exploring every new corner and wanting to join in the game. The play came to an immediate stop when the two older children spied their sister. With cries of delight they ran down the path to her, and she flung her arms around them. Agnes had also recognised Hannah, and made an unsteady dash towards her. She gathered her baby sister in her arms and gave her a hug.

'Daddy come,' Agnes gabbled.

Hannah's face dropped. Rosie stared at her, but immediately realised the answer. The joy of meeting her sister immediately turned to tears as Hannah shook her head. Tom seemed confused and looked down. Harriet remained calm, not letting her sadness show through, but her embrace for her eldest grandchild was intense, as was her kiss for Nancy.

'Thank you so much, Mrs Clough,' Nancy said. 'I don't know how you cope so well looking after the three of them.'

'Oh, they keep me young at heart. And Rosie is so sensible and helpful. It's like having another grown-up around. She's so good at keeping young Tom happy and occupied and out of mischief. I only have Agnes to watch over most of the time.'

Nancy had taken Rosie's hand and was being led inside the small, neat house. 'I'm sure Agnes makes up for all three.'

'You're right there. Yon little lass has a mind of her own, you can be sure of it. Too much like her oldest sister, I can vouch for that!' She winked at Hannah, who gave a little smile and followed them in.

The children walked back home through the park. Nancy followed behind, carrying Agnes, while Rosie attached herself to her older sister. When they stopped to feed the ducks with crusts their grandmother had supplied them with, Agnes was delighted by the mallards and shelducks waddling up the bank and crowding round them in their greedy, noisy demand for food. Then she spoiled it all by running at them, stamping and shouting, sending the small flock scurrying back to the safety of the water.

'Naughty Agnes, no,' complained the disappointed Tom, but she wasn't to be thwarted, and laughed and giggled at the others. Nancy lifted her back into her arms, and shook her head in resignation.

The little party trooped out of the park and headed back home to Bowling Park Road. They found the curtains drawn and Annie alone in the house, busy tidying and dusting the furniture. After the family's absence dust and damp seemed to permeate every corner of the house, and she was determined to restore a vestige of normality. A fire blazed in the hearth and a saucepan of soup was simmering on the stove, its welcoming aroma greeting Nancy and the children at the door.

'Sit down and have a rest,' urged Nancy. 'I'll help you with everything that needs doing, and if you want I'll stay over the weekend to give you a hand. And Sophie will be back on Monday.'

'Oh, how can it ever be back to normal?' sighed Annie. 'And I'll have to dismiss Sophie. We can't even afford her wages now.'

'I'm sure Hannah and Rosie won't mind helping,' Nancy suggested. 'You seem to have grown up so much in the past weeks.' She took the dustpan and brush out of Annie's hands and proceeded to clear up some ashes and cinders that had fallen onto the hearth. 'You know what, it might be a better idea if you all moved back to Wakefield Road. There's just Mother and me in that big house now, and we rattle around. There's plenty of room for the children and it would save you a lot of money.'

Annie nodded. 'I've been thinking about that myself. If we *have* lost Walter . . . ' She bit her lip, and tears came to her eyes again. 'If we've lost him that would be a sensible move. Though how Mama would stand our noisy lot I don't really know . . .' She broke off as there was a loud knock at the front door. The sound echoed round the house, bringing Rosie and Hannah running back downstairs. 'Oh, I hope it's not another of those reporters. There's already been one young man with his notebook while you were out. James dealt with him, and I hoped it would be the end.'

Nancy strode into the hall and opened the door. Her fears were realised. An older man, with a black bowler hat, wire-rimmed spectacles and an earnest expression, lifted his hat. Nancy noticed a notebook and pencil in his other hand. 'I'm so sorry to bother you, Mrs Clough, at this sad time,' he began, in a well-rehearsed introduction, 'but I wonder if you could give me a few details about your sadly departed husband and the circumstances of his demise. I'm sure that as he was a well-known and respected figure here in Bradford many people would be interested . . .'

'Too many people are interested in other people's business!' barked Nancy. 'And it's Miss Ackroyd, not Mrs Clough. It must be obvious, even to you, that she and her family are far too upset to speak to the local papers.' With that she slammed the door in the reporter's face and marched back into the parlour. Hannah edged towards the window and watched the man as he hesitated, clearly thought of knocking once more, then thought better of it and beat a hasty retreat down the garden path.

'Thank you, Nancy,' Annie whispered, giving her sister a hug. 'You were wonderful. I don't think he'll come back in a hurry.' She turned to her eldest daughter, who was still looking out round the edge of the curtain. 'Hannah, come away from there. You don't want him or anyone else to see you gawping out into the street.'

Hannah reluctantly let the curtain fall back and made her way to the stairs.

'Not so fast, young lady,' her mother commanded. 'I've a job for you. We've run out of potatoes. You can go down to Holmes's and get me a stone. And mind *you* choose them: don't let that old rogue foist any mouldy or soft ones on you. He wouldn't try it on me, but he does with those who don't keep an eye on him.'

'Don't worry, Mummy, I'll watch out. No one's going to push us around.' She glanced at her aunt, who gave her a secret smile.

'Can I go as well?' begged Rosie.

'I suppose so.'

'Thank you, Mummy.'

Rosie put her coat on and skipped off after her sister, catching her up on the pavement outside. She may have been her rival at times, and more ready to assert herself now she was older, but she had missed Hannah during their week apart and was happy to be back in her company.

Nancy watched them from the doorway before returning to her sister. 'You know, Annie, you've got two girls there you can be right proud of. And Hannah seems to have grown up a lot. Hard though it may be, we'll come through in the end. We Ackroyds are a tough lot. We'll always stick together.'

Annie put her arms around her sister. For the first time in many years she felt close to her once again. She seemed different somehow. Nancy was still confident, principled, zealous, but now she seemed caring, more selfless, more vulnerable.

Nancy's eyes had not been the only ones that watched the two girls step outside, nor were theirs the only footsteps down the street. Behind them, more than thirty yards away, a figure moved out from behind a tree and slowly followed them, carefully keeping his distance. When Hannah and Rosie turned at the end of the road he hurried on, lest he should lose sight of them. He stopped at the corner, noted the direction they were going, and lit a cigarette before going on, his shoes treading softly so as not to arouse any suspicion. The girls vanished into the greengrocer's, and he walked past, glancing in to confirm their presence. Stopping at the next shop window, he looked intently at the blouses, skirts and linens displayed, glancing sideways from time to time to keep the greengrocer's under observation.

After a minute the two girls emerged, a heavy hessian bag slung between them. They walked slowly back home, stopping from time to time to catch their breath and rest their aching arms. Stumbling on, they chatted and complained about their heavy load. The man followed, quickening his pace. By the time they reached the corner of their street he had almost caught them up. They stopped once more to rest, moaning and breathing heavily. Now was his chance, before they reached the safety of the front gate.

Chapter Five

That's a heavy bag for you young girls to carry,' the young man said. 'Let me give you a hand.'

'Thank you, sir,' Hannah replied. 'That's very kind of you.'

He took a handle from Rosie. 'Have we far to walk?'

'Half-way up Bowling Park Road. Those houses by the lower park entrance,' said Hannah.

'Not the one with the curtains drawn? I noticed it on my way down.'

The girls fell silent for a moment. Rosie slowly nodded. 'Yes, that's the one.'

'Oh, I'm so sorry – your grandma, or a dear uncle or aunt? Don't say it's a brother or sister.'

'It's our father,' said Rosie, tears in her eyes.

Oh dear, oh dear,' sighed the young man. 'As a new neighbour I must pay my respects. When is the funeral? Do you know?' The girls remained silent. 'Don't worry. I won't bother you or your family. I'll find out from the local papers.'

Hannah's voice trembled. 'There won't be one, not for now anyway. You see, he went for a walk on the sands at Morecambe.'

'And he didn't come back.' Rosie's voice faltered and she broke into tears.

They all stopped and Hannah put an arm around her sister. 'All they found was his jacket washed up on the tide.'

'Oh I'm sorry, so sorry. I seem to have brought back the pain of it all. But sometimes it's better to talk about it, you know, even if it's difficult.'

Hannah turned to face the stranger. 'Thank you for your concern,' she answered. 'He was a wonderful daddy, so full of fun. He cared for us so much.'

'What can have made him do such a dangerous thing?' the young man asked in a low, gentle voice, as if to himself.

'He didn't do silly things,' Hannah answered. 'Oh yes, he loved adventures and trying out anything new. But he was thoughtful and careful

29

as well. We stayed at Arnside a year last summer. He made friends with the fishermen and went right out onto the sands with them. He even took me once.'

'He never took me,' cried Rosie.

'That's because you were too young,' comforted her sister. 'I'm sure he'd take you now you're older and more grown up.'

Rosie realised her sister's kind words were true. She wiped her tears away, and turned to the stranger. 'He always loved to go on walks. He enjoyed beautiful scenery and interesting places, and he wanted us to enjoy them as well.'

It seemed a relief to talk about it all. Chatting to the kind and sympathetic stranger made the walk seem less tiring. With his help the heavy bag seemed much less heavy, and the load on their minds seemed lighter too.

'It must have meant a very sad end to your holiday,' the stranger sighed.

'Oh no,' replied Hannah, now completely at ease with the man's searching questions. 'It wasn't on a holiday. Daddy was a sales representative and he visited Morecambe in his work.'

'He sold Field's soap and soap flakes,' added Rosie, keen to talk about her wonderful father.

'Well, we're nearly there,' the man said, offering his side of the bag to Rosie again. 'I'll let you both carry the bag to the house. We musn't let your mummy know someone's helped you all the way, or you may not get any sweets or pennies for it. She'll think you're such strong and helpful girls,'

Hannah and Rosie gave a little wave, then walked on until they reached the front gate. The stranger turned and walked back towards the park entrance. He strolled in for a few yards, then leaned against the trunk of an oak tree whose new tender leaves glowed a bright fresh green in the early summer sunshine, took out his notebook and pencil and scribbled furiously. He had got the scoop that a keen, up-and-coming reporter always wanted. His editor would be pleased.

* * *

'How in heaven did they find all that out?' gasped Annie, staring at the *Bradford Observor* spread out in front of her. She looked up, disbelieving, at her mother and brother, and sank back into a comfortable armchair in the drawing room at Wakefield Road.

'These reporters are too clever by half,' said James. His round features and clean-shaven face made him seem much younger than his thirty-three years. 'I'll ask Victor to have a word with them and ask the papers to leave it for now. He's got a bit of influence with most of them, and he enjoys throwing his weight around a bit. You know me, Annie, I like to play second fiddle and let him take the glory.'

Annie turned to look at James as the wagon full of her family's belongings and furniture drew up outside the front door. 'It was good of you both to arrange for one of the firm's wagons. It's one less expense. I won't forget it, or any of your other kindnesses.'

'It's nothing. It's the least we can do for our little sister.' James hugged her. Annie had always been much closer to James than Victor. He had been the brother who played with her and Nancy as children, climbing the apple trees or finding the best places for hide and seek in the large garden, while the studious and solitary Victor had been more interested in his stamp and butterfly collections. James reminded Annie so much of her father. Tears welled up again for a moment. Her father was gone so soon, and now so was her husband. Life did not seem at all fair. She pulled herself together, got up and closed the door behind her, preparing to greet the men with their load of furniture.

Mary Ackroyd sighed. She had bided her time, but now Annie had left the room she would have her say – as she always did. She would never have stopped Annie moving back to her house, but, oh, those children! They were so noisy and full of life, and with her headaches and aches and pains . . .

'It'll be nice to have children in the house again, won't it, Mother?' James began.

'As long as they keep to the garden and back parlour,' she complained.

'You'll get used to it. Didn't we get up to tricks or make a hullabaloo when we were children?'

'Not Victor, and Nancy only sometimes. It was you and Annie who were the liveliest. And there were only two of you. I don't know how I'll stand it. They're not like Victor's two, so well behaved and quiet.'

'Just like our Victor,' laughed James, 'and that miserable wife of his.'

'I blame Walter,' his mother went on, ignoring her son's comment. 'Not that we should speak ill of the dead, but it's been nothing but trouble since she married him. His evil cousin Albert and what he did to Nancy. The shame of it! How can we ever forget?'

'That's in the past, now, Mother, and Nancy's got over it.'

'Has she? Will she ever really forget? Somewhere there's a child, a boy called Gideon, and it's hers – and his. The memory will always be with us. It was Walter, remember, who introduced Albert to our family, to my daughter. If it wasn't for all that she wouldn't have decided to work at that vile little church down in the slums, with all the criminals, drunkards, trollops and Irish.'

'It's her calling. She's always been religious, Mother.'

'But to do what she's doing, looking after those sinful, wicked girls . . .'

'You can't blame Walter for that.'

'Oh yes I can, him and his fancy modern ideas. And what did he become? A travelling salesman! You know from the people you meet in the wholesale grocery trade what kind of people they are, and what they get up to far away from home. It wouldn't surprise me if he'd taken a leaf or two out of his cousin's book.'

'Walter was a decent chap,' James insisted. 'They're not all like that, you know. Most salesmen are good blokes earning an honest living.'

'Perhaps he was,' Mary admitted, sensing her son's animosity. 'But how do we know, what with his wild, modern ideas about bringing up children? Thinking they should appreciate beauty, express themselves and develop their talents. Children should be seen and not heard! That's how it should be, quiet and respectful to their elders, especially those who have so much to suffer.' James opened his mouth to speak, but his mother would brook no interruption. 'And now he's gone and done such a daft thing. He's left those children fatherless and dependent on the charity of our family. He thought he knew all about those dangerous sands just because he went out there a couple of times with a fisherman when he kept a public house. A public house, mind you! Oh, what kind of man did our Annie marry?'

'But our uncle's a publican, and a finer chap than Sam you'll never meet,' James insisted. 'I know the Mason's Arms isn't in one of the nicer parts of Bradford, and it gets one or two rum characters in there, but there's hardly any trouble. One of the magistrates told me they wished all pubs and inns in the city were run as well.'

'But it's still a public house. And this family's abhorred drink, been a sober, God-fearing family. It was your father's side that thought different . . .' Mary stopped as she heard the front door close and her daughter's steps in the hall.

On the other side of the panelling the listener strained to catch some more snippets of conversation, but her grandmother's shrill voice had tailed off. Hannah had found the cupboard in the back parlour a perfect place during a game of hide and seek. Hidden in a small space behind the bric-a-brac, rugs and old cushions, she was sure Rosie and Tom would never find her. Rosie had once opened the door, but Hannah had survived undiscovered. It was in the long silence that she had realised that the cupboard, set into thick walls, could reveal more secrets than she would ever have imagined, especially if you listened carefully. But there was no need to tell her brother and sister of it; not just yet. She clambered out, quietly closed the door and slipped out into the extensive garden. Rosie and Thomas were at the far end searching behind a hedge. She sprang out from the middle of a bush.

'I've won!' she triumphed.

'But I looked there,' complained Tom.

'You can't have looked hard enough!' snapped Rosie. 'Hannah's too clever for you.'

'But I did look, I did look,' he wailed. 'Hannah's cheated. She wasn't there.'

Although saddened by the apparent loss of their father, moving home had at least provided a little dash of interest and excitement for the children, which had taken their minds away from the overpowering sense of sadness that had gripped them. Few changes had been made to the family house in the last seven years during which only Mary and Nancy had occupied it. The rooms were gloomy, with dark, heavy furniture and curtains, but they were large, and with a back parlour for their own use there was space to play. Agnes slept in the same bedroom as her mother, for the present, while an old box room had been cleared out and made into a small bedroom for Tom, and Annie's cavernous old bedroom was reserved for Rosie and Hannah. The bay window looked out on the busy road and Hannah often retired upstairs, curled up on the wide sill and occupied herself with her sketchbook, depicting the ever-changing characters, vehicles and dramas below.

Downstairs the wide mahogany table in the parlour afforded the children room to draw, read, make scrapbooks, do jigsaws and occupy themselves with peaceful pursuits – except when Agnes was on the rampage, but she seemed to be less annoying since the move. Perhaps, like her brother and sisters, she realised that this was not her home: they all had to pay court to the formidable Mary Ackroyd's foibles, complaints and illnesses. Even so, the four children had settled in well and were prepared to make the best of it.

Their new life was sadder, and slightly more restricted, but it was not without its new discoveries and opportunities. Best of all was the garden, much larger than the one at Bowling Park Road. It was surrounded by a brick wall and there were bushes to run round, hedges to hide in, a wide lawn to play on and a few old apple trees to climb. To Hannah it had all the mystery of one she had read about in a book. James promised he would send his gardener to cut the lawn and tidy the place up, and showed the children the secret corners and hiding places that he and Annie had enjoyed in their childhood. He even told them how to climb the largest apple tree and peer over into the neighbour's garden. Hannah was fascinated to learn of the tricks and scrapes Annie had got into as a child, gaining a picture of her mother that she had never had before, of a happy, carefree childhood that had been so quickly ended by her dear father's death. Their uncle became even more appealing and funny when, demonstrating how to get down the tree, he tore his trousers on a sharp branch that he swore had not been there when he was a child. Hannah found it hard not to laugh when he faced opprobrium and censure from the women of the house.

'James, what have you been up to?' Annie gasped in consternation.

'You ought to be teaching those children how to behave, not getting into mischief yourself,' his mother moaned.

Tucked up tightly in the large bed next to Rosie, Hannah could not sleep. The wind rushed past the windows and shook the trees, and the window frames suddenly creaked as if a giant hand were gently shaking them. What had seemed a welcoming new home now seemed dark and forbidding. But it was her thoughts that kept her awake, thoughts about that conversation she had heard through the cupboard wall.

Had she heard it right? Nancy had a son called Gideon? But Nancy was not married. And how did Albert, of whom she had only vaguely heard, come into it? Why did he have to run away to Liverpool? She recalled a funeral long ago at a strange house over a butcher's shop, close to Grandma Harriet's. She remembered Mummy, Daddy, Grandma, grumpy Grandad Enos and Nancy. Or was it grumpy Grandad's funeral? Or a baby that Mummy and Daddy had, who had died? It was all so confusing, so far in the past, when she was little. And she was angry with all those nasty things that Grandma Ackroyd was saying about her father. That it had been his fault that Nancy met Albert, his fault that Nancy was looking after those terrible, sinful girls at the Mission church. What did it all mean?

Suddenly she sat bolt upright. She almost woke the sleeping form beside her, but Rosie turned over, put her thumb in her mouth and settled down again. A thought had struck Hannah, a terrible thought, one that was almost impossible to understand. Nancy had been a mummy and had borne a child, but in shameful circumstances. But it was only mill girls and poor people and wicked women that such things happened to, wasn't it? She shook her head. And you never spoke of such things! Their babies were taken away so that they might have a good start in life, not tainted by Sin and Wickedness. And this had happened to Nancy . . . and Uncle Albert was the daddy, but he had run away and they hadn't got married. But Nancy was a very good woman. She tried to stop people drinking. She was a Christian. She helped poor, unfortunate girls, who lived in sin, who did wicked things . . . just as she herself had done.

Hannah's sense of deep unease was mixed with a slow realisation that she had stumbled on a dreadful secret, one that she could not share with anyone, least of all her mother and certainly not with Nancy. Was it all to do with Daddy's disappearance or nothing to do with it? Did that hold another secret just as terrible, a secret that Nancy knew but wouldn't tell?

The howling of the wind and the creaking and rattling from the house were replaced by another noise. A drunken man was making his unsteady way along Wakefield Road. He was singing loudly and his words were slurred. 'Come into the garden, Maud, for the black bat night has flown.' His voice rose in a crescendo. 'Come into the garden, Maud, I'm here at the gate alone.'

He was not alone. As he staggered to his front door it opened, and a shrill voice called, 'Be quiet. What will all the neighbours think, you drunken fool?'

* * *

In another part of Bradford another drunk was making his way home, but he was not singing. His gait was just as tottering and wayward, but he was silent. He was as full of remorse and guilt as he was of drink. Lem Metcalfe staggered slowly homewards. This was not an unusual predicament, but tonight it was different. He too had seen the headline in the *Bradford Observer*, and it had started a train of thought as dreadful and worrying as the one in young Hannah's head. 'Not my fault,' he muttered to himself. 'They can't blame me. I didn't know he'd go and kill himself.'

His slurred, mumbling speech was incomprehensible to anyone except himself, certainly to the policeman he met at the corner of the street who knew him well. The tall, muscular constable eyed the hopeless form, gave a cursory wave and continued on his way, twirling his moustache. Lemuel Metcalfe was a pillar of the community, a man of some substance, a respected local businessman: so what if he drowned his sorrows? He was respectable when sober and harmless when drunk. And being married to a dragon as he was would turn any good man to drink.

Several pints at the Duke of Wellington followed by a few whisky chasers had done nothing to remove the worry and guilt from Lem's mind. The drink had confused him, muddled the details in his head, but not removed the nagging doubt that his threats might have caused another man's death. But it had resolved him on his course of action.

'I'll see the young bitch in the morning,' he mumbled under his breath. 'If it wasn't Walter Clough who spilled the beans . . . and he so insistent he didn't. And why should he? Him in the same boat with that Eliza. No, it must have been Madge. She let it slip out. No other man had touched her before me, and she had to tell someone about us.'

Lem's mind wandered as he thought of his affair, of his hands on Madge's firm young flesh. The spindly spinster of the accounts office had dolled herself up quite a treat, especially if you paid for a couple of nice dresses and a hair-do. A twisted smile turned to a leering laugh as he remembered their first night together at the Imperial in Blackpool, of the virgin intacta, the uncut diamond. Then there were the regular outings: the Piccadilly in Manchester, the Queen's at Southport, the Adelphi in Liverpool . . . His grin was cut short. That was where they had bumped into Walter and Eliza. That was the source of all his misfortunes and the end of his affair.

'I'll sort the bitch out tomorrow,' he promised himself.

A sober morn found Lem with less resolve, and it was with some trepidation he approached Madge's desk. 'Miss Dobson, I wonder if you would bring me last year's March accounts for South Yorkshire.'

It was the usual code for 'Meet me upstairs in the attic where they store the old paperwork.' In the past it might have meant 'I'm keen for a bit of hanky-panky and I can't wait for the weekend,' but the hanky-panky had finished long ago and now it was 'I've got something private to tell you that I don't want all and sundry to hear.'

'It'll have to wait half an hour,' she replied loudly, giving him a hard stare. She would never have dared address Lem like that in the old days, but now she had a hold over him and could speak to the senior sales manager of Ledger's Wholesale Drapers as she liked. A few faces in the office turned away, scarcely able to conceal their mirth, and sly winks shot across the room from one desk to the other. It was the best show in town, and had been for the two months since the affair had leaked out.

A red-faced Lem puffed and panted as he climbed the steep winding staircase at the back of the building to the storeroom. As in many large shops and warehouses, the space between the beams and roof had been floored to provide additional storage. It was not an ideal space and each week, or after storms or high winds, an office junior was dispatched with a broom to sweep up the dust and crumbs of cement and horsehair that had been dislodged. He opened the door tentatively. Madge was facing him, pale and apprehensive. 'What the hell do you think you're up to?' she whispered. 'I told you it was over.' He walked slowly up to her until they stood face to face. She stepped back, breathing heavily. 'Don't try those tricks on me again,' she snapped. 'I'm not so innocent and naïve as I was a couple of years ago. I know what men like you get up to.'

'I wouldn't dream of it, you conniving little bitch,' Lem snarled. 'I just want to show you the end result of your gabby little tongue, telling all and sundry about our love affair.'

'Love? Is that what you call it? Pawing me all over with those sweaty hands of yours in those hotel rooms, and half the time not able to perform like a real man? A few too many drinks and the unsteadiness doesn't just go down to your legs.'

Lem's face turned a deep red. The veins stood out on his neck and he sweated in the warm, stuffy air. His inclination was to give her a hard slap, but for all his bluster he was a coward at heart.

'Me let it out?' she continued. 'I'm the joke of the office! Do you think I'd want to tell anyone that the only man who'd ever had me was the fat old sales manager? And don't think it's just me. You're the laughing stock of Ledger's as well, and you're too daft to even realise it. God knows what'll happen to either of us if young Mr Ledger ever finds out.' She paused for breath. 'How you can accuse me I've got no idea. We know it was Walter. And he let the story out because you sacked him.'

'Then what about this?' said Lem, regaining his composure. He handed over the folded page for her to read. It was a few seconds before Madge took in the significance of the headline, but when she did it seemed to paralyse her. She stood motionless for over a minute, her face turning paler every second. Finally she trembled, and collapsed on to a pile of curtains. Shocked by her reaction, he sat down beside her, supporting her in his arms and offering her a swig of brandy from the small silver flask he kept in his pocket. Tears filled his eyes and he shook his head. After a minute the brandy did its work and she sat up.

Lem released his hold on her and they turned towards each other. 'Oh my God! My God! What have we done?' he whispered.

'We've taken revenge into our own hands, without heed of the consequences. Vengeance is mine,' she continued, as if she were chanting the words in a church. 'Vengeance is mine. I will repay, saith the Lord.'

'But I didn't tell his family,' moaned Lem. 'It was a threat, that was all. Even I wouldn't do an underhand thing like that. Madge, you must believe me.'

'I can't stay here. We can't see each other ever again. I'll get a job elsewhere and you'll write me a reference. And make sure it's a damn good one!' Lem nodded silently. 'At least I've not had to bear the ultimate humiliation, thanks to your inadequacies. That would have been the last straw!'

Lem winced, and Madge rose, walked over to the door and tiptoed carefully down the stairs. He sat in silence, idly shaking the flask. It was empty. There was no consolation to be had.

Chapter Six

His kisses were becoming more intense and she longed for more. They had moved from her lips, her neck, her shoulders and were now all over her body. It was like a fire inside her. She returned them just as passionately and clasped his smooth body close to hers. She stared into the bright, blue eyes. She observed the round, perfectly formed face. She could read his lips mouthing 'I love you,' and she replied 'I love you too.'

She lay back and let him slide on top of her, pulling the bedsheets away so that he could see the whole of her naked body. And it was happening again: that intense, pleasurable mystery that no one spoke of but everyone desired, and it was happening to her for the first time, and it was wonderful.

Nancy woke up and stared around. Something had disturbed her nightmare. The dream was just as it always was, but without the usual ending – her lover's departure, and that intense feeling of pleasure slowly turning to a deep, nagging pain, growing and growing inside her until it burst out in the shape of another blond and handsome lover. He did not resume where the other left off, but slowly vanished, as all round the bed she saw many faces that had been watching her ecstasy and with their eyes condemned her monstrous, lustful sin. And the pain turned to burning shame, so deep she could not look at the faces she knew: her family, her friends from church, Pastor Robinson from the Mission, the drunks, whores and vagabonds from Silsbridge Lane. It always seemed as if the whole world had been watching her act of love.

And now there was still someone watching her. The small dark eyes were real, not a dream. 'Were you having a nightmare too, Aunt Nancy?' a small voice said. 'I had a terrible one about Daddy and this sea monster which grabbed him and ate him up. Oh, I wish he would come back.'

Nancy lifted Rosie on to the bed and gave her a warm and comforting hug. 'There, there, Rosie, he'll come back one day, I'm sure of it.'

'It was so horrible, and I couldn't wake Hannah to tell her. I could hear Mummy so I went to her bedroom, but it wasn't Mummy's bedroom, it was yours – and you were having a nasty dream too.'

So much had happened to Nancy in the past few weeks. Here she was comforting a sobbing child, hugging and loving her almost as a mother. All her barriers of formality and deliberate aloofness had been swept away, if only for a short while, and it seemed so natural to her.

'Let's go back to your bedroom,' she suggested, when the sobbing ceased. 'We'll see if we can get you back to sleep. I'll stay with you, I promise.' Nancy put the girl down on the floor and took her hand. Rosie, as she always did, obeyed, and they tiptoed across the landing and into the girls' room.

As Rosie climbed back into bed she turned and whispered, 'Aunt Nancy, who's Albert?'

'Oh, someone from long, long ago.' Nancy lightly held Rosie's hand until she slowly withdrew it and put her thumb in her mouth, falling deeper and deeper into oblivion beside her sleeping sister. Nancy closed the door behind her and returned to her own room, where she lay awake, no tears in her eyes but deep in thought, until the curtains paled and the silence faded away with a crescendo of small sounds from the streets below.

* * *

'And who's that, Grandma, next to Mummy?' asked Tom.

'I know,' interrupted Hannah, 'it's Aunt Nancy.'

'Isn't she pretty?' gasped Rosie. 'Look at her long hair and her lovely white dress like Mummy's. I wish she'd make herself pretty now. Then she could have a husband.'

'Where am I in the picture?' asked Tom.

Harriet smiled and the girls laughed. 'It it was a long time ago,' answered Rosie, 'before we were born. Mummy and Daddy were getting married, and you can't have babies until after you're married.'

Hannah bit her lip. She was about to say something but stopped. Even the thought made her blush.

'There's you, Grandma,' said Tom, pointing to a younger, smiling Harriet.

'And your granddad, Enos Clough,' added Harriet, pointing to her departed husband, a square-faced, lantern-jawed man, forcing a smile through gritted teeth.

'And who's that?' asked Tom, pointing to a slim, handsome, fair-haired young man, standing close to the principal bridesmaid.

'That's the best man,' interrupted Harriet. 'He's the one who helps the bridegroom on his important day and sees things go well.'

'But who is it?' begged Tom. 'I want to know.'

'I know – it's Albert!' exclaimed Rosie. Both Hannah and Harriet stared at her in amazement, then for a brief second at each other. Hannah turned away and flushed a deep red. She had caught her grandmother's look of surprise and embarrassment. Oh how could she ever keep the secret to herself?

Harriet was disturbed. It had seemed a good idea to show the children the wedding photograph and to let them talk about their father, even if there had been a few tears. To shut it all out was not the way. They had to remember, to know. But it had all turned in a strange direction. And that look on her oldest granddaughter's face had surprised her.

'Let's play weddings,' suggested Rosie. 'You can be the groom, Tom, and just for once,' she turned to look at her elder sister, 'I'll be the bride.'

'I'll see what I can find for you in Grandma's dressing-up box,' said Hannah, keen to change the subject. She delved into the box Harriet kept for them, busying herself among old hats, dresses, material and pieces of old curtain.

'Oh dear, I've thrown quite a few things out,' said Harriet. 'They were getting so old and tatty. I'll tell you what, why don't you help at my bookstall on Saturday, as you used to? And while you're there you can go round the fent stalls and beg a few pieces for the box.'

'Yes, Grandma, I'd love that.'

'It must be three months since you've been down to the market to help me. Marie will be pleased to have Saturdays off again, and Charlie on the pottery stall will be glad to see you back.' Hannah's face brightened. It was just what she needed. 'I know the pocket money will come in useful. Your mother won't be able to give you much these days, and I'm sure you have to share a bit with the others. It can't have been too good for them either.' She looked towards the little bride and her even smaller groom.

Hannah smiled. 'Thank you, Grandma,' she said, and gave her a big hug.

* * *

'Eee, are you back again, lass?' The kindly old man wandered over from the china stall that adjoined Clough's Book and Magazine Emporium and rested his elbows on the edge of the counter. 'I think we'll have to watch ourselves a bit if you're in charge again, Miss Hannah.' He winked at Harriet.

'I'm not in charge, Mr Hargreaves, just helping Grandma and Marie.'

'Well you should be, lass,' the jolly neighbour commented. 'I'm sure you're the best sales assistant on the whole of Kirkgate Market. You're always helping the children to choose their books and comics and you never get your change wrong.' The red-faced man gave a laugh and threw his head back. His bald pate shone under the electric lights.

It was good for Hannah to be back, busy all day, chatting with friendly people and the many children who asked for her help. It was helping her forget her troubles and worries, if only for a day.

'I'll tell thee what, Harriet,' Charlie began again. 'If thee doesn't want her any time, she can come and work on my pitch. I bet she'd learn about t'pottery business in no time. Yon's a grand lass, you can be sure of that. And I bet she's as sharp and charmin' as her grandma any day.'

'Oh, Charlie, you are a one,' laughed Harriet, 'I don't know how you've got the cheek!' She too was glad to be back at her business. Marie had held the fort for the last two weeks, but there were displays to tidy up, shelves to replenish and out-of-date stock to shift. It was wonderful to have her granddaughter back with her as well: Hannah was so good with the children, who had been asking Marie every week when she was coming back.

'Aunt Harriet!' On hearing her name, she turned round. She was surprised to see Nancy in Kirkgate Market. 'You remember what we discussed?'

'Yes, of course.'

'I've brought some of those books with me, and a few penny magazines. It's kind of you to agree to have a section for Bible stories and Christian books for the children. And giving your profit to the Mission is more than we expected.'

'You're more than welcome, lass, though you haven't brought many. We're a bit light on stock at the moment. It's because I've been away these last few weeks.' She lowered her head and spoke in a whisper. 'Marie, bless her, can handle the selling, but when it comes to business she's not much idea, I'm afraid.'

'We have some more down at the Mission. They could help to fill up your shelves until you get more of your regular supplies.'

'It's children's books and penny magazines we're particularly short of. A bit of Christian preaching among the adventures won't come amiss, with children as they are today!'

'May I go down to the church with Aunt Nancy and help her bring some books back?' asked Hannah.

For once her grandmother hesitated. Silsbridge Lane was one of the most squalid and unpleasant areas of Bradford.

'I'll bring her back within the hour,' Nancy said. 'She'll be safe with me.'

41

Harriet nodded. 'I know you'll take good care of her, but within the hour, mind.'

Hannah linked arms with her aunt, and together they wandered off down the crowded aisles. The market was certainly busy that Saturday morning. Children were milling around the toy stall, examining wooden dolls with painted hair, Tommy talkers, lead soldiers and a host of musical instruments, from tin trumpets to drums and tambourines. Two younger children recognised Hannah from the bookstall.

'Eh, Miss 'anna, wilt thee be at t'bookstall today?' a girl asked.

'I'll be back in an hour,' she replied, as she gently pushed her way through the crowd.

'See you then. Hast thee got some new uns for us?'

'I'm bringing some new books back with me,' she shouted after them.

They had reached the front of the market, but before they got to the street Nancy dragged her niece over to the sweet stall. 'I think you deserve a treat for helping me, and we'll be too loaded up to stop and get anything on the way back.'

Hannah didn't object. In the last few weeks, what with the trouble surrounding her father's disappearance, the lack of money in the household and the overwhelming feeling that indulgences were not a priority, neither she nor her brother and sisters had been given any sweets or treats. But this was different. It was a reward. She stood in front of a bewildering array of colours and shapes, and an intoxicating mixture of odours: peppermint, aniseed, liquorice, coltsfoot and an overlying perfume of cloying sweetness. She stood dazzled by the array, first thinking she would choose butter drops from a row of great bottles on the shelf, then toasted teacakes made of coconut and marzipan. She finally settled on striped humbugs from tins at the front of the stall. 'Thank you, Aunt Nancy, thank you very much.' She offered one to her aunt, and when this was declined she popped one into her own mouth and put the bag into a small patch pocket sewn on the front of her dress. 'Don't worry,' she added, 'I'll save some for the others.'

They descended the steps to Kirkgate. The crossing sweeper moved out and swept a clear path across the cobbles for them and for two other ladies who were venturing across the dusty, manure-covered street. After fifty yards they turned into Westgate. Hannah asked her aunt to stop a moment as she had noted a pretty dress in a shop window. It was far too old for her, but, as Nancy remarked, even at the age of twelve she had a keen eye for fashion. They turned left again between two tall and elegant sandstone buildings, and in seconds were in a totally different world.

Silsbridge Lane ran south-west towards the factories of the Goit Beck. Although some newer houses had been built near its junction with Westgate, the houses gradually became smaller, meaner and more dilapidated as they descended the lane, taking care on the rough stone sets.

The air became more pungent, with the smells of cooking onions and fish, mixed with the stench of drains and rotting matter, together with acrid smoke rising from the old mills further down the valley. The inhabitants seemed to have taken on the hopeless aura of their surroundings. A few wretched barefoot children sat on a step watching the only one with clogs practising a little dance, no doubt for a performance round the pubs that night. A young woman in stained and ragged clothes emerged from a pawnbroker's carrying a bundle under her arm. As they passed her the two could see it was a dress, no doubt her only decent garment, which she wore of a Saturday night and redeposited on the Monday morning, as was often the custom.

'Begorra, 'tis Miss Ackroyd from the Mission coming to save our poor Irish souls from drunkenness and sin,' a voice rang out.

Nancy stared straight ahead. Any attempt Hannah might have made to turn and see where the voice was coming from was forestalled when Nancy quickened her step, determinedly ignoring the group of young men around the door of the Slaymaker's Arms.

'Is that another girl with you that Jesus has saved?' another man called.

'Ask him to save one for me next week,' yet another drunk shouted.

Hannah did not understand what it was all about but sensed the hostility and hurried on, tightly grasping Nancy's arm. The cobbles sloped more steeply, as they were nearer the valley bottom. Suddenly Nancy turned right through a gate, up a short flight of steps and into a simple brick building with narrow windows and a plain white cross fixed to the gable end. They were greeted by a round, florid, smiling face, framed by a mop of grey hair on which was perched a small white bonnet. 'Dear Jesus, this is a young one to be out on the streets . . .'

'This is my niece, Mrs Mullarkey,' interrupted Nancy. 'She's come to help me collect some books for her grandmother's stall in the market.'

'And me thinking I'd have an extra pair of hands to swill the floor this morning,' the old lady laughed. 'I'm getting little help from those girls. It's a right rum lot you've got in the hostel at the moment, apart from her who's always got her nose in one of your books.' She nodded towards a group of girls at the other end of the hall, intermittently engaged in dusting and sweeping but stopping to chatter and engage in horseplay as often as they could. On seeing Nancy they resumed a semblance of work. They were older than Hannah, she guessed between fifteen and seventeen. One sat away from the others, reading. She was smaller than the rest, hardly taller than Hannah herself, and was steadfastly ignored by the others. The cloth she was supposed to be using was draped over the back of a chair, and she had taken a book from on top of a pile that lay nearby under the window sill.

'Those are the books we need,' Nancy said, indicating the pile near the solitary girl. 'We can't carry them all so I'll let you choose some. About two dozen will be enough.'

Hannah went across the hall, to where the solitary figure had resumed her dusting. 'Hello. My name's Hannah.' The girl bowed her head and ignored her. 'Do you like books? I help out on my grandmother's bookstall in the market, and I've come with Aunt Nancy to choose some.' The girl stared at her with empty, expressionless eyes. 'I need someone to help me choose some. We need some with nice pictures for little children and some for older ones. Old Testament stories go down well and there's got to be something for boys, of course. Heroes and battles like Samson, David and Goliath, that kind of thing.'

'I can't read all that well . . . But I want to,' the girl mumbled in a voice so soft that it seemed to come from deep within her.

'You choose the easier ones then, for the young children.'

'Thanks, Miss.'

'Not at all . . . What's your name?'

'Deborah.'

'Here, Deborah, would you like a sweet? They're humbugs from the market.' She offered the bag to the thin-faced blonde girl, who tentatively slipped one into her mouth. 'Where did you live?' Hannah asked.

'I come from Wakefield. I ran away from home. I got caught and then ran away again from an orphanage. I got a job here in Bradford. They said it was a housemaid, but it weren't what they said.'

"Ere, what you doin', givin' sweets just to 'er?' a rough voice broke in. 'We share 'n' share alike 'ere. Don't be taken in by Miss High 'n' Mighty, Miss Deborah "Keep Yourself to Yourself". She's just the same as the rest of us, you ought to know. Been in the same business, has the same shame as every girl here.'

'But some of us feel the shame more than others, Charlotte.' Nancy's quiet but stern voice broke in. 'That's what learning about God's love is. Trying to understand and love everyone. Not just your friends. One day even you may learn that.'

Hannah offered the bag to the hard-faced girl, who quickly took one, then grabbed three more which she handed to the others.

'It's more polite to let my niece offer one to each in turn,' rebuked Nancy.

'No offence, miss. Just wanted to make sure we all share. That's what it's all about. God's bounty, isn't it, miss? We all get a share of it.' Nancy ignored the taunt.

After the girls had wandered back to their tasks, Nancy examined the books that Hannah and Deborah had laid aside. 'You two have chosen well,' she said.

Deborah's face lit up like the soft glow of a lamp. She had rarely received praise for anything before.

'Will you get some string and scissors, Deborah? Mrs Mullarkey will show you where they are. You'll need to tie the books up in two bundles for us to carry back.'

Deborah obeyed, and hurried back a minute later with string and scissors. Hannah showed her how to make a secure bundle and tie it with a neat double bow. The older girl was clumsier and not very confident, but watched her mentor carefully and eventually presented her with a securely tied pile of books.

'That was good,' said Hannah. 'Would you like me to come down here and help you to learn to read better? I can ask Aunt Nancy if she can bring me down sometimes.'

The thin, pale face turned towards Hannah, making sure that none of the others could see. She blushed and nodded, and a faint smile crossed her lips. For the first time in her miserable existence she had found a friend.

Chapter Seven

It surprised everyone at Ledger's when they heard of Madge Dobson's sudden impending departure. It was even more surprising when they heard she was going to Brown Muff's as senior secretary to Mr Brown himself. The rumour mill was rife – Madge Dobson of all people, who had been with the firm more than twenty years!

Madge's impending departure surprised Vera Binns as well. The thin, grey-haired, bespectacled spinster was the one friend Madge had at Ledger's. She was not a close friend, but someone she could chat to and occasionally gossip with. But there had been no contact between them since the shocking story of Madge's relationship with Lem Metcalf had spread round the office like influenza. How could she comment on this woman or that when she knew that the one big story was her own affair, and that she herself was the main object of gossip and tittle-tattle.

It came as a surprise to Madge when Vera spoke to her after a month during which she was either ignored or received a perfunctory nod and an enigmatic smile. Then one day she found herself alone with Vera in the drapery stockroom.

'I'm surprised to hear that you're leaving us. Still, it's a very good promotion. I'm sure a superior firm like Brown Muff's will pay better money than you get at this place.'

'Let's not beat about the bush,' said Madge tartly. 'You know as well as I do why I've got to leave this place. I've no doubt you've enjoyed my embarrassment as much as anyone, and I'm sure you've not been averse to passing the story on. Still, if that's what being a friend means to you then so be it.'

Vera was shocked, and pangs of regret stirred within her. 'I'm sorry, Madge, particularly if you think I've been the cause of some of your pain. I hope we'll meet from time to time again in the future. Perhaps lunch hours would be convenient?' She was met with a stone cold stare. 'We might have some tea and fancies over in the restaurant at Brown Muff's. They say it's quite the nicest place for afternoon tea in Bradford these days. I could tell you what's been happening over here at Ledger's and you . . .'

'Personal secretary to Mr Brown is a very responsible position. It means *confidential* secretary. You won't find me passing on rumour and gossip. Perhaps some social chit-chat and the latest fashions – which you won't see at Ledger's for years. It all depends on *you*.'

'What do you mean?' asked Vera. 'What depends on me?'

'Who let the cat out of the bag?' Madge whispered. 'I want to know. Who found out about my friendship with Mr Metcalf? That's all it was, Vera, a friendship: no more. And if I accompanied him on some of his business trips it was to help him with his paperwork, to take notes, to help him secure contracts. For the good of the firm. Nothing improper. Do you understand?'

'Oh yes I do, Madge. I'm sure it was. You'll never hear another story from me.'

Madge stepped closer. Small she may have been, but she was determined and intimidating. She may once have been the office mouse, quiet, accommodating and at the beck and call of anyone and everyone, but circumstances, experience and need had turned her into a different creature. 'Be that as it may, Vera. What I want to know from you is who found out, and how they found out.'

'I don't really know.' It was a lie, and obvious at that. Madge stepped even closer, and her sharp blue eyes at last penetrated Vera's defences. She had to confess.

'Well . . . Miss Naylor from the ladies' retail department told me . . . but I'm sure someone else told her, someone from the shop floor or even from window dressing. Perhaps I can find out for you.'

'Do that!' Madge's stern gaze transfixed her again.

Vera had never seen her friend like this before. She was panicking. She suspected it was Maude Naylor, but how could she hide the trail and put what seemed a very determined bloodhound off the scent?

Madge smiled. She could get to Maude Naylor long before Vera, and would prise the truth out of her.

* * *

The rain tapped relentlessly on the windows of Silsbridge Lane Mission Church. The small hall was empty except for two girls. Charlotte and the others were out at work, either in the local mills or as part-time servants in houses on Westgate or Thornton Road. Nancy was in the city distributing posters for the Band of Hope, having promised to pick up Hannah and return her home in an hour.

For the first time in many months Deborah felt a small glow of happiness deep inside. She rarely showed this to the outside world, and never to the other girls, who taunted and bullied her: her silent isolation was the shield she used against the burdens of this world, the horrors of her early childhood and the shame of the recent past. Even now, sitting with her one friend, she did not laugh or giggle, and there was just an occasional shy smile or a sparkle in those dark eyes that betrayed her innermost feelings.

'"They brought Jacob back with them and Joseph came out to meet them in his chariot. He kissed his father because he was so happy and Jacob wept tears of joy and praised God because he had pro . . . prot . . ."'

'Protected,' said Hannah.

'That's it, "pro . . . tec . . . ted . . . protected his son. And they all came to live in . . . Egypt"! I remembered that word even though it were a funny un, and it don't sound like it writes.'

'Well done. You're really reading well.' Hannah gave her companion a little squeeze, her arm around Deborah's shoulders – which were much less bony, thanks to a diet of plain but wholesome food from Mrs Mullarkey's kitchen. A simple but smart dress, regular washing and some neat snips of her hair by Nancy was turning her from a thin, dirty, wretched waif into a surprisingly beautiful young girl.

Deborah turned to Hannah. 'I love that story. It has such a happy ending. Joseph forgives his brothers, Jacob finds his son again and they all live happy together. That's how it should be . . .' She bowed her head. 'But it'll never be like that for me . . . It was once with my dad. He were all right, bit of a laugh really. Got drunk sometimes. Only ever belted my brothers if they was really naughty. We was poor. He were only a delver.'

'What's a delver?'

'He worked in the quarry, cutting and hauling stone, until it fell on 'im one day and killed 'im. Then Mum took up with *him*. Said he'd look after us, he did. Evil he were. Even my mum got scared of him, the beast. What he did . . .' Deborah's voice tailed away and tears filled her dark eyes.

'There's no need to talk about it if you don't want to,' whispered her companion.

'Want to tell it,' she mumbled. 'Not the worst bits. But I got to tell somebody.'

Hannah felt as if the burdens of the world had been thrust on her shoulders, but who else could her friend turn to? 'All right. You tell me.'

'Ran away from *him*, I did. I went to Leeds, slept under railway arches and begged on the streets. Then I were so hungry I stole bread from a shop. Got caught and were sent to this home. That were terrible too. They beat you for the slightest thing, locked you up by yourself and starved you. They were even worse to the boys. Not that we were supposed to mix and meet, but we did. The lads stole food for us. All of us got beaten terrible if we were caught.'

'So why are you here?'

'Got wind of them sending me back home. Bobbies must have found out who I was. Couldn't go back. Not to *him*. So I ran away, far away, here to Bradford.

'And you found your way here?'

'Not straight away. I looked for work as a servant, but it weren't what it were supposed to be. Gentleman wanted more than scrubbing and cleaning. I got by. Did things I couldn't tell you. Really ashamed I was, but it kept me alive. Put a crust in my belly. Then I heard about the Mission from another girl in this pub.'

'It can't be nice for you here. The way the other girls treat you.'

'Na, it's all right. If all I get is teasin' and tauntin', and the odd thump from that Charlotte, I can put up with it. That's nothin', that is. I keeps myself to myself. And your aunty's a reyt good un. Seems a bit sharp but underneath she's got a heart of gold . . .' Deborah's voice started to break up. 'I don't know what would 'ave 'appened to me if she hadn't been 'ere. They'd have found me dead down a ginnel, perhaps, or gone mad out of my head and put in Menston or some other loony bin.' She burst into tears and for five minutes was inconsolable. Hannah offered her a handkerchief, and she dried her eyes, blew her nose loudly and handed it back.

Hannah delicately put it back in her pocket, without showing any obvious disgust. 'I think we'll try some writing now,' she suggested, picking up the slate and chalk from the floor beside her.

'I know,' burst out Deborah, 'I'll write what Miss Nancy's got on one of her banners. "Jesus saves us all".'

'All right.'

'Jesus begins with a big J 'cos it's a proper name like Hannah or Nancy or God.' She took a minute to carefully write down the words, then showed it to her young tutor. 'Jesus savs us all.'

'We need an e after the v. It changes an a into an ay.'

'Oh yes, I remember.' Deborah snatched the slate back and corrected the word. 'It's like gav becomes gave with the e on the end.' She wrote another sentence below her first effort and showed it to Hannah. 'He gave His lif for us.'

That's very good. I suppose we'd better choose another book for our lesson next week.'

'I've seen the book I want,' Deborah interrupted. 'It's here. It's called *Gideon Soldier of God*. Funny, that is. They had a young lad at the home called Gideon. Smashing lad he was. Always a laugh, and so good looking with his curly blond hair and blue eyes.' She grabbed the book, not noticing the look of blank horror that had come over Hannah's face.

* * *

'Ah, Miss Naylor, Mr Metcalf asked me to send last month's sales returns to your department. Between you and me I don't think he's too pleased with them. Heard him say to Mr Ledger about "more effort", or was it word "changes" I overheard?' Madge's opening move was designed not just to put Maude Naylor on the defensive but also to instil a little fright into her adversary. She hovered round Miss Naylor's counter, silent and menacing, pretending to look at some blouses piled on the counter, then a display of lace gloves. The expression on Madge's face was one of vague disapproval. There were no customers around so she made her move. 'I was talking to Vera Binns today,' she remarked casually.

'Oh really, Miss Dobson? Is she managing well in the office?'

'I think so. Now she knows who her real friends are and has learned who to avoid, especially those who spread rumours.'

Madge had stopped casting a spurious glance over the displays and was now facing a nervous Maude Naylor across the counter. Although the two women were the same height, Madge Dobson seemed to her hapless victim to have grown a few inches taller. Confident and self assured, so she cared little whom she might upset or what mayhem she might cause, as she was leaving the firm at the end of the week. Her small eyes outstared the slighter, younger woman, who turned away to tidy a drawer of aprons – but when she turned round again the eyes were still on her, and the gaze was just as hard and intimidating.

'I really don't know what you mean, Miss Dobson.' Maude lowered her head, trying to avoid those eyes. She was proving a harder nut to crack than Vera, and Madge decided to adopt a more direct attack.

'Don't come that, Maude Naylor. I know what game you've been playing. I'll be going back to Mr Metcalf's office directly . . . Doesn't look a very good display on your counter to me. It wouldn't attract me if I were a customer. She fingered the gloves with disdain. We're still friends, Mr Metcalf and me, just good friends. Don't forget that, Miss Naylor. He still listens to what I say or think about people. He values my judgement. Says I've got a lady's taste.' Madge seemed to tower over the helpless figure before her, and moved in for the kill. 'Who told you, Maude Naylor? Who saw me with Mr Metcalf on those buying trips? Who spread those rumours when all I was doing was helping the sales manager with his paperwork?'

'Well . . .'

'Yes, Maude?'

The senior sales assistant reddened and her voice shook. She knew that before Madge left the firm she might exact a terrible revenge. 'If I was to tell you what I know, you wouldn't say anything to Mr Metcalf, would you?'

'I might not. No, I don't think I would, unless I found out you weren't telling the truth.'

'Well . . . Miss Dobson, you know I've been at Ledger's for over six years.'

'Yes, I do.'

'I started at the same time as this girl in accounts. We knew each other at school.'

'Yes . . .'

'Eliza, she was called. We stayed friends for years, and when she left the firm we stayed in touch, wrote to each other. It was in one of her letters she said she'd seen you.'

'All right, all right, I understand.' Without another word Madge turned and headed for the stairs. She was no longer angry but puzzled, very puzzled. It all came from that chance meeting at the Adelphi Hotel in Liverpool. But why would Eliza let it slip? She was there with her own lover, Walter Clough, the one who drowned himself out on Morecambe Bay. It was all very mysterious.

'Better not let Lem know about this,' she said to herself, as she took the lift up from the shop floor, 'not for the present at least.' Returning to the office, Madge resumed her work, but her mind wasn't on it. She made some mistakes, which was unusual. She ignored those around her as she thought about Eliza. There was definitely more to this than met the eye.

Chapter Eight

A small, sad party tramped along the path at the edge of the cemetery, bent against the wind which was coming from a winter-grey Irish Sea. It roared over the dunes, scattered sand over the promenades, desolate hotels and pleasure palaces, wreaked havoc in the shopping parades and suburbs of New Brighton, stormed the rising ground up Rake Lane and battered itself against the tombs of Wallasey Municipal Cemetery. It was all to no avail: it failed to disturb the thousands who slept below, or move the square vaults guarded by stone lions, or topple the indulgent Gothic towers and giant pillars that commemorated the passing of the wealthy and powerful.

The determined little band was not deflected from its purpose, either by the wind or by the tombstones' shadows, but marched on relentlessly along a straight track laid out between smaller and less imposing gravestones, memorials to the modest and insignificant. A tall, sandy-haired man led the little group with a grim determination, carrying the tiny coffin in his arms. There were no tears from Walter that terrible day, just a blank face and empty eyes that stared at the ground ahead of him. Eliza clung to his arm, her wide, dark eyes stained red with tears, her black hair blowing out behind her. The neighbours, with only passing acquaintance of the young couple who had recently moved into the large terraced house, followed them. The procession was brought up by the vicar and a youthful figure who, despite his black suit, solemn expression and grave demeanour, seemed too plump, fresh faced and bright eyed to be an undertaker's assistant; he was more suited to be a butcher or baker. He hung on to his black top hat for dear life: it would cost him too much out of his meagre wages if he lost it to the elements.

52

They stopped at an unmarked plot beneath the cemetery wall, where there was some respite from the incessant gale. Walter laid the small pine box down on the edge of the hole that had been freshly dug in the sandy soil.

'Man that is born of woman,' the vicar began, 'hath but a short time to live.' They bowed their heads in prayer or contemplation. 'He cometh up and is cut down, like a flower . . .' From time to time they listened to the words of the intonation, which rose above them and vanished in the gale or merged into their own thoughts. Eliza's were of the child she had lost so soon after giving birth. It was a pale-faced, black-haired little thing, who, too weak even to cry, would not suckle, and had died ten hours after coming into this life. Eliza had been exhausted by the long hours of her first labour. Walter had been with her for some of the time, as had their kindly neighbour, Mrs O'Connor. It was she who had comforted the anxious mother-to-be, and brought them drinks from her house next door.

Albion Street was quiet. The newly built terraced houses all looked the same, except for a few grander ones at the end which boasted bow windows, tiled and recessed entrances or decorative brickwork arches, like Eliza's parents' new house in the avenues of Cottingley, on the edge of Bradford: they were built of Yorkshire stone, but in all other respects were the same. Boasting respectability, relative wealth and new-found confidence, they were born of isolation. Unlike the narrow, meaner streets of Manningham, where with her sisters and brothers Eliza had been brought up, she had few friends and neighbours she felt able to call on. And now, far away from home, she did not even have a baby to love, cherish and care for. Despite her deep, intense love for the man who was the father of her child, she felt desolate, and the grim surroundings and raging weather only served to confirm her isolation.

'In the midst of life we are in death: of whom may we seek for succour, but of thee, O Lord?'

Eliza took no comfort from the words of the short service, only from memories of how it had all begun. For the first few days together she and Walter had been so wrapped up in each other, as lovers, friends and explorers setting out. It had seemed like a holiday. As it was summer the shops and streets of New Brighton were thronged with holidaymakers. It had all been a new adventure. Walter had resumed his job with Field Brothers, having explained his short absence by claiming he had fallen ill on his travels and had had to stay over in a small hotel. His employers had seemed to accept his explanation without question. But that was the trouble. It was all based on lies. They were not Mr and Mrs Adams. They had not come from Halifax. They were not married, either in the eyes of God nor under the law of the land. It was as if they were acting out a story, one that ended in bitter tragedy.

'Thou knowest Lord, the secrets of our hearts; shut not thy merciful ears to our prayer . . .'

In Walter's tortured mind were glimpses of past memories: his arrival at their rented house in the anonymous suburbs of Wallasey, and the tender, joyous welcome from his new 'wife' some six months before. At weekends there were walks along the promenades, shows and dancing, ferry trips across to Liverpool and a lift ride up Britain's newest and tallest tower to view the docks, and nearly all of the city of Liverpool. They even saw a new ocean liner moored across the river at the Pier Head, preparing to sail that afternoon. With the aid of a small telescope affixed to the rail they saw people swarming around it, carts and wagons loaded with the trunks of the emigrants and provisions for their voyage. They saw lines of people crowding the quayside and ascending the gangways. The magnificent ship dwarfed the buildings and the ferries and tugs alongside, its three blue funnels standing proudly above the mêlée. Walter and Eliza had even talked for a time of joining the voyagers one day, on an adventure to lands far away.

But it had all come to this. For Walter there came with it the memory of another child long lost, a first son who did not even come to his term. With it also came pangs of guilt, feelings that resurfaced; despite all his efforts he could never drive them away. He filled his mind with the last happy months of Eliza's pregnancy, the shopping trips for all that they needed for their new family. He recalled his over-protective care and consideration for Eliza, as with Annie before her first child.

'Thou most worthy judge eternal, suffer us not at our last hour, for any pains of death, to fall from thee . . .'

Walter remembered how he had watched with Eliza as the small bundle in her arms fought for hours, then gave up her struggle. He remembered his sad journey to the registrar's in Birkenhead where, in sombre, dark-panelled surroundings, the even more sombre clerk took down the details and received the letter Walter's doctor had given him. Walter registered both the birth and death of the daughter he would never see again, and duly received both certificates. The second one, like the first, told two lies: that he was Walter Adams and that Eliza was his wife. It did not lie, however, when it stated that the reasons for death were exhaustion and breathing failure, and that the father and informant was present at the death.

'Forasmuch as it hath pleased Almighty God of his great mercy, to take unto himself the soul of our dear sister here departed, we therefore commit her body to the ground . . .'

Walter was awakened from his reverie by a hand on his shoulder that gave him a gentle shake. He knelt on the small green mat that had thoughtfully been placed on the edge of the grave, and lowered the pine coffin down with the help of the round-faced youth.

'Earth to earth, ashes to ashes, dust to dust; in sure and certain hope of the Resurrection to eternal life, through our Lord Jesus Christ; who shall change our vile body that it may be like unto his glorious body . . .'

The frozen earth and pebbles rattled on the box as they fell. Walter succumbed to his grief, and wept along with Eliza and the two older ladies from Albion Street. Was he weeping just for the tiny infant in the grave?

The party disbanded. Two burly gravediggers slipped out of the shadows as the mourners walked away and began to fill the grave, affixing a simple wrought-iron grave cross with the words 'Martha Adams R.I.P. 11th November 1899' painted around its centre.

As they reached the cemetery gate Eliza turned. 'I don't want to go home just yet, Walter. I think I'd prefer to walk along the promenade.'

'All right, my darling, if you feel able to.'

The couple politely refused their neighbours' kind offer of a cup of tea, and Mary O'Connor, the older of the two women, nodded. 'I understand, my love. If you'se wants to be on your own a bit we can understand that.' Her round and florid face burst into a sympathetic smile. She took the arm of her companion and walked away along Rake Lane towards New Brighton, while Walter and Eliza turned down one of the many gently sloping streets that led down to the promenade. The sun was shining but the fierce wind still bent the trees and bushes, and they were glad for the shelter of the terraces and boarding houses along the deserted winter streets. As they turned along Egremont Promenade in the direction of the tower, which even at this far distance seemed to dominate everything around it, there was again no shelter from the wind, which blew up the Mersey, turning even the river into choppy, white-crested waves and jumping foam.

'Walter.' Eliza stopped. 'Do you think . . .'

'What, my love?'

'Do you think this is . . . a kind of judgement?'

'What do you mean?'

'That we're living in deceit and sin, and in the name of man and wife unlawfully, and so God has sent this to punish us.'

'How can that be? Why would he want to punish an innocent new-born child with our misdeeds? These things happen. I once thought, like you, that everything had a reason, a purpose. But if there is a God, I don't think he interferes like that in the running of this world. Things just happen to the good *and* the wicked. And there's nothing wrong with our love. It's true and kind. You still love me, don't you?'

'Of course I do.'

'And you know I love you?'

'Indeed I do.'

'And we've been so happy these past months, until this?'

'I've never been happier in my whole life.'

They gazed out across the choppy waters. Walter bent down to kiss her. There was not a soul to watch them on the wide-open, windswept promenade. Across the river a squat, two-funnelled ferry chugged from the Liverpool side towards them. It slowed to give way to a much larger vessel, making its way gingerly downstream in the teeth of the gale. As it drew level with them they could see that the decks beneath its two giant funnels were lined with passengers, enthusiastically waving handkerchiefs at them. Walter took note of the name on the side: it was the *Oceanic*, a transatlantic liner of the White Star Line, similar to but larger than the one he had seen so many years before at Liverpool Pier Head, on one of his last visits to see his dying cousin Albert. The memories came flooding back: the sunny day by the docks, his panoramic journey on the overhead railway, the slum tenements where he found Albert, the tragic waste of a young life. He raised a hand in salute and Eliza joined him. It was a solemn greeting, a wish for a safe journey to the hundreds of people lining the rails, rather than an enthusiastic celebration.

'The next time those people see land,' he murmured, 'it'll be the New World, America, or Canada perhaps.'

'Do you wish you were going too?'

'I don't know. Perhaps.'

'We could put the past behind us, Walt. A new beginning, proper marriage vows, no old life to catch up with us.' Eliza turned to him. 'There's still some of the old life left in you. I can tell when you get these silent moods. I imagine it's your family, your children.'

He stayed silent, and they resumed their walk towards the dark, brooding tower that was silhouetted against the weak winter sunshine. The ship vanished for a time behind the dark, grey mass of Fort Perch Rock, bristling with guns which pointed to the far shore. The liner appeared again on the other side, smaller, less significant, then gradually became a black blob on the horizon.

The cafés on the Ham and Egg Parade were all closed, their shutters rattling in unison like a discordant, angry choir. As the couple turned the corner the wind blew stronger, right into their faces. Instinctively they descended the stone steps on to the sands and wandered towards the water's edge. The blast almost blew them back to where they had come from, but they grabbed each other's arms, clinging close as if they were one body, bent their heads into the gale and struggled towards a line of black, jagged rocks. At the end of them was the old lighthouse, the last thing the voyagers would have seen before they vanished into the roaring expanse of ocean.

The clouds raced headlong towards them, while the grey sea foamed in white, jagged lines as it surged in their direction. The spray flew through the air, shooting from the dark waves as they hammered constantly against the rocks. At times it showered above even the lighthouse, and sent clouds of fine white mist towards the couple, drenching them to the skin. They pressed on to the water's edge, and stared out at the black dot on the horizon until it finally vanished from view.

Walter pressed his face close to Eliza's, so he could be heard over the shrieking chaos of air and sea. 'Six months from now, by the summer of 1900, we'll have done it. We'll take a ship over the Atlantic to America, to a new life. We can leave everything behind and really start anew, with no baggage from the past. Just me and you.'

She held her face against his. 'Promise?'

'I promise!' he shouted. His words resounded against her cheek, then were lost in the maelstrom above and around them.

Chapter Nine

It was good to get away from it all: the cheery, patriotic messages displayed in shop windows, the ringing church bells and the convivial mask that seemed to be a necessity on every face you met. There was also the tendency for every stranger to greet you as a friend, then regale you with their thoughts about the momentous victory – and how the relief of Ladysmith heralded a new dawn, and imminent victory over those dreadful Boers.

Here, among the sand dunes that flanked the strangely calm Irish Sea, Walter was out on his own. It was the perfect day to take a walk on a lonely sea shore, something he had always loved. It was a grey, melancholy day, which was trying its best to defy the mood of xenophobic rejoicing that seemed to pervade every soul and street. In this first week of March it had tried to snow, but it ended up as it always did on the Wirral: a soft, watery mess of slush and puddles.

How he missed the winters of deep snow in his native Yorkshire. The pure white streets and roofs only remained like that for a day, before the mill chimneys covered them with millions of specks of black soot and the silent beauty was gone – but at least for a short while the city looked pristine, almost purified. The lads and lasses would be out on the streets, sledging, sliding, building, throwing snowballs and whooping with joy at the new and delightful playground that nature had made for them. Walter remembered it all, and the faces that came with his recollections: the chubby cheeks of Abraham Harvey; Herbert Craven, the rubber-faced comedian who died under Ripley's mill chimney; one-eyed Isaac Butterfield; and the cheeky grin and fair, tousled locks of Albert, his cousin and dear friend. The memories came flooding back, and a few tears nestled in the corner of one eye. He felt their passing even more keenly than that of the brave soldiers whose bodies had, a few weeks before, littered the slopes of Spion Kop, plunging the nation into an orgy of grief and despair.

Walter smiled again. He recalled breaking the welcome news to Eliza and showing her the newspaper, but she had news of her own, far more important than any great national event. She had managed to book their passage to America four months hence. They were to have a cabin on board the White Star Line's largest and finest ship, the *Oceanic*, the one they had seen eight weeks before.

He walked on over damp, firm sand until the dunes thinned out and he neared the road again by Leasowe Castle. The octagonal stone tower was now a hotel surrounded by gardens, the trees and bushes lurking menacingly around it. The only greenery left was ivy spreading over one side and on to the adjoining building. The garden was empty, and would see no sign of life till the early summer. For a few minutes Walter sat and rested on a wooden seat, contemplating the tower. He remembered another tower, a ruined one high above Morecambe Bay, three years ago: the three children scrambling with him up a steep path, the silly games they all played, and a view over the bay on a bright warm summer's day.

Walter got up, to walk along the straight Leasowe Road, back to civilisation and people. A few farms lay to the right, and then, after a railway bridge, elegant terraces of large, new, pebble-dashed houses flanked both sides of the road. He was back in the world again, and the ugly present intruded into his thoughts. A milk cart passed him on its way back to one of the farms, its churns empty and the measuring cans hanging from the handles clanking against them with every bump and cobble on the road. The horse looked tired. It was not like the magical, silver-grey mare that he remembered from his childhood, delivering around the streets of West Bowling and stopping to perform its circus tricks to the delight of every child. That horse could count, pinch the caps of cheeky boys, pick out him as the cleverest boy – and select Emily Lumb as the prettiest girl in the village. Ah, Emily! The memories came flooding back.

'Afternoon, sir.' The smiling milkman greeted him, cheering Walter slightly.

'Good afternoon. On your way home now?'

'Aye, that I am. But 'tis a momentous day for us all, is it not?'

Oh no! The comment instantly depressed Walter again, as the milkman was revealed as yet another homespun philosopher, intent on spreading joy. He did not deign to reply, but raised his hat as the victory procession of milk churns passed by.

But he remembered the face. It was round, reddened and sported a luxuriant moustache which drooped down at both ends. It reminded him of that wily old fox Lem Metcalf. Walter's eyes followed the retreating figure on the milk cart. Lem, you old devil. You caused all this, didn't you? Upset the apple cart right 'n' all. But did you ever tell Annie's family? I didn't hear from you at all after we met at the station. I wonder what happened to you. What happened to your affair with that scrawny little mouse from the office? Miss . . . Dobson. That was it!

Walter's thoughts took him past a row of shops, some of their windows decorated with Union Jacks, a few with placards announcing the famous victory, lavishing gratitude on the brave soldiers and praising General Buller, the field commander in Natal.

At least the paper boy was doing business. '*Echo*,' he shouted out. 'Want an *Echo*, guv?' Walter's cold hands fumbled in his pockets for some coppers. 'Thanks, guvnor. It's all in about the victory over those Boers. Great day for us all, ain't it?'

Walter nodded, pretending that his elation had reduced him to silence. The news on the front page wasn't news; rather it was outpourings of exaggerated praise from all and sundry, including a message from the Queen to the hero of the conflict. 'Thank God for the news you have telegraphed to me,' it began. 'I congratulate you and all under you with all my heart. V.R.I.'

He pretended to read on as he walked, hoping to shield himself from anyone he might meet until he reached home. But one voluble soul was determined to deliver his verdict to all and sundry. 'Is it in about our great victory, wack?' he called as he caught up with Walter. 'It's a great day for us and the whole nation, isn't it?'

'Indeed,' murmured Walter, and made a sudden, deliberate turn to the left down a side street, completely wrong-footing his would-be companion, who went on for a few yards talking to the empty air. Walter was already wondering who else might have seen Lem and Miss Dobson, and might have spread the rumours that had caused him so much trouble. He knew that the two unlikely lovers would have tried to keep their tryst secret. He gave up, and put the speculation from his mind. Down the next street was their house, and Walter thought fondly of the welcoming arms of Eliza.

* * *

The last strains of 'The Day Thou Gavest Lord is Ended' faded away into the vaulted recesses of Bradford Cathedral. The funeral for Samuel Ledger, once owner of Ledger's Wholesale and Retail Drapery and eminent and respected businessman, was drawing to a close. Some cried openly, some hid their tears in their handkerchiefs, others stayed to talk, but most quietly and reverently dispersed.

Two figures, one a large man resplendent in black coat and top hat, the other small, female, her face well hidden behind a black lace veil, slipped away quietly from the crowd and into the back streets. He led the way into a small public house down a short narrow street. She looked around, furtive and distrusting, before vanishing out of sight into the almost empty bar.

He took her through to a small back room and closed the door behind them. A few seconds later the barman entered, nodded to the woman, who had removed her veil, and took the order from her companion, returning a minute later with a couple of brandies. No money changed hands: it would be on the slate later.

'We'll not be disturbed here, Madge, you can be sure of that,' said Lem, 'and a drop of brandy will help take off this winter chill. Now what is it you want? I must say, lass, I was surprised to hear from you. I thought you never wanted to see me again.' He opened his arms in a welcoming embrace.

Madge shrank away. 'No, Lem. We're not resuming that again. Those days are finished. Forever!'

'Then what in God's name do you want to see me about, woman?'

'We've got some unfinished business. For a start, I want you to cough up ten pounds.'

Lem almost choked on his brandy. His worst fears were realised. The nasty little bitch was going to blackmail him, or tell his wife everything.

'You can go to hell if you think I'm going to . . .'

'Shut up and listen just for once, Lem Metcalf. It's not for me.'

'Then who the bloody hell is it for then?'

'A private detective.'

'What? Why in God's name do you need a private detective? They don't come cheap, you know. I can tell you that now.'

Madge sighed and shrugged her shoulders, then rose to her full height of five foot nothing, half-intending to leave the dingy back room, and fired her parting shot. 'Will you ever listen to me, you big, blundering fool?' she whispered in a quiet but angry tone. She glanced around, not knowing how thin the walls might be in the drab and seedy pub, nor who might be listening at the door.

'All right. Sit down and tell me. What do you mean by unfinished business?' Lem was shocked by her manner, her confidence, her determination. This was not the shy Madge Dobson he had seduced. He was in awe, and secretly beginning to admire her.

'It's a long story.'

'Then let me order a couple more brandies,' he begged, getting up to summon the barman.

'When I've finished you're going to need one.'

The barman returned with the drinks, placed them on the table and departed.

'I wanted to find out how knowledge of our affair got back to Bradford,' Madge continued, 'and how it got all around the office and shop. It had to be deliberate, as we were so careful about our meetings. At least I was. I always checked no one was following us, and I even suggested not taking the same railway carriage out of Exchange station.'

'Yes, I know. You were good at arranging things, making sure no one . . .'

'A woman has her reputation to consider, Lem, much more than a man.'

'And what did you find out?'

'More than I bargained for. Vera Binns let slip it was Maude Naylor in the Ladies' Department who told her. And, of course, once you've told Vera Binns you might as well tell the *Bradford Argus*, the *Yorkshire Post* and the *Pudsey News* to boot.'

'How did Maude know? You know, now you mention it she's been acting very strange to me lately. Since you left Ledger's she's been very friendly whenever our paths have crossed, very polite, almost frightened.'

Madge smiled a smile of deep satisfaction. 'Who do you think put the fear of God in her? I made it clear you'd give her the chop if she didn't tell me what she knew, you daft ha'porth.' Lem leaned back, his eyes open wide and drew a deep breath. His respect for the woman before him was growing. 'Now listen to this. It was Eliza herself who told Maude – in a letter.'

Lem's eyes opened even wider. He took a large swig from the brandy in front of him, almost finishing it in one gulp. 'Eliza herself? I can't believe that!'

'From what I could gather, Maude didn't know anything about her friend's affair with Walter Clough, so I didn't let on. We'll keep it like that for the present.'

'Why would she deliberately tell Maude Naylor, knowing it would be all round Ledger's?' asked Lem. 'It doesn't make any sense. Especially as Eliza could have guessed I wouldn't stay silent about her and Walter's goings-on. She knew what I'd be like. I don't take anything lying down. And that Eliza, she were no fool, brightest girl in the whole of the firm she was, by a long chalk, and the prettiest. And she knew how to handle blokes. Very clever she was. Most of 'em never got a chance with her, except Walter bloody Clough.'

'If you'll let me finish . . .'

'Sorry, Madge.'

'On the last day I was at Ledger's I collared Maud for a second time. Put the fear of God into her again. I tried to get something more out of her, but she hasn't seen or heard from Eliza Smith for over eight months. She thinks she might have moved away. Left that business she built up. It was all in a rush, and even her family don't know where she's gone.'

'Really?'

'Yes, Lem, and that's why we've got to find her. There's more to this than meets the eye. There's definitely something fishy about it. And it may be to our advantage, or at least a chance to get our revenge.'

'Leave the detective to me. I've got a few contacts. I'll sort that out.'

'All right.'

Lem bent forward to give Madge a peck on the cheek, in the hope it might lead to a longer, more passionate contact. He was disappointed when she rose and held out her hand in a distant, frosty manner. There would be no resumption of the *status quo*.

* * *

'George Sugden – Private Enquiries Undertaken. Complete Discretion Assured. 27b Darley Street, Bradford.'

The card looked impressive. The location certainly did not. Number 27 was an ironmonger's shop, which cluttered the pavement outside with its wares. It was no better inside the shop, where buckets, lamps, pans, baths, plate carriers, toilet sets and Parisian jugs filled almost every spare inch of the floor space. Lem had to negotiate an obstacle course to the counter to ask the surly old proprietor where he might find the elusive Mr Sugden.

'Oh, it's him you want. Down the alley at the side, turn right, up the iron staircase.'

'Thank you very much, my good man,' Lem replied, noting the display of housemaids' gloves at the end of the counter. His wife had been nagging him for a week to get some for the scullery maid: he would buy some after concluding his business upstairs.

The ironmonger frowned. He was none too pleased that his first customer of the afternoon was another fellow wanting to see the suspicious Mr Sugden, who rented the first-floor office at the back. 'Private detective indeed!' he muttered to himself when Lem was out of earshot. 'Another bloke wants his missus spied on 'cos of her goings on.'

Lem reached the safety of the doorway after nearly tripping over a tin bath and a pile of hearth fenders. He turned down the alleyway and puffed and wheezed his way up the steep iron staircase to an anonymous dark wooden door. He knocked, and the door was opened by a small, bald man with wire-rimmed glasses and a tired-looking moustache. He could not have been more than five foot five inches tall. Lem nodded and strode in, carefully perching himself on a small rickety chair in front of a chipped wooden desk. There was nothing else in the room apart from a chair on the other side of the desk, a few dusty files on a long shelf and some peeling brown patterned wallpaper.

George Sugden took out a notebook and pencil and laid them on the desk. 'Mr Metcalfe. I think for the purposes of this enquiry we'll write you down as Mr Jones, in the interest of discretion. You do understand?'

Lem nodded. 'You say considerable police experience,' he said doubtfully, eyeing the little man up and down.

'I wasn't in the serving uniformed force, Mr Met – Jones,' the little man answered. 'I was chief clerk for some fifteen years in the Leeds Metropolitan Police Department.'

Yes, thought Lem, until one day someone found you with your hand in the petty cash. That's why you've resorted to this little racket. 'No matter, Mr Sugden. You come well recommended.' From some right dubious characters, he thought to himself. 'I want you to find the whereabouts of this young lady. I've written a description and her last known address on this paper. The name's Eliza Smith.' He handed the sheet over. The detective's small, thin hand stretched forward to take it. Lem noticed the fingers were excessively brown. The whole office smelt of cheap cigarettes.

'You describe her as a young lady of exceptional beauty, large dark eyes, black hair and slim figure. Was there some understanding . . . entanglement between yourself and the lady, Mr Jones?'

'Certainly not!' shouted Lem, banging his fist on the table. 'I'm a respectable married man, a well-known businessman.' He calmed down. 'She's . . . the daughter of a good friend of mine, a fellow businessman who's well known in the city. It's of some embarrassment to the family, so I want utter discretion.'

'So who are they?' the detective asked. 'It would be useful to know.'

Lem was beginning to panic. He didn't want enquiries about the Smith family rebounding on him. Smith's haulage firm was one of the biggest in the city. It held the contract with Lister's Mills and Ephraim Smith, once a simple carter, was wealthy and well known. But Lem had dug himself in too deep to extricate himself. Hesitantly he gave the detective the details.

George Sugden sucked in his cheeks. Even he had seen the name emblazoned on the wagons that constantly rolled out of goods yards to the biggest mill in West Yorkshire. He nodded. 'I understand, Mr Jones. You can rest assured there'll be complete discretion on my part.' His eyes grew brighter, imagining a pile of sovereigns, even fivers. With wealthy families like the Smiths or Listers involved, he could see his income doubling.

'All we need to do now is settle the fee, Mr Jones,' he said in his most business-like manner. 'For such an important and lengthy inquiry I would expect twenty pounds.'

'Twenty bloody pounds! You must be stark raving mad.'

'Twenty pounds. She may be anywhere in the country, which might necessitate a lot of travelling. Then there are my contacts. They don't give information for nothing, you know. And as I can't make enquiries directly to the family, a wealthy and influential family, I might add, that'll add to my time.'

Lem was trapped. It was he who had mentioned the Smiths. He could see there was no room for negotiation. 'All right. Ten pounds now and ten on successful completion of the investigation.'

The little man eagerly shook his hand, Lem's stiff, unfriendly response conveying all the suspicion and doubt that he felt for George Sugden. He made his awkward and hurried exit down the steep staircase.

Chapter Ten

H, O, P, E. That E at the end makes it hope not hop, doesn't it?'

Hannah was trying to choose some more books for her grandmother's stall, but the interruption from Deborah was not unwelcome. 'What are you doing?' she asked, noticing the pencil her friend was holding.

'I'm writing a letter. The very first letter I've ever written.'

'Who's it to?'

'It's to May.'

'Who's May?'

'She was my friend in the orphanage in Leeds. Now how do they spell Bradford?'

'Why are you writing to her?'

It was Miss Nancy's idea. She suggested that we write to people who are more unfortunate than us. A few of the girls are giving it a try.'

'And who's more unfortunate and miserable than you?' interrupted Charlotte. 'You should be writin' a letter to yourself!' She laughed, snatched the letter from Deborah's hand and began to read it aloud. '"My dearest friend" – your friend – you've got to be lucky to have any friend, 'cept Miss Bookstall 'ere. And she's only sorry for you.' She tugged Deborah's hair sharply. For a second her victim's look of pain and submission flashed to hate, but it instantly subsided. 'There's only one letter I'd write. That's to a nice millionaire or a rich toff. Don't matter how old or ugly he is. I'd ask 'im to look after me. A nice apartment in Kensington. He'd take me to the south of France, like the Prince of Wales

66

does with 'is fancy women every summer. Monte Carlo, Biarritz, posh hotels, casinos, big yachts. That's the only reason I'd write a bleedin' letter.'

'That's wicked,' burst out Hannah, 'to say things about our dear Prince like that.'

Charlotte roared with laughter. 'God bless you, little Miss Innocent. If you wants to think that then think that. Becky's worked in London, and she knows what the toffs and royals are really like. Morals no better than us, but they can hide it, see? Papers don't print owt about *them*, just about us poor sods at the bottom of the pile.'

'That's quite enough, Charlotte. Give Deborah her letter back. Now!' Nancy's commanding voice could persuade even the rebellious Charlotte to submit. Nancy hadn't caught anything of the conversation, but instinct told her that Charlotte was bullying again, and she was determined to put an end to it. She was not pleased at the influence the girl held over the others. 'May I see your letter?'

'Of course, miss. It's to my friend May.'

'Oh, I remember. Mmm, it's good so far.'

'What should I put in it?'

'Tell her that you're well, and what you do here at the Mission, and that you've learnt to read and write. And ask her how she is and if anything's happened to her.'

'Can I mention my friend Hannah?'

'Of course you can. And don't forget to tell her you've become a Christian, about God's love, of how you pray and how you hope for a better life through His salvation.'

'I'll need to ask Hannah for a lot more words.'

Both Nancy and her niece smiled. 'I think it's a good idea, Aunt Nancy, to write to those who are less fortunate. Could I write to someone, perhaps another child at Deborah's orphanage?'

'Certainly, Hannah, but keep it simple. Remember you're very good with long words that other children won't know. You'll find the paper and pencils on the desk in the back room.'

'Thank you, Aunt,' Hannah replied. She was back in a minute and sat down in the corner to compose her letter, well out of everyone's way – even Deborah's.

> Dear Gideon,
> I'm sorry to hear that you are in an orphanage.
> From what I hear from Deborah, who was once
> there with you, it's not a very nice place.
> Deborah tells me that although it's not a very
> nice place you are always happy and cheerful
> and you and some other boys help the girls and

the little ones by getting them some food. You
seem a nice and kind person and so I decided to
write to you.

My aunt Nancy works at a mission church
here in Bradford and together with Pastor
Robinson and his wife does good things for
people and children as well. My aunt runs a
hostel for girls with no home. I help her and
teach some girls to read. That's how I met your
friend Deborah. She is writing to her friend
May and so I am writing to you. Perhaps if the
orphanage is such a terrible place my aunt could
help you find a new, nice home, maybe here in
Bradford.

Please write back to me. I have put in a
spare stamped envelope and paper. Send it back
to me at my home in Wakefield Road, Bradford.
I have written the address on the envelope.
Please keep this a secret. Don't tell anyone or let
the people at the orphanage find the letter. They
may come to take Deborah back and that would
be terrible.

Your friend, Hannah

P.S. I hope you like my drawings

She finished the letter, and thought for a moment before she set pencil to
paper again. He definitely wouldn't like girlish drawings of bunny rabbits,
dolls or ribbons. Better to put in things a boy might like. She spent
the next five minutes filling the edge of the paper with sketches of
soldiers, footballers, clowns, trains and ships. Oh, and just one
small rabbit: for luck.

Hannah had just completed them when Deborah came over. 'I'm
ready to post my letter,' she began. 'Isn't it exciting? My first letter. Miss
Nancy said you'd help me with the envelope. How to address it right.'

She was about to seal the envelope when Hannah stopped her.
'Would you put this inside your letter?' she asked.

'Of course.' She caught the name on the front. 'To Gideon? You don't
want others to know you're writing to a lad then?'

A faint smile crossed Hannah's lips. 'No.'

'Don't worry: I won't tell. Mind you, lads and blokes mean only one
thing, Miss Hannah. Trouble. You mark my words.'

Hannah's smile broadened, and she blushed.

Deborah sealed the envelope and copied the address as Hannah had showed her. She was about to stick the stamp on when she looked at it closely. It was a penny red, with the Queen's head looking disdainfully to the right. 'I wonder if her son does take all those lady friends to the South of France, like Becky said?' Deborah giggled. 'Can't say I fancy him, though. He's old, bald and whiskery, and you couldn't call him good looking in a million years.'

Hannah's smile changed into an infectious giggle, and the two girls collapsed in uncontrollable mirth.

* * *

'Why have you brought us here, Walter?' asked Eliza, stepping down from the cab they had taken from the Pier Head. They had had a busy morning sorting out passports, visas and tickets for their journey to America two months hence. She was surprised that after lunch, instead of taking the ferry back to Wallasey, he had insisted on a ride in a cab to Liverpool's pleasant suburbs.

'It's a surprise.'

'A pleasant one, I hope.'

Walter smiled. 'I'm sure you'll find it so.'

They were before an impressive park entrance, its large ironwork gates mounted on magnificent marble pillars. It spoke of the city's grandeur and elegance, far removed from the grimy industry of the docks or the squalid hovels of its slums. Beyond was a long, straight drive flanked by trees on the left and extensive beds of primulas and tulips to the right, which seemed to stretch as far as the eye could see. The couple linked arms and strolled into the park. It was a fine but breezy May day, so Eliza decided not to raise the parasol she held in her right hand. In the distance, straight ahead, she caught the glint of something reflected in the midday sun. It disappeared behind some trees as the path sloped down to a series of winding lakes, edged by willows and chestnut and adorned by a series of stone follies and quaint carved mock- boathouses. As they reached a carved iron bridge, a small sign announced that they had reached the Faerie Glen.

'It's lovely, darling, but there are parks in Birkenhead and Wallasey nearer home.'

He led her on across the bridge. They followed the path out of the glen and through a gap in the trees. Almost immediately it came into view.

'Oh, it's a glass palace, like the Crystal Palace in London, but much more beautiful,' Eliza exclaimed. They were dwarfed by the building, which seemed to hang above them in the air. The Palm House was octagonal in shape, an elegant mass of curved glass more than twenty feet in height. It was surmounted by a large dome, itself topped by a smaller one, and the sumptuous curves of glass and iron rose almost fifty feet above them. They walked towards the entrance.

'A wedding cake!' she exclaimed. 'An eastern pagoda!' Then, remembering a story she had heard as a little girl, 'The Ice Queen's Palace!'

'You like it then?'

'Of course. And knowing the way your mind works, there's got to be another reason.' She thought for a second. 'I'll bet it's got a section with plants and flowers of the Americas.'

'You're too clever for your own good, Eliza. Is nothing a surprise for you?'

She was about to mount the steps to the arched glass entrance, but he led her first to one of the corners, where there was a bronze statue raised on a plinth.

'Who is it?' she asked.

'Can't you guess?'

The figure, in cap, doublet and breeches, held a telescope in one hand and pointed to the far horizon with the other.

'I know. It's Christopher Columbus.'

'Yes. If you think about it, he's the one who's made it all possible for us.'

Eliza gazed at the figure. 'Do you know, I feel like an explorer too, setting off into the unknown, to the other side of the world. Let's not stop in New York when we reach there, Walt. Let's go on to more exotic parts of America, and to warmer places too. No cold winters, no rain-swept cities. Let's journey on to wild country with beautiful strange plants and flowers and amazing scenery, totally different from anything we've ever seen before.'

'Florida,' Walter said. 'Arizona, Louisiana, New Mexico, California.'

'California,' she sighed. 'That sounds like the place I want to go.'

He squeezed her hand. 'Let's go in, then, and visit the American section to find what awaits us in California.'

Once they were back behind the front door in Albion Street, they stopped to kiss long and passionately. Walter took her slim body in his arms and carried her upstairs, gently lying her down on the bed. For him it was as if they were new lovers again, flitting from one hotel to another to indulge their passion. To Eliza it was as if they were to start their married life once more; but this time, half a world away, there would be no shame, no-one to deceive, nothing to hide. She embraced him, and he kissed her passionately. She responded ecstatically to her lover's promptings, as he did to hers.

After half an hour the two lovers, tired, satiated and blissfully happy, lay in each other's arms.

'Darling Walter, that was the perfect place to visit. It was a wonderful idea of yours,' she whispered.

'I'm glad you enjoyed it so much. Just think, in less than two months our dream's going to be reality.'

'How will we get to California? What will we use for money?' Eliza asked sleepily.

'Don't worry, my darling, I've made provision. And I'll be getting a good final bonus in the next month. Sales on my patch are doing well. Field's appreciate the work I've put in and they'll see me right, you can be sure of that.'

But she wasn't listening. A hectic day and their passionate love-making had taken their toll. She was fast asleep, dreaming of sunny skies, open prairies, strange people and exotic scenery. He gently lifted her arm and laid it on the pillow, then tiptoed over to the window. Darkness was falling so he quietly drew the curtains. He took little notice of the small, bowler-hatted man by the gas lamp.

But that didn't mean the small, bowler-hatted man hadn't noticed. The small, drab figure had been hanging round all day. He smiled to himself, and wandered away through the near empty streets to a dilapidated lodging house down by the docks. Once back in his dingy little room, which overlooked a brewery yard, he lit a cigarette from the dim and flickering gas lamp, and took out his notebook. The room stank of brewing beer, mustiness, unwashed sheets and cheap cigarettes. That did not bother him. For an hour he wrote, detail after detail: times, places, people, names, snippets from conversations. It was just as he had learnt from copying countless reports for the Leeds Metropolitan Police, before his hurried departure to the anonymity of Bradford. Such an unfortunate misunderstanding it was, and over just a few pounds at that! Still, tomorrow he would be on his way back to pick up the rest of his well-earned fee.

* * *

'Do excuse me, Mr Metcalf, but there's a gentleman to see you.' Vera Binns was excessively polite and deferential, as she had been for a month, since Madge had spoken to her. Having guessed from the sales manager's attitude that Madge had told him she was the one who had spread the story of the affair around the firm, she realised she had to watch her step: one wrong move and her vindictive, lecherous old boss would not hesitate to take his revenge and sack her.

'Who is it, Miss Binns?'

'He says he's a Mr Sugden from the Keighley Co-op drapery department. Wanted to speak to you personally about some enquiries he was making on certain lines.'

The penny dropped. 'Oh yes, Mr Sugden. My word, a highly valued customer. Known him for years, Miss Binns. Show him into my office.'

She smiled, a sycophantic, nervous smile, and walked back down the corridor. Lem surveyed the retreating figure. Tall elegant frame, well-coiffured hair, thin waist, nice hips . . . but a face that would frighten a ghost and a gob that was never shut.'

After a minute she returned with his visitor. Lem greeted him warmly, and shook his hand with the enthusiasm of meeting a long-lost friend. 'George! How nice to see you! I hope you liked that new line in bed linens we supplied you with last month.'

The little man, rather bemused, nodded.

'I told you they would sell well, didn't I?'

The office door shut with a bang, and the rest of the conversation was inaudible to Vera. She walked back to the general office. But what should have been a run-of-the-mill visitor didn't seem quite right to her. The man doesn't look like any buyer I've seen in the drapery trade, she thought to herself. He's far too scruffy. The brown suit's wrinkled and shiny. Most blokes in the trade dress smart. And no orders from Keighley Co-op have crossed my desk: they've got their own suppliers. She pondered for a while, but by the time she got back she had put it from her mind: there were far better items for gossip. Like the new woman who had taken Madge's place. What a taste in hats! She looked utterly ridiculous.

'What the hell do you mean coming here?' Once the office door had closed, Lem's tone changed. 'This is my office. Them women can sniff a wrong un like a bad piece of fish. Why didn't you send me a bloody note like I told you?'

'Calm down, Mr Jones.'

'You can cut out that claptrap for a start! If anyone here hears you calling me Jones they'll know summat's up. I'll tell you now, you could use one or two of them in *your* business. Got noses that bloody long they can poke your eye out, never mind sniff their way into anyone's affairs.'

'Mr Metcalf,' the detective began, 'I came because I've got some information and it might be important. So I needed to tell you urgently, rather than wait for notes to pass around.' George Sugden also had another reason. He doubted whether Lem would pay him the full amount, and reckoned he wouldn't risk a blazing row at work.

'Information? That quick? You can't have had that hard a job finding out about her if you're back so soon.'

'Believe me, it was hard, Mr Metcalf. I've traced her to Lancashire and Cheshire, and a lot of work has been involved.'

'Go on then, tell me about it.'

'I'll not only tell you about it, Mr Metcalf, but I've written a full report. You'll have that on completion of all payments.'

'All right, but it had better be good. I'll not give a penny till I know you've come up with the goods.'

'You needn't worry, Mr Metcalf. I think you'll be more than pleased.'
Lem relaxed slightly, leaned back and lit a cigar. He didn't offer one to
George Sugden. 'I first made general enquiries in the Bradford area,
discreet and careful. I know a man in the haulage business, and he put me
on to a wagon driver who works for Smith's.'

'Hey, I hope you're not stirring it up with Smith's.'

'No, no. This man didn't ask any questions, and he was well paid for
what he did. He got his information by other means.'

'He nicked it, you mean.'

George slowly nodded. 'He's been in prison but Smith's don't know,
so he's not going to blab anything or he'd get the sack. Anyway, I asked
him to find out about the work she did, accounting and bookkeeping. He
was able to supply me with a list of firms she'd worked for before she
disappeared, and he also managed to purloin a photograph of her. That
was very useful. You're right, she's a good-looking lass.'

Lem smiled. He was already quite impressed with the down-at-heel
little man in front of him. He didn't seem as stupid as he'd first thought.

'I didn't enquire with any of the Bradford firms she worked for,' the
detective continued. 'Too close to home. It might arouse suspicion or get
back to her father. There are too many friends together in high places, you
understand.'

'Quite right there. Too much business and pallying behind closed
doors in this city.'

'So I visited some other firms a bit further out, mostly small mills and
businesses, Huddersfield, Ossett, Heckmondwike. Places like that. Found
she'd packed up work for them last spring and hadn't been seen since.
There were a couple of firms in Manchester on the list, so on the off
chance I took the train over there, gave them a visit and asked a few
questions. Pretended I owned a small firm who needed the bookkeeping
checked out, and I'd heard she was very good. I got nothing with one firm
but the other came up trumps.'

'She's in Manchester, then,' interrupted Lem.

'No, not Manchester. She had to finish checking off some accounts
after she'd left Bradford, and she arrived there on the Liverpool train. The
manager met her at the station. Now this firm has an associate company,
Morgan's in Bootle, and she was recommended to them.'

'So she's in Liverpool?'

'Not precisely. I went down there last week. I managed to get friendly
with one of the clerks. Had a few drinks. Money changed hands. He told
me she'd done some accounts work with them for a few months. Called
herself Mrs Adams. They were impressed with her. She sorted out a lot of
their bookkeeping problems. They were sorry when she had to give up.'

'Give up? You mean she's moved on again?'

'No. She had to give up on account of her condition.'

'Her . . . So that's why she did a flit. Got one in the oven and didn't want to face the music.'

'And I got an address. It's on the other side of the river in Wallasey. So I stayed on. A small private hotel isn't cheap over there in the holiday season. And I've tracked her down.'

Lem's face was a picture of concentration, curiosity and utter delight. He sat there spellbound, like a child listening to his favourite story. 'I dug a bit further. Seems as if the baby died, but she's still living there with her bloke, pretending that they're married, calling themselves Mr and Mrs Walter Adams. He's a tall, fair-haired bloke, smart dresser, travelling salesman for that big soap firm round there. Now what is it? Hudson's? No . . .'

'Field's bloody soapflakes,' whispered Lem. His face had turned as white as the chart on the wall behind him. 'And I, stupid bugger that I am, thought he'd drowned himself 'cos I threatened to tell his wife's family.' It seemed for a minute as if he had been drained of life. His arms appeared stuck to the desk in front of him and he sat rigid in his chair, staring past the detective into a world of his own. George wondered whether to escape. After all, he didn't want to be involved in the death of a client, especially if he was the only witness or suspect. Then he thought of summoning help, but before he had made his mind up colour returned to the ashen face before him. Lem slowly withdrew a flask from his pocket. One swig was followed by another, and the erstwhile corpse returned to life.

'The crafty sod,' Lem whispered, almost to himself, 'and her too!' He focused again on George Sugden. 'Thank you very much, Mr Sugden. Now let's see. How much do I owe you? Ah yes, ten pounds more and worth every penny.' He withdrew the money from his bulging wallet and received the thin typed report in exchange, before showing the detective to the door with an undue haste. 'And here's something for a few drinks tonight. You've deserved them. You'll get my recommendation any time, and my opinion goes a long way in this city.'

George was relieved. He had not had to fight to get his money, and there was a tip as well. He could pay off his protectors and have a bit left for the next few months. Things did not look too bad after all. 'If you want to contact them yourself, or her family does, you'll have to hurry up. By all accounts they'll be on a ship to America before the next few weeks are out.'

Lem's delight turned to shock, and then worry. This was something he didn't want to hear.

Chapter Eleven

I'll give that detective his due, Madge. He didn't look up to much but he's good, very good. He's got contacts all over, knows how to get information out of people, and how to bribe them when he can't.'

The tea shop was quite empty but Madge felt uncomfortable. It was Lem's idea to meet that Saturday in Harrogate. Although the café was not on Station Parade or Happy Valley, where all the world strolled and took afternoon tea, there was still a risk. Harrogate was not Manchester or Liverpool: it was still too near to home. And she knew his agenda. An afternoon out might become a suggested overnight stay next time. And their affair was finished as far as she was concerned. As personal secretary to Mr Brown, she was of too high a status to get herself mixed up in a sordid little affair with an older married man, especially one employed by one of Brown Muff's competitors. She feared she might be risking too much, yet Lem was tempting her with new information. The chance to get revenge on that pretty young trollop who had spilled the beans on her own misdeeds was too much to miss.

'Who'd have believed it?' she whispered. 'Making up a plan like that. Getting people to think he'd drowned and then running off to set up home with her as man and wife. It takes some gumption.'

'Well, we have 'em now,' interrupted Lem. 'Faking a death, fraud, abandoning his family, perhaps even bigamy.'

'The police would have a field day,' she gloated. 'The trial would be in all the papers – the *Bradford Argus*, the *Yorkshire Post*. It might even make the national press.'

'No, wait! There may be time for that later, but I think a bit of

75

personal satisfaction is due first. After all, finding all this out has cost us a bit, me in particular.'

A bell tinkled on the door as an elderly couple entered the teashop. Madge turned her head away and spoke in a low voice. 'If I know what you're thinking, Lem Metcalf, that's criminal. Blackmail. We could end up in jail as well.'

'No chance. Just a one-off, then let them fly away to America. Then we let the police know, anonymous of course. They wouldn't dare admit they were being blackmailed, and then when the scandal does come out they've gone. Their reputations are shot to pieces. They won't dare ever come back.'

'I'll give you this, Lem, you've got a right cunning and twisted mind.'

'But we've got to cover our tracks.' He paused while the waitress passed on her way to serve the couple at the other side of the room. 'I'll get an accommodation address, one of those little shops up the Manchester Road. They asks no questions and says nowt to anyone, the police included.'

'How much do we ask?' she whispered, her voice rising with tension and excitement. The thought of doing something illegal and with a hint of risk appealed. Her staid, dull life had been turned upside down in the last two years and she had got the taste for adventure and danger, though not if it meant sharing a bed with the stout, whiskery man opposite.

'Twenty-five pounds? Should cover what I've spent on this lark plus a bit over. Best not be too greedy. It'll frighten them, but not too much. If I know him, he'll have planned things out, put a bit aside for when they reach America. And they'll have been selling up as well. They still might have something to tide them over, but it'll make things a bit harder.'

'Make it thirty, Lem, and that'll really get them on their uppers.'

Lem nodded. 'All we need to do is write a letter. What do you think I should put in it?'

'Leave that to me, Lem. I'll write, woman to woman. Though she won't know which woman it is.' Madge chuckled. 'I'll think of something. I can make it more subtle. If you wrote it Walter might recognise your writing, and that would be dangerous. No, this might shift the blame, widen the field, make her think it could be anyone from Ledger's who's cottoned on. Teach her not to have blabbed about us.'

Lem sat wide-eyed with admiration. 'I'll give it to you, Madge, you're a clever lass. We make a reyt good pair when we're working together, whatever you say.'

'I'll want that address. We'd better get on with this quick, before them two flit quicker than we expect. I'll give you a copy of the letter, but for God's sake hide it with your life. And I'll have five pound on account out of this. I saw a lovely new dress at Belle Madame on Regent Parade.'

'I'll come round with you and pay for it myself,' suggested Lem. Then perhaps we could stay at the Clarendon for a few drinks and . . .'

'And nothing, you daft thing,' she whispered. 'The last thing we need is to be seen together. I want you on the next train back to Bradford.'

* * *

The letter dropped on to the doormat. It was the only one that day. The letterbox clanged shut and the sound of footsteps receded down the path. She walked down the hallway and picked up the envelope. It was addressed to her. She was surprised, not expecting a reply so soon, if at all. Hannah was relieved she had got to it first. With luck no-one else would have heard the postman. She tucked the letter inside her dress and made her way to the bedroom. Rosie was doing a jigsaw with Thomas in the back parlour. Their mother was out shopping with Agnes. Nancy was about her church business. Only Mary Ackroyd and Susan, the servant, were in the house, and as long as the children were quiet the grumpy matriarch wouldn't bother them.

Hannah found her favourite spot on the bedroom window sill, where she could peer out and see what was happening in the world of Wakefield Road. As ever her sketchbook was at her side, so she could capture any scene, character or happening that took her eye. She snuggled into the corner and carefully took out the letter, sliding her fingers between the flap and body of the envelope and making a rough tear. She took out the sheaf of paper, folded the envelope and put it into the pocket in her apron. Had her message reached its intended target? Would the reply be from Gideon? Was it too much to hope that he was the right one? She could hardly wait . . .

The door burst open. She only just had time enough to slide the letter underneath her. 'Hannah, this jigsaw is ever so hard. We're really stuck. Can you come and give us a hand?'

'I'm just in the middle of a sketch. The bread man's cart and horse. It'll be gone down the street in a few minutes.'

'You can finish it when he comes along tomorrow,' pleaded Rosie. 'You're so good at jigsaws. You can pick things out that me and Tom can't see.'

'Tomorrow's Sunday, you nincompoop. He doesn't deliver on Sundays. I'd have to wait another week. Ask Susan to help you.'

'I can't do that. Nana Ackroyd would be ever so cross if she found out.' Flattery had not worked. She gave her big sister a hard stare. 'What are you up to? There's nothing in your sketchbook.'

'Looking and thinking about it. If you tried to do that you wouldn't have to ask me to help you with your jigsaws. Now go away and don't stick your nose in other people's business.'

Rosie stamped her foot, stuck her tongue out at her sister and departed quickly, slamming the door behind her. She expected to hear Hannah's footsteps close behind her and, if she didn't get down the stairs quickly, to get a box on the ears. But there was none. She returned to the parlour, gave up the jigsaw, much to Thomas's disappointment, and found a book to read.

'What are you children up to?' Mary Ackroyd's shrill voice echoed round the house. 'What a row! Don't you have any feelings for your grandmother and her nerves? When your mother's back you'll have a piece of my mind and hers.'

The house was silent again. Hannah picked up the notepaper and began to read. She was surprised: although there were a few spelling mistakes, on the whole it was well written. Despite his circumstances this Gideon had learnt to read and write.

> Dear Hannah,
> Thank you for your letter. I'm glad your friend Debra told you about me. Since my parents died three years ago I've been in this place and life hasn't been very good. We get very little food and if you complayn you get shut up in the tower. It's a little room up a fliyt of stairs. You sometimes get beaten and nobody's ever nice to you. They call you charity kids. It was different when my mum and dad were alive. They were good to me. It was lovely. We weren't rich but we were happy. We lived in a little house in Leeds. My dad was an engine driver on the railways. I would have loved to be one lik him. I liked your picture of the train. That was great. I liked the rabitt too. I hop he doesn't get run over by the train. I would love a rabit or cat or some animal to care for. Have you got any pets?
> My mum and dad died of diptheerea when a lot of people got it. Then I found out they wasn't my real mum and dad. They adopted me when I was a baby. I still loved them though and I miss them. I found out my real mum was from Bradford but nothing else about her. The rest of the family wouldn't have owt to do with me cos I was adopted so they sent me here and here I am all alone. Don't worry about writing

to me. The people who run this place don't read any letters. To be honest I don't think they can read and write that good and they think if we've got someone to write to and get letters from then we'll be less trubble. I think your idea of finding me a nice home here in Bradford is just what I want. I'd miss a few frends here but life is so awful, I don't think I can stand it for much longer. I feel I want to run away even work in a factory or as a servant for some family. Write to me again. You cheered me up no end with your letter.

Your friend Gideon

Hannah rested the letter on her lap and stared out through the window at the horizon of houses, factories and trees. She cried. Only a few small drops fell on to her dress, but deep inside she was hurting. How unfair life could be, that a boy of twelve, who had to be her cousin, should put up with so much misery in his life, tragedy far worse than hers and deprivation that made her family's hardship insignificant. What was a reduction in sweets and treats in comparison with being half-starved? What was the loss of your father, even, when you still had your mother, sisters, brother, grandmother and aunt to love you? Gideon had no one: just a couple of friends and a letter to comfort him. And yet here was the mother who had given him away for adoption, as well as his aunts and uncles, his cousins and even a grandmother, who might grow to love him. It all seemed so unfair.

She read the letter again, more slowly this time, taking in every word, imagining, thinking, planning. It had started to rain and the drops started to tap on the large window panes. The irregular staccato music of the pattering rain, one moment intense, the next lighter, caused her to move to the bed, to avoid leaning against the rapidly forming jewels of condensation. As she got up she noticed her mother opening the gate and struggling with the impetuous Agnes, who was keen to get up the path and to the shelter of the house.

Hannah thought for a minute then put the letter back in the envelope, looking round the room for a place she might hide it. Too late: there were already footsteps on the stairs: the excited, scurrying steps of a small boy followed by his sister's slower, more measured tread. Hannah opened the middle drawer and stuffed the envelope between her clothes. At the first opportunity she had to find a more permanent place to hide it, away from her mother's and Rosie's prying eyes. She was just in time. As she closed the drawer Tom burst in, closely followed by Rosie.

'Mother met Grandma Harriet in the village, and she's invited us to tea,' said Rosie. 'That means jelly and some of those lovely jam tarts she makes. I think she's got a surprise for us. It might be a toy for Tom and Agnes and new books for us two. Isn't that nice?'

Hannah smiled. The altercation with her sister was forgotten. 'If you want, as it's raining and we can't go outside, I'll help you both with that jigsaw,' she said.

* * *

'Is that another letter you're writing, Deborah?'

'Yes, Miss Hannah. I got a reply from May. Weren't very well written, though. Lots of spelling mistakes and funny words. I reckon she could do with some of your magic help.'

'You haven't asked me for any words, though.'

'Nah. I've got to try it on my own. And Miss Nancy's lent me her dictionary. She even showed me how to find words, quick like.'

'I reckon there'll come a time when you won't need my help at all. You'll be able to read and write as well as anyone.'

'Yes, but I'll still be your friend, won't I? And talk to you and help you choose the books. I don't want that to stop.'

Hannah smiled. 'Of course not. And what if sometimes I can't help on the bookstall? Do you think if I asked my grandma she'd let you take my place?'

Deborah's face was a picture of pleasure. Her smile was wide, although there were one or two teeth missing. The eyes, once so pale and insignificant, were large, dark and bright. Little wrinkles of sheer happiness appeared around them. She gave a little yelp of delight. 'Waaw, that would be great. Do you think she would? I'd help all the children, like you do, keep the stall tidy, choose books, make sales, give change. I'm good with money.' She closed her eyes, and for a few seconds was in her own, sublime, happy world. 'I'd love to be a shop girl. No working ten hours a day in noisy, filthy mills, no scrubbin' and moppin' and livin' below stairs. I'd be standin', no, *standing*, behind a counter in a clean white blouse and smart black dress and making polite conversation. Would sir care to try this? Or that does suit madam.'

'No,' said Hannah in a disdainful voice. 'I think I prefer that skirt in a blue. Fetch me one immediately.'

'Yes , madam, of course, madam. Just as madam wishes.' They laughed at the little scene they had acted out. 'That would be the perfect job for me, and if I did get it I'd have you to thank for teaching me to read and write proper, no, properly ey mean.'

Hannah laughed at her friend's attempt at a posh voice. Where was the shy, frightened mouse she had met just a few months ago? Here was a girl with spirit, wit, a ridiculous sense of humour, at least when Charlotte and some of the other girls weren't around. What Charlotte had once said was true. Hannah had felt sorry for her, that was why she had befriended her, but not any more. The new Deborah, or perhaps the real Deborah, was her true friend. 'Don't close your letter yet,' she confided. 'I've got another one to write.'

'You've got something to send to Gideon, then? Told you he was a charmer, didn't I? Reckon you're stuck on him a bit.'

Hannah made no reply, but blushed slightly.

Deborah winked. 'It's not a love letter is it?'

Hannah pretended to be even more embarrassed. Her friend's giggles were infectious and she had caught them. Could she tell Deborah the real reason for the letter, and her plan? No, not yet. She wandered off into the side room of the church, which was used as an office and store room. She knew the cupboard where her aunt kept the writing paper and envelopes: Nancy wouldn't mind her taking some. She opened the cupboard and took two sheets and an envelope, but the latter was marked with a brown water stain. Lifting the pile to see if others were also marked, she found three sheets of penny stamps underneath, eighteen on each sheet. She stood for a few seconds, thinking, then slipped one sheet of stamps between the envelope and paper. With luck it would not be missed. She knew now what she was going to do, and how she would help the unhappy boy. She felt both guilty and yet strangely justified by her action.

Hannah began to write.

> Dear Gideon,
>
> Thank you for your letter. I didn't write back straight away because I wanted to think carefully about what you wrote. It upset me to hear that you are unhappy and are not treated well by those people at the orphanage. It made me cry when I heard that you once had a happy home but that your mother and father both died. I have no father, he died at the seaside, but I have my mother, brother, sisters and grandmothers. I also have my Aunt Nancy who runs that home I told you about for lost girls here in Bradford where Deborah is staying. But my aunt, Pastor Robinson and his wife and Mrs Mullarkey (she's the cook and cleaner) are all very kind to the girls. They are all well fed and clothed and they find them jobs with people

who are kind and understanding to them. I'm sure if you came to Bradford, my aunt or Pastor Robinson could do the same for you. Obviously you couldn't live at the hostel with the girls, but they might be able to find a home for you where people could be kind to you and you could get a nicer job.

I have no money to help you make the journey but these stamps might help to pay for a train fare and buy you some food for your journey. There's one shilling and sixpence worth there. It should be enough. If you get to Bradford don't come to my home. I work for my grandma on her bookstall every Saturday, so if you get here meet me there. It's called Clough's Book and Magazine Emporium and it's in Kirkgate Market in the middle of Bradford. Give yourself another name, Peter perhaps, just in case they come looking for you. I promise we will do our best to make you happy again and with luck you'll meet new friends and kind people and life will be much better.

Your good friend Hannah

Hannah folded the stamps in the middle of the letter and sealed it inside the envelope. She had done wrong, she knew that, but she was trying to right a greater wrong, and if she succeeded it would make things a lot better. It was at times like this that she really missed her father. If only he was around to confide in, to guide her. He would have known what was the right thing to do.

'You finished already, Miss Hannah?'

'Please, Deborah, if we're to be true friends call me Hannah.'

'Right, Mm . . . Hannah. You know, no matter how good I got writing letters I don't think I could ever write as good as you.'

Hannah popped her envelope inside Deborah's, and with a sly smile put a warning finger over her lips. Deborah giggled and did the same. It was their secret.

Chapter Twelve

My dear friend,' the letter began, 'I am writing to warn you of some danger you might be in.' If receiving a handwritten letter came as a surprise to Eliza, the first sentence turned it to a deep anxiety. She looked at the envelope again, and to her horror realised it had a Bradford postmark. She picked up the letter again and read on.

I am afraid someone has discovered your whereabouts and wants to do you harm. They also know of your sham marriage to a man named Walter, the manner of his disappearance from his wife and family and that you gave birth to his child. I was indeed sorry to hear that it soon departed this earth. I know how much pain and suffering this must have caused you.

It was only with some difficulty that I have been able to dissuade this person of evil intent not to go to the police. After all, faking a death, false claims, fraud and perhaps bigamy are all serious crimes and could result in jail terms for you both. If you add to that the embarrassment of a public trial with all the shameful details being published in the newspapers, I am sure you must realise you stand in great danger. Fortunately I have persuaded this person not to

inform the police for the present. It has taken a
great deal of persuasion to do this and a promise
to them of a substantial financial inducement. I
don't think it would be untoward in asking you
for the sum of thirty pounds to prevent this
malicious person from wrecking your life and
that of your 'husband'.

There was a sudden knock at the door. Eliza stuffed the letter behind a
cushion and hurried to open it. Mrs O'Connor's smiling face greeted her as
usual. It was all Eliza could do to keep herself under control, and not burst
into tears before her neighbour.

'You'se all right my love?' she asked, noticing the pale complexion and
red eyes.

'Oh, it's just that you caught me napping. I've been tired recently, and
the business of getting ready for our voyage must be catching up on me.'

'Don't you worry your pretty little head about it, my duck. My
cousins in Ireland went over five years ago, and they're doing very well.
And you two being both that clever and with so much energy, you'se
bound to succeed and do well. Anyway, I've come about those table-cloths
you've got, the ones you said you'se hardly ever used.'

'Oh yes, I've got them upstairs on the blanket box. Do step in. I'll get
them for you now.' Panic had set in. For once Eliza felt she could hardly
cope. The contents of the letter were racing around in her head, and as she
attempted to make sense of them here she was talking about table-cloths.
After a minute she returned with them and thrust them into Mrs
O'Connor's arms.

'And how much will you be wanting for them?'

'Oh, I don't know. You think of a fair price and pay me tomorrow.
Would you excuse me? I need to take some powders for this headache.'

'My poor dear, I can see you aren't that well. Don't worry, I'll give you
a good price. Wouldn't want to rob a lovely couple like you two, who need
every penny they've got for the start of a new life.'

The door closed. Eliza retrieved the letter from behind the cushion.

I would caution against any rash action on your
part. After all it was such an action, in ensuring
the whole of Ledger's knew of a certain liaison,
that led to the suspicions regarding your
disappearance.

I would also advise prompt action with
regard to sending the financial 'compensation'.
Delay might make this person think again. I

enclose a name and address to send the money to. Do not try to have it traced. I have to keep my whereabouts and identity secret. It is only an accommodation address.

Yours sincerely,

A well wisher and friend.

Addressee: P. Jones, 236 Manchester Road, Bradford, Yorkshire

For a full half-hour Eliza remained hunched over the kitchen table, sobbing. Her tears dripped down on to the table-cloth making dark spots on the white lace. Sadness turned to despair, to anger, to incredulity. How could this have happened? And if someone had found out about them, so could the police, even without the information from this blackmailer.

She was in no doubt that the writer was indeed the blackmailer. There was no other 'person'. That was just a front from someone determined on an act of revenge, but who? Maude Naylor would surely not do such a thing. They had been friends for many years. And yet friendship could change, turn sour. If Maude had done her job well, and told all Ledger's about the affair between Lem and Madge, then perhaps she might have let slip the source of her information. If so it could be anyone: a shop girl once envious of her position and popularity, a spurned lover, the jealous wife or girlfriend of an admiring employee, even Lem Metcalfe in an act of revenge. She was about to examine the letter again when there came a knock at the door and a shout of 'Milko, milko'. In all this confusion she had forgotten to put out her jug.

'Mornin', my little love.' The leering face greeted her, eyeing her carefully from head to toe. 'Got up a bit late to put something out, eh?' His disappointment at seeing her fully clothed was evident. Eliza felt uncomfortable, as she always did, facing the ogling eyes and suggestive banter of this young man. No doubt he had his way with a few female customers, particularly if the bill needed to be paid.

'I'll pay you now for the month ahead.'

'All right by me, darling.'

She hurried back to the front room to find her purse and could feel the eyes following her, examining every step, every movement and every part of her body. Thank God, with luck it would be the last time she would ever see this abhorrent man. She would not tell him that they were moving. Let him find out for himself.

'Thank you, darling,' he said on her return.

The gloating eyes followed her until she slammed the door. That was all she needed on a terrible day like this. Eliza picked up the letter again and examined it more carefully. It was definitely a woman's hand, a woman's style, unless it had been deliberately crafted to deceive. It spoke of an immediate reply. Did the writer know they were emigrating to America? Did she want to get some money from them before they were out of reach? If so, it would be wise to be prompt and not invite retribution. There was only one thing to do. She would have to use the twenty pounds, their America money, which was stuffed in an envelope inside the kitchen clock. If Walter's final bonus was generous, and if they were able to sell most of their household items they would replace most of it, and she could make up the remainder of the blackmailer's demand from her own meagre savings.

Eliza carefully replaced the envelope in the back of the clock. By the afternoon she had thirty pounds. Purchasing a stout envelope, she addressed it, wrapped the money in a folded piece of paper and posted it at the main post office in Wallasey.

On Walter's return she complained of a headache and cold, to explain her pale appearance and red eyes and ensure that contact was at a minimum that evening. After his dinner he remained at the kitchen table reading the newspaper, while she sat alone in the front room with her thoughts and retired to bed early. But she couldn't sleep that night. She dreaded another letter from Bradford dropping through the letter box.

Before he turned out the dim gas light and went to bed, Walter took a sovereign from his pocket. He lifted the wooden case clock off the kitchen mantelpiece and opened the small brass door at the back, lifted out the key, then searched with his fingers for the envelope. It had slid further down under the mechanism. That was strange. He pulled it out, and to his surprise found it empty. He thought for a moment. Eliza had said it was too obvious a spot to risk hiding such a large sum as twenty pounds. No doubt she had found a better place. He wouldn't bother her now. He would ask her where she had hidden it in the morning.

Walter wondered what it would be like in New York. How long would they stay there? Where would they change into dollars the money they had saved? What kind of job would he get? They said it was easy to set up business there. That would suit him, being his own master and not being at everyone's beck and call, making his own decisions, being responsible for his own future. If the final bonus Field's had promised him was generous, he might be able to set up straight away, once they had reached California and assessed the opportunities. Or perhaps that wouldn't be such a good thing. Best to get a job, any job to start with, then get a better one. Mr Fieldhouse had promised him a written reference, and a good one too. He could use that. Possibly try the soap giants Procter and Gamble for a sales position, or that new washing machine company, Acme Electric. That was the market for the future. Just think: American women wouldn't have to dolly-peg their washing in a tub; they could let a machine do all the work for them. Now that was America, the land of the future!

Eliza still could not sleep. She lay awake, eyes wide open, with her body turned to the wall. She heard his footsteps on the landing, the bedroom door open, the splash of water in the bowl, the rustle of his nightshirt as he got ready for bed, the gentle creak of the springs and the slight lurch of the mattress.

'Won't kiss you tonight, my love. Don't want to get that cold of yours,' he murmured as much to himself as to her. His hand lay around her waist for a few seconds, slipped lazily down over her thigh, then moved away.

She pretended to be fast asleep but was still wondering. Had he checked the envelope? No, he would have woken her for sure. She remained awake with her thoughts, which became fears, and as she slipped deeper into the realms of unconsciousness they turned into silent nightmares. Eliza slept on until the first glint of light filled the curtains, then, half in slumber and half awake, resumed her contemplation. She was working out a plan. It was not a good plan but it might suffice. She was dreading his discovery, further letters, a heavy knock on the front door in the middle of the night. She would not sleep soundly until they were on that ship and over the horizon. What had seemed like a new beginning, a chance to put everything behind them, had turned into a nightmare, with a host of new dilemmas and problems.

She woke late. Walter was already dressed and boiling a kettle on the kitchen range. He made her a cup of tea, cooked two eggs and made some toast. She sat at the table looking at him with doleful eyes. How could she deceive him, when he was without doubt the most wonderful, considerate and loving husband in the world?

'I know you weren't happy with hiding the America money behind the clock,' he began, 'so come on, my dearest, where is it?'

She stared at him. 'I haven't.'

'But where is it?'

'You mean it's gone?'

'It's not there! Don't tease me, Eliza. It's not funny. It's not funny at all.'

'Oh my God! I told you it wasn't safe. People always hide things behind or inside clocks. And there were, yes, there were . . . two people in this kitchen yesterday, Mrs O'Connor and that milkman, you know, the one I don't like. I left both of them in the kitchen alone. I went upstairs when Mrs O'Connor was here, to fetch those table-cloths she was going to buy from us. And I went in the front room to find my purse to pay off that odious fellow.'

Walter's face turned pale. 'But that's the money for America. To keep us going when we get there. It could have helped us set up that business we dreamed about. What will we do?' He got up from the chair and vanished into the hallway, returning with his hat and coat on, and made his way to the back door.

'Where are you going, Walt?'

'To the police. It can't be Mrs O'Connor. She's given us so much to help us set up home, and she was kindness itself when Martha died. It must be that evil blackguard. He's had his lustful eyes on you since we moved in here, and he's taken some kind of revenge because you're one young woman who hasn't succumbed to his charm. I'm going to get him arrested.'

'You can't! Think, Walt. We can't bring in the police, risk being found out, identified. We can't throw away our future together for the sake of twenty pounds.'

Walter slumped into a chair, and buried his head in his hands. 'What will we do without that money?' he groaned. For a few minutes there was silence, except for the ticking of the clock, the empty clock.

'I know what I'll do,' Eliza whispered. 'I'll sell some of my dresses and hats. We'll go with half the things we intended, and pawn or advertise the rest. And then there's your final wages, your commission and the bonus you've been promised. If Field's are as good as their word that'll see us through. Some poor folks emigrate with little more than five pounds in their pockets. They find it hard but they survive. America's the land of opportunity. Your reference will stand you in good stead. You'll walk into a job easily, I'm sure.' She put her arms round his shoulders, devastated to see him in such despair.

Walter's spirits began to revive. He returned Eliza's embrace, and gradually a smile spread across his face. He rose, took off his coat and hat and put them on the kitchen table. For once she didn't mind, and didn't chide him as she sometimes did.

'Then when we get there,' she continued, 'we can raise the money before we go to California. Don't you see?'

'But I wanted us to go straight there. Set up a business, be my own boss. With you at my side.'

'With my help and contribution,' she interrupted. 'I'll throw myself into any enterprise as much as you. I want us to succeed as well.'

'We could make it big over there, I'm certain . . . You're right, Eliza. We can't risk it all by going to the police. Let that vile man have his money. And much good may it do him!' Walter put his arms round her. Her tears ran down his waistcoat. She would not raise her head to kiss him or look him straight in the eyes, but he didn't mind, or suspect why.

* * *

Walter felt justified in taking the money from Field Brothers. He had picked up his reference from the desk, and had noticed a key peeping from under the pile of papers. He knew it was the safe key. He had entered the manager's office angry, very angry. How he had managed to keep his temper he didn't know. Mr Fieldhouse had explained that they couldn't give him a final bonus, and because of the difficult situation even the sales commission had been drastically reduced. The excuses went over his head. 'Trade not as good as expected . . . Hudson's new product that's edging Fresh Toilet Soap off the shelves . . . Forty workers to be sacked, because of the slump in sales . . .' Mr Fieldhouse had wished Walter well for the future, handed over his final disappointing and inadequate salary envelope and thanked him for his efforts for the firm. He told him that it was a good reference, that it spoke well of his sales ability, his knowledge and expertise, his attitude and his prompt and tidy paperwork. He apologised again for the lack of bonus, and asked Walter to pick up the reference which he had left on his desk. When Walter walked into the office he found himself alone and very bitter. He knew it was wrong, but he had worked so hard for that bonus over the last few months. He was scared but strangely determined. Thirty pounds would not be missed for some time: there was over five hundred in that safe. And he would return the money he took, with interest, when they had made their start in America. On that, as much as anything, he was determined. The next day they would be setting sail, and by the time the loss came to light he would be on the high seas, or in another country over two thousand miles away.

He would not say anything to Eliza. She had gone through so much and still had so much to think about – making the final arrangements, disposing of the items they could not take with them, organising the wagon to the Pier Head, returning their keys to the landlord. He knew she was worried about the missing money from the clock. It had upset her terribly, so he had not dwelt upon it. She had reproached herself unnecessarily about its loss, and the less she knew of the thirty pounds for now the better.

Walter put the notes inside his pocket, locked the safe and returned the key to the desk. He stepped out of the office quietly, shutting the door behind him and walking straight out of the building, not saying a word to anyone. It would be the last he ever saw of Fresh Fields.

Chapter Thirteen

A summer mist hung over the river. As soon as the *Crocus* had chugged out into the middle, the grey buildings of the landing stage and the hotels and houses of Egremont quickly disappeared, and to the two figures gazing out over the port side of the small ferry it was as if they were already in the midst of a wide ocean. They held hands and looked out across the water into grey emptiness. Beside them their two trunks stood on the deck, where they had been deposited by the waggoners. To Walter and Eliza it was as if they were alone. The two hundred or so other passengers did not belong to their world, but were about their daily business, working in the shops, warehouses and offices of the great city or out on shopping trips; a few were even travellers themselves, going on by train or packet to their destinations.

The *Crocus* had drifted slightly in the ebbing tide, so that the first they saw of the other side were the warehouses and cranes of Stanley Dock, the strange six-sided dockers' clock and the overhead railway running behind. This seemed to give the little ship a reminder of where it should be heading, and it swung hard to the right. The engines rumbled into life, pushing it upstream against the strong river current which always flowed along the Liverpool side. It seemed determined to reach its destination, the Pier Head, and gave a sharp blast of its hooter, startling one or two unwary passengers. It awakened another two or three ships' sirens into life, like an echoing chorus, but not the leviathan resting at the seaward end of the Pier Head. This loomed into view suddenly, a black wall of steel appearing out of the mist, topped by two enormous funnels and three even taller masts.

Eliza squeezed Walter's hand as they caught the name *Oceanic* painted on the white strip of the top bow. The vessel dwarfed the tiny ferry, and they had to crane their necks almost vertically to see the excited faces looking down from almost forty feet above.

'That looks like our ship,' she whispered.

'That's definitely it. And in just over five hours we'll be sailing on it all the way to America.'

She turned. 'No regrets?'

'There'll always be some,' he whispered. 'But this is the way forward, for us.'

The *Crocus* wallowed and rocked as it edged into the side of the floating dock. Its engines rumbled and roared again to keep it steady in the turbulent water, then died as soon as strong hands had secured the ropes to the wooden bollards. The passengers rushed off down the gangway intent on their business. Walter followed them, and soon secured the services of a couple of burly porters, who despite the cool of the morning glistened with sweat on their brows from their exertions. They hauled the trunks off the ferry and on to a hand cart, the second trunk with some difficulty.

Eliza smiled. 'Please be careful with that one,' she begged. 'It's got some delicate things inside.'

'Seems like you'se got half of Birkenhead an' all, luv,' quipped the smaller of the two porters as they laid it carefully on the cart. 'You'se not goin' into the export business is you?' She smiled again, having come to like the Scouse humour: it was witty, but not unkind.

'Don't worry, my luv, I'll look after your stuff,' replied his mate, obviously taken with Eliza's beauty and charm. 'An' if he don't, I'll break him into as many pieces as are in that flippin' trunk. Now it was the *Oceanic* you'se goin' on?'

Walter nodded. 'That's the one. The biggest passenger ship in the world.'

'That's right,' replied the smaller man, 'but from what I hear not for too long, wack.'

'What do you mean?'

'That Mr Ismay, he's got three more lined up, bigger than this one. First one should be coming over to the Pool next year. It'll be launched in Belfast in a few months, then a further six months fittin' out. And there'll be no steerage on these new ones. Even the third class passengers will have cabins. Mind, I do hear they might be asked to help with the stoking.'

'And they'll soon be so big they'll have to build the Pier Head across to Ireland,' joked his mate.

They had reached the ship's embarkation point, and by now all four were laughing. They deposited the trunks alongside the gangway and Walter paid them off.

The smaller man gave Eliza a wink. 'If you'se wants to push him over half-way across, then you'se can always come back for me. Have a good journey and I hope you'se does well.' He and his companion waved goodbye as a young officer in an immaculate white uniform approached.

'If you're ready to board, sir, madam, you can do so now. I'll arrange to have your trunks taken to your cabin. It may take some time but don't worry, we don't sail for five hours yet. Please have your papers ready for inspection when you arrive on board.'

Walter took some folded sheets from his inside pocket. 'Oh, Eliza, there's something missing. We must have left it behind.'

'What is it? Surely not your passport or ticket? We checked them before we left.'

'No, no. It's that job reference. But I'm sure I've got time to go back and get it.'

The ship's officer nodded. 'We don't sail until three. I see you lived in Wallasey. Providing you get back to embark before one, there should be no problem.'

* * *

Gideon stared down the aisle at the girl by the bookstall as she leaned over to help some younger children choose from a small pile of books. She had a thin, freckly face. You wouldn't call her beautiful but there was a happiness in that face that made her instantly appealing. She was a bit taller than him, and tidily dressed – but not in a girlish, soppy manner: no frills, pink flowers, ribbons or bows. He liked that. But could she help him? Would she be true to her word and get him a nice home, where he could start his life again, without being starved, locked up or humiliated? Respect and a little kindness, that's all he wanted. He didn't even ask to be loved. She looked all right. The way she spoke to those little ones showed that. He stopped in the aisle, behind a crowd at Hargreaves Glass and China Fancies, not daring to approach.

There he was. She had looked up for a second and knew it was him. He didn't look as Deborah had described him: he looked scared and forlorn. His clothes didn't fit him very well, and they were obviously well-worn hand-me-downs. But it was definitely him: thin, wavy blond hair, fresh face, bright, blue eyes. And he was staring at her. She collected the two pence from the little girl, gave her the book, smiled at her, then wandered slowly down the aisle. She led him away from Charlie's stall, but looked at him the whole time. He bowed his head, not daring to meet her gaze.

'Gideon?'

'Yes. I thought you said . . .'

'Let's call you Peter, then. I'm Hannah.'

'Nice to meet you, Hannah. Look, I'm sorry if I surprised you. I know I've turned up unannounced like, but . . .'

'You were desperate to get away. You couldn't stand any more.'

'You're right. In a way it were easier for t'others I left behind. Some of 'em have known nowt else but t'orphanage.'

'But when you've had a family, one that loved you,' Hannah whispered, 'when you've lost them, it's different.'

'How do you know?'

'Well, I've still got my family, but . . .'

'Your father died. I remember you telling me in your letter.'

'You look cold.'

'And I'm hungry too. I haven't had a bite hardly fer two days.'

'But the stamps. I sent you those stamps in the letter.'

He turned away suddenly, silent and embarrassed. 'I couldn't go without doing summat for t'others. They'd have to put up with all the fuss and trouble when they found I'd gone. So I got them some food with it. Sneaked out and bought cakes, pasties, pies. We had a party, like. Didn't tell them where I was going, though.'

'But how did you get here with no money?'

'I got a lift in a barge to start with, from Leeds basin all the way to Rodley. Then I walked again through a few villages. Farsley, Thornbury. Then down a long straight road into Bradford. I've worn a hole in my shoes. Started off at six o'clock this morning.'

Hannah took a silver threepenny bit from her apron pocket. 'Have this. Go over to Joe's café at the side of the market, to the right of the main door. Say Hannah from the bookstall sent you, and that she says it's the best place in the market. He'll give you a mug of tea and a sugary bun, and will probably throw in a pie as well.'

Gideon didn't know what to say. 'Thanks,' he mumbled.

'Wait there until I come to you,' Hannah ordered. 'Both Grandma and Aunt Nancy know I've been writing to a boy in an orphanage called Peter. Aunt Nancy will be here later to deliver some books. I'll tell them you've turned up unannounced, that you were beaten or locked up and starved, and that you were so unhappy you decided to run away. You can say that I told you in my letter I worked here on Saturdays, and so you came here to ask for help.'

'Got it,' Gideon replied, and for the first time he gave her a wink and one of his cheeky smiles.

* * *

'So you're Peter.' The tall dark-haired lady smiled at him.

He hadn't seen such a kind smile since his mother's three years ago, after he had brought in the coal to keep the room warm when she was so ill and couldn't do it herself.

'Yes, miss, that's me all right.'

His shy grin immediately endeared him to Nancy. She could see behind the half-smiling face and sparkling eyes that there was a propensity for innocent mischief, but he had such an endearing charm that she couldn't resist him. 'I think I might be able to help you. From what Hannah says, you seem to have had such an unhappy time at that terrible orphanage. I know Pastor Robinson from our Mission church has the addresses of some families who might help in such a situation. They are people who will care for you but will also employ you. You needn't worry: they are all Christian families who would never be unkind to you and will always be fair. But you must do your best for them. Will that help you out of your troubles for the present?'

'Ooh yes, miss. That would be smashing. I don't mind hard work. I'll do my best. For a warm bed, and some decent food and a kind word or two, I'd never let you down. Thank you, Miss Nancy, and you too, Hannah. You've been a real friend.'

'I'll be going back to the church and seeing Pastor Robinson to sort things out for you. You can come down and see me after three o'clock. Hannah can tell you how to get there. I've no doubt she'll draw you a map, with everything you can imagine on it.'

Both children began to laugh.

'No rabbits on this one,' he joked, 'not in the middle of a big city like this. They'd end up as rabbit pie.'

Nancy descended the steps outside Kirkgate Market and made her way to Silsbridge Lane. There were the usual insulting comments from the drunks outside the public house, but they didn't bother her. Her Christian charity was helping a young boy out of his troubles, and a lovely boy he was at that.

* * *

Eliza woke. A dull rumble was shaking the whole cabin. She had been so weary, having hardly slept the night before, because of the excitement of the day ahead and because of the endless packing. She reached out to touch the sleeping figure beside her. There was no one there. She looked at the bunk. The sheets and coverlet were flat, untouched. No one had lain there. Surely it wasn't time for sailing? She got up and poked her head out into the corridor.

'Steward?'

'Yes, ma'am.'

'What time is it, please?'

He took a pocket watch from his white waistcoat pocket. 'Three o'clock, ma'am.'

'But that's sailing time.'

'Yes, ma'am. You can tell that from the sound of the engines. They're not up to full power yet. They're idling, to help the tugs pull us into the channel and out over the Bar. Then you'll see what a fine ship she is. She can make nineteen knots when we're at full . . . What is it, ma'am? Are you ill?'

Eliza had turned pale. Panic was surging inside her, taking the strength from her legs and turning her stomach into a sharp churning ache. 'My husband! Where is he? Where is he?'

'He'll be around the ship, ma'am, watching us pull away, waving goodbye to Old England.'

'No, no. He had to leave the ship to collect something. He was going to be back by one o'clock. The officer said there would be no problem. I embarked, and we agreed to meet at one o'clock in our cabin.'

'Don't worry, madam. A whole crowd came on board at that time: late arrivals, last-minute tickets and all the steerage passengers. We don't let them on until after twelve, and there's seven hundred of them. Then they have to check them all out and allocate cabins and spaces below. It can take up to four hours sometimes, long after we're under way. He'll have to wait his turn with them.'

Eliza heaved a sigh of relief. The steward must be right. She remembered how long it had taken that morning when she had come on board, and one of the trunks hadn't arrived at the cabin even now. She recalled waving to Walter from the gangway as he dashed down the quay towards the Wallasey ferries. The job reference *was* an important piece of paper. How had they managed to leave it behind? It might be the key to their success in America, despite the good bonus that Field's had given him. He would need a job at first, thanks to that blackmailer, whoever he or she was. But that was all behind her. From now on there would be no deceit, no lies. It was a new start to their lives and to their relationship and their marriage. Marriage! The word meant so much to her. It would secure her for ever the man she loved above all others.

The steward had finished his visit to the adjoining cabin and manoeuvred his way past with a laden tray. 'If you want, ma'am, you can come down to the purser's office with me and wait for him there. Or perhaps they'll have finished with the queue and he'll be on his way up. I'll call in and check for you.'

She smiled. He was such an obliging and charming fellow – and he had fallen under the spell of her smile, as all men did. She followed him down the stairs, along endless corridors, stepping carefully over bulkhead thresholds, and eventually they arrived at a large foyer. In front of her a wide staircase swept upwards, adorned with chandeliers, mirrors and sumptuous decoration. A sign at the bottom indicated it was for 'First Class Passengers Only'. She had seen it that morning when she registered at the purser's office, and had imagined herself one day walking down, to the first-class lounge or even the captain's table, dressed in all her finery. The foyer was full of people queuing into or emerging from the purser's office, where passenger registration was taking place. Some were being escorted by stewards to their waiting cabins, while other poorer and ill-dressed people, who carried their own meagre cases and bundles of possessions, were being hastily directed through a narrow doorway and down steep iron steps into steerage compartments in the bowels of the ship.

'What's your husband's name, and can you give me a description?' the eager steward asked.

'He's a tall fair-haired gentleman. He's called Walter.'

'Just wait a minute, ma'am. I'll go in and enquire.'

He vanished through double wooden doors into the office, skilfully weaving through the waiting crowds. Five long minutes later he returned. 'There is such a gentleman there,' he announced, 'and his name's Walter. I think your worries are over. He's at the head of the queue and should be out in a couple of minutes. If you don't mind, ma'am, I'll be on with my duties.' He hesitated a moment, waiting awkwardly at her side.

'Oh, wait a minute.' Eliza fumbled in her purse and eventually retrieved a sixpence which she handed over to him.

'Thank you, ma'am. I hope you both have a pleasant voyage.' He vanished through the crowd.

A tall fair-haired man emerged from the office. He had a ruddy, weather-beaten complexion and carried a scuffed and battered suitcase. His suit was obviously borrowed from someone else, as it was a size smaller than he was. He looked round the foyer, spied Eliza and wandered over to her. With excessive politeness he bowed. 'I really can't imagine why you want to meet me. I can't recall us ever having met, but it's Walter Flynn at your service, ma'am, from Tipperary. In Ireland, it is.'

'But you're not Walter . . .'

'Indeed I am, ma'am.'

He was not near enough nor quick enough to catch her as her legs collapsed underneath her, and her head hit the deck with a sickening thud.

* * *

Walter could not believe his eyes. He had retrieved the letter from the sideboard drawer, or rather from behind it, after first pulling the drawer out. It was only when he removed the envelope, now a bit creased but still serviceable, that he saw the other pieces of paper that had vanished over the low back lip of the drawer and into the depths beyond. Instinct told him to look through them in case there were any others that might prove useful in America. It was only when he read the third piece of paper that he sank down into a chair and drew a deep breath. The letter said it all, but it took him ten minutes and two slow readings to realise all its implications. Suddenly everything became clear. It was Eliza herself who had let the information slip about Lem and Madge Dobson. But why? Of course! She was pregnant, and she knew that they, well, he, would have to make a choice – that things couldn't go on as they had for many months. And she would have anticipated Lem's reaction: his threats to tell Annie's family, which would frighten her lover into her arms. Doubt and suspicion clouded his mind. He knew she loved him, that was never in doubt, but would she take steps like that to secure his love? How could she be so devious? How could he have been so gullible?

There was a knock at the door. He rose, went back through the kitchen to open it, and was confronted by the worried face of Mrs O'Connor. 'Whatever's the matter, Mr Adams? Why are you here? Where's Mrs Adams? What's wrong? Has anything happened?'

Walter realised that the curtain-twitchers didn't miss a thing on Albion Street. The news would be down the whole street by now, and half-way to New Brighton Tower. 'It's all right, Mrs O'Connor. There's nothing to worry about. Mrs Adams is on the ship. I just nipped back to find an important letter we left behind. See? It's here. I've found it. Fifteen minutes' walk to Egremont, a ferry back over and I'll be back on our ship within the hour. You can be sure of that.'

'You're sure it's all right?'

'Yes, certainly.'

'Then I'll leave you to your business. And best wishes to you both.'

'Thank you.'

Walter closed the door, and returned to the armchair and read the letter again. It all became clear: the missing money from behind the clock and why Lem hadn't carried out his threat to tell Annie's family. Blackmail was far more profitable. He didn't recognise the handwriting on the blackmail letter, but he detected Lem's wicked hand behind it all. How he would like to exact his own revenge – but it was all too late. Now he was faced with the worst dilemma he ever could have imagined. Should he hurry back to the ship and forget it all, or confront Eliza with the evidence? Or should he let it rest, leave it until they had settled in America and then work everything out in a sensible, measured manner, away from all threats, deceits and dangers? Should he return to the ship at all? Would this mean the end of their life together? How could he decide all these things in one moment? This was the worst dilemma he had ever faced, worse even than his journey across the sands. How could things get any worse?

Someone was knocking on the back door again. 'That woman,' he said to himself, 'can't she ever mind her own business?' He got up and made his way to the kitchen.

The knocking resumed, heavier this time. 'Open up! We know you're in there! Open up in the name of the law!'

Chapter Fourteen

I t's a trip in the old queen's carriage for you, now,' the sergeant informed him, peering in through the bars.

'What's that?' asked a dejected Walter, blinking as a shaft of light lit up the darkened cell.

'My, my, you are a new one to this thieving lark, aren't you? Don't worry, you'll learn it all soon enough when you're convicted and sent to prison.'

'I told you I was going to pay it back,' pleaded Walter.

'You can tell that to the magistrate tomorrow morning. That's where the black maria's taking you, to the remand cells at Birkenhead police station. Going to pay it back, were you? And you with a ticket for America in your pocket! That's going to make the beak laugh, that is. And the crowd who come down to the court, they'll love that one. It'll be a spell in Walton for you. Stealing thirty pounds . . . it's more than some poor souls earn in a year.'

There was the sound of a key grinding in the lock. The heavy door swung open and Walter stepped out. Singing from the end of the dark corridor ceased. A young policeman of about Walter's height stepped forward in front of the sergeant to clamp on a pair of heavy iron cuffs. They immediately dug into the flesh on his wrists, causing the skin to chafe and turn red where they had gripped him before. The party proceeded through the door at the end, into the prison yard where the van was awaiting them. A brief moment in the afternoon sunshine revived Walter's flagging spirits. Those three hours in the cell at the police station had been the longest of his life.

His mind had been racing the whole time. How could he get a message to Eliza? What would happen when she realised he wasn't coming on board? Would they ever be together again? If he pleaded guilty, and got a light sentence for a first offence, would they eventually be allowed to resume their passage to America? And why had he done such a stupid, reckless thing in the first place?

Two black horses, immaculately groomed, stood motionless in the yard, attached to the shafts of a black prison van. A gold VR crest surmounted the small black door and a couple of iron steps hung down at the back. Both the policeman and Walter had to crouch as they climbed in. The first impression Walter had was of a foul stench that wafted out down the steps, a mixture of urine, vomit and other bodily odours. Obviously cleaning the vehicle was not as high a priority as grooming the horses. There were six tiny cells, three each side of the narrow central passage, and he was shown into one of the two at the back; from the other came the sound of snoring. The handcuffs were removed as soon as he was sitting on the plank seat, and the cell door was shut and bolted with a bang.

'Two for the remand in Birkenhead, driver,' announced the young policeman.

'Two for Woodside lock-up it is,' repeated the smaller and tubbier of the two drivers. He took two pieces of paper from the station sergeant, signed one and returned it before climbing up to his seat with some difficulty. He shouted 'Move!', his companion whipped the reins and the whole contraption lurched forwards over the cobbles. Walter heard the iron gate bang behind them. They were out on the street.

As Walter was a tall man, he had to crouch forward in the tiny cell, hardly able to move under the low curved roof. Being in the end cell, he could just catch a glimpse of the passing street if he pressed his face on the bars, which also afforded a small amount of fresh air. He could not imagine what would have happened had he been penned further into the van, but he feared he would have vomited or even passed out.

They were climbing the gentle slope of Rakes Road. The horses made slow progress, even with only two passengers on board. The weight of the heavy wooden frame and iron panels and doors meant even the mildest incline was a mountain to them, but patiently they plodded on. The van passed the cemetery, which looked almost like a park under the blue summer sky. Walter's eyes filled with tears as he remembered Martha, whose tiny body lay there in its final rest. At the top of the hill the road bent to the right, and squinting to the left, through two sets of bars, Walter caught a brief glimpse of the Mersey. The early summer mist had vanished, and the view was clear. A ship was out in the middle of the river, being hauled by two tugs up the channel and out to the Bar. It was enormous, with two enormous funnels and three taller masts. Anyone on the street who cared to listen could have heard the sound of sobbing from the last cell in the back of the prison van.

'Eeh, lad, what's up with thee?' The snorer had awoken, and was pressing his face against the bars to see what the commotion in the cell opposite was all about. It was hard to hear him above the clattering hooves and rumble of the wheels along the cobbles. Walter looked up and stared across the two foot of space between them. Up to that moment he had taken little notice of the figure in the opposite cell. The first thing he saw was the bear-like paws grasping the bars, then as a shaft of sunlight came through the outside grill he caught a clear glimpse of a giant of a man, with a face that seemed to fill the entire barred window. It was an almost clean-shaven face, with a bent and broken nose, scarred with long-ago and recent battles. It did not, however, seem cruel, evil or even terrifying.

Walter stopped sobbing, dried his eyes and swallowed hard. 'You're from Yorkshire, aren't you?'

'Aye, lad. Though you speak a bit posh you sound like one of us too. Round about Bradford, I'd say.'

Walter was surprised to say the least. This apparently rough, uneducated thug had more than a keen brain and quick ear. 'Right first time! And you're from . . . it's difficult to say. You sound a bit like Leeds, Bradford, Halifax, almost anywhere.'

'That's 'cos I am. Anywhere and everywhere, that's me. Born on t'canals and lived my whole life on 'em. Me and me missus run a boat on the Leeds to Liverpool. Except for the time I've spent in jail. She's not going to like this. Got drunk with some scousers and decided to go on this little jaunt to a tobacco warehouse over in Birkenhead. One of 'em reckoned he'd bribed t'watchman. T'coppers were waiting, though. The scousers got clean away but I didn't know where to run. Got chased all the way up to Wallasey before they got me. I guess this'll mean another three months in't clink.' He gave a huge sigh. 'God knows what she'll say. She'll have to run t'barge hersen and look after t'kids an all. I'll get hell to play when she finds out. Oh God, I'm hungry. Coppers didn't feed me at Wallasey. I reckon it was 'cos I gave one or two of 'em summat to remember me by. Mind you, they did return the compliment, and wished me a happy birthday as well.' He grinned, and pressed his forehead against the bars to show a couple of large, swollen bruises.

Walter fished in his jacket pocket. The paper bag was still there: the police had not removed the pasty he had bought at the baker's shop that morning. 'You can have this if you want. I'm afraid I took a couple of bites of it, but I'm not hungry any more.'

'Thanks lad, you're a good un. My name's Caleb. Caleb Stone.' He demolished the pasty with his second bite.

'Walter Adams.'

'What you in for?'

'Stole thirty pounds from my employers. Needed it for a journey to America. I was going to pay it back, though.'

'First time?'

'Yes. How did you know?'

The big man roared with laughter. 'Can tell easy like. If you cough, and with you being new and promise to repay, you might get off with a couple of months. Mind you, some of 'em don't like better-class thieves and conmen. It all depends who you get sittin' on t' bench. You should end up in Walton, same as me. It's a new built one, not too bad. Prison can be hard though, first time round, but I'll look after thee. You're all right, Walter Adams, and we Yorkshire lads 'as to stick together.'

The van drew to a stop. They heard a gate close and the sound of footsteps on the cobbles.

'Two prisoners for remand,' a voice called out.

'All right,' was the reply, 'Let's have a look at them.'

* * *

Crying and shouting filled the court room and drifted out into the corridor outside, and Walter listened apprehensively as he sat between two burly constables waiting his turn. The doors flew open, and he saw two more policemen holding them back.

A voice rang out. 'Mary White, I find you guilty of common assault on George Gittins, pawnbroker of Woodside Road, Birkenhead. I hereby sentence you to one month's imprisonment with hard labour. You are a nuisance and a danger to all decent people and tradesmen with whom you come into contact. Take her away!'

'I'll have two months in clink then, if you don't mind, you syphilitic old sod,' bellowed the prisoner as she was grabbed by two more police constables. 'Now don't you dare let those bastard bizzies lay a hand on me. I'm a lady an' can make my own way down to my cell.'

Walter saw the pantomime unfolding through the doorway. The young woman, her face scarlet with rage and, no doubt, the effects of drink, hung on for dear life to the spikes fixed around the top edge of the dock. One policeman left his post by the door and proceeded to help his colleagues wrench her hands free. For such a slight woman she seemed to possess reserves of enormous strength, for it took all three of them to prise her grip away. One constable caught his hand on a spike and it dripped blood, much to the delight of the crowd, who cheered and booed at the sight.

'Goodbye, your honour,' the woman shouted as she was eventually hauled through the door. 'You can come and visit me in my little cell any time. Same service, same price, if that's what takes your fancy.'

The audience in the gallery roared with laughter. Some made gestures and threats at the retreating policemen, and one or two leaned over and spat in their direction. For a second Walter caught a close-up glimpse of the woman as she was dragged past him. Her face was square and bloated, with full cheeks and a large jaw. Bruises and scratches covered all parts of her forehead, and her thin straggly hair hung down, lank and knotted. She caught sight of him and gave a salacious wink. 'Like to share my cell with you, darling,' she chortled. As she reached the steps she shouted, 'Give that old bugger a hard time for me, will you, love? We don't want 'is lunch to settle too quickly.'

There was a pause as the courtroom calmed down again, and an expectant hush as the audience awaited the next item of entertainment. The magistrate drank from a glass of water to clear his throat. 'Call in the next prisoner.'

Walter stood up with his escort. Their touch on his arm was light, as they seemed to sense that the smart gentleman in their charge would offer no physical resistance. Slowly they marched into the light and airy room. From the ceiling two light fitments hung from long poles, each with four lamps attached. Once lit by gas, they had been converted into newer electric lights. The windows were large but high up on the walls, no doubt to deter escape. To Walter's surprise the people in the gallery were mostly women, respectably dressed but rowdy and brash in their manner. A sense of latent hostility filled the courtroom – not, he sensed, towards him but towards the magistrate and other officials, and especially to the four policemen.

Walter felt many eyes on him, and he glanced around as he reached the dock. Some of the crowd seemed contemptuous; most of them were curious and a few even welcoming. He noticed a couple of women giving him the glad eye, and one even pursed her lips. Above the clerks and officials of the court, he stood facing the magistrate's bench, which was raised to the same height. It all seemed to be set out like a theatre, and he guessed that by the end of the day the gallery would have had their fill of free entertainment and high drama.

The magistrate cleared his throat. 'You are Walter Adams.'

'That is correct,' Walter replied.

'Walter Adams, you are charged with the theft of thirty pounds from your former employers, Field Brothers, soap manufacturers of Liverpool.'

The crowd drew a collective breath. This was different from the run-of-the-mill drunken assault, opportunistic pilfering, wife-beating, husband-battering and burglary that were the norm for this court. And the defendant was a well-dressed, handsome young fellow, who was drawing the admiration of many of the women. They stopped chattering and listened intently.

'Good on you!' came a voice from the back of the court, followed by a shout of 'That should clean 'em out,' which drew a laugh from the gallery.

'Silence in this court!' demanded the magistrate, 'or I will have you all ejected.'

For the first time Walter looked at the man facing him. It was not a pleasing or welcoming sight: dark eyebrows, an aquiline nose, high cheekbones, thick old-fashioned side whiskers and a contemptuous look, which ended in the downward turn of one side of his mouth, did not bode well. Caleb had warned him that Benjamin Hardcastle ('Hardcase' to most of his victims) was the beak to avoid at all costs. From Caleb's description, Walter began to realise that he had drawn the short straw.

'How do you plead?' the magistrate continued.

'Guilty.'

'In that case it is my duty to pronounce sentence . . .'

'If it please Your Honour, I would like to say a few words in mitigation.'

'But you have pleaded guilty, young man. It is an open and shut case. What need is there for any statement from you?'

'Let 'im 'ave 'is say,' a voice rang out from the back of the courthouse.

'Yes, let 'im speak,' another joined in.

'Silence!' shouted a flustered Benjamin Hardcastle. 'I have made my decision. If the plea is guilty then I will proceed with the sentence.'

'Then I change my plea. I plead not guilty,' interrupted Walter. 'I *will* have my say in this court.'

It was as if the blind prejudice of his judge and the injustice of his decision had stirred Walter from his state of terrified lethargy. Anger had risen inside him, and a defiance that roused him into action. He was not going to be trodden into the ground by this myopic, biased and ignorant excuse for the power of justice. He stood up straight and stared at the magistrate with contempt. There was mayhem. People were both booing and cheering, and the officers of the court looked rather embarrassed. The clerk of the court approached the bench and whispered a few words into Benjamin's ear.

'Since you are changing your plea, it seems we will have to allow you an opportunity, however inadvisable or unnecessary, to address the court in your defence.' His voice was scathing and sarcastic. He was furious that an open and shut case might now last the rest of the session, thus precluding his afternoon drink or two at the Merchants Club around the corner in Hamilton Square. Besides which, his lunch was lying heavily on his stomach: he was beginning to regret the extra portion of sherry trifle. 'We will proceed with the case, then.' He eyed the defendant suspiciously. 'You will have the opportunity to address the court when later this afternoon you come to defend yourself.'

'I do not think I am being unreasonable, sir, in stating that I am still willing to change my plea to guilty, if I am given the opportunity to speak in mitigation,' Walter insisted. 'It is surely my right to let everyone know the circumstances surrounding my actions. If you were to allow this, it would surely prevent us from wasting a lot of the court's time.'

'You tell 'im,' yelled a voice amid the cheers from the gallery.

The clerk whispered again. Benjamin Hardcastle's face began to turn purple with rage and frustration. 'It appears that despite the fact that you are changing your mind yet again, like some demented woman, I must let you have your say, though for the life of me . . .' The rest of his words were drowned by cheering and stamping from the crowd. 'Silence in this court! I will not have this court treated like a music hall or fish market. I will clear the room, and none but myself and the officers of the court will hear him.'

The court settled down again, and when Walter spoke in a quiet, clear voice, the whole room was reduced to silence. 'Yes, I did take the money. But from the outset I intended to pay it back. I had worked for the firm for over three years and I always did my best for them in my work as a travelling sales representative.'

'You broke the trust of a good employer,' interrupted the magistrate. There was a quiet hissing from a few in the audience. He looked wildly round to spot the culprits but was unsuccessful.

'I thought that Field's was a good employer,' continued Walter, 'until I gave in my notice. Their attitude changed. I had booked a passage to America for me and my wife. Since the death of our baby daughter last year, we wanted to make a new start in life, and America seemed the perfect opportunity.' The gallery sat in stunned silence, and one or two women wiped their eyes. 'I asked if they would give me a final bonus, as reward for my efforts. I was one of their most successful salesmen over the years, and never gave anything but my full commitment to the job. They agreed, and during those last two months I worked harder than ever. I did not slacken off, and was the top salesman in the whole company for the month of April. When I came to leave they went back on their word. They didn't award me that final bonus, and only gave me half of the commission I might have expected.'

'Shame!' came a voice from the crowd. The rest murmured in agreement.

'I needed that money for the voyage, and for the first few months over there. It would have helped while I was getting a job. We planned to set up a business and to work hard to make our way. Before I left, the opportunity to take some money fell into my lap, so I took just thirty pounds, which I felt was the amount I was owed. I took only that amount, and as soon as I could have done I would have sent it back to clear my conscience.'

'You expect the court to believe that?' interrupted the magistrate. 'When you were arrested you had your ticket to America. If the police had not been so vigilant you would have escaped, and it would have been the last your employers would have seen of the money.'

'That's not true,' protested Walter. 'The opportunity occurred on my last day at the firm, and there was over five hundred pounds in that safe. I could have taken much more and no-one would have discovered it immediately. If I had stolen a couple of hundred it would have meant I could have started in America a rich man. I had a perfect opportunity, but I only took what I felt was owed to me.'

'You tell 'im, mate. Greedy bosses, they never give you what you're due.' The interruption was greeted with approval from the gallery.

By now Benjamin Hardcastle was oblivious to the interruptions. 'And where is your wife now?'

'I don't know.'

'Don't know? How can you not know?'

'I went back to the house from the ship that morning to retrieve something I'd forgotten. It was sailing from the Pier Head mid-afternoon so I knew I'd got plenty of time. I was in the house when the police arrived, and I was arrested.'

'So where is she?'

'I can only assume she waited on the ship for me and it sailed.'

'Oh no!' shouted a woman in the gallery.

'She must be half-way to America by now, worried and frightened by my disappearance. My poor Eliza, she must be out of her mind with worry.'

The court went quiet, and some women gasped in astonishment.

In the silence Benjamin Hardcastle saw his opportunity. He rose to give his verdict. 'I find your excuses feeble. You are obviously trying to spin some kind of yarn to get the sympathy of this court, but I can see through your story. It is a tissue of lies. The maximum sentence I can give in this case, as this is your first known offence, is three months in jail. That is what I commit you to.'

There were cries of 'No, no,' and the crowd began to voice their displeasure. Above the seething discontent, Hardcastle determinedly continued with his verdict.

'Walter Adams, you are a deceitful rogue who has contrived to cheat his employers by an act of blatant theft. Take him away!'

The court was in uproar. Rubbish pelted from the gallery in the direction of the bench. The room did not quieten down until the police and court officers had cleared it. All thought of any more cases that afternoon was abandoned. Benjamin Hardcastle retired to his chambers and vindicated his decision with the help of two or three glasses from a bottle of Madeira, which he kept in a cupboard for that purpose.

Chapter Fifteen

I t had been a long time since Gideon had tasted sweets, and such
lovely ones at that. They were sugary, slippery, striped humbugs that
rolled around the inside of his mouth, releasing a torrent of sweet
juices and intoxicating vapours. He had worked hard for a couple of
hours, helping Hannah's grandmother dust and tidy the returned books,
and this was his reward. Hannah had taken him to Heaton's sweet stall in
the market, the biggest and best in the market, in Bradford, in the world!
It had taken them over twenty minutes, and on their return Harriet
pointed to the large, white-faced market clock which hung above their
heads and was already showing five past three.

'I think it's time for you to go down the Mission and find out what
Miss Nancy and the pastor have sorted out for you. Have you got that map
Hannah's drawn for you, Peter?'

Gideon patted his jacket pocket and smiled.

'Can't I go down with him and show him the way?' asked
Hannah.

'Certainly not,' replied her grandmother. 'You must never go down
Silsbridge Lane without a grown-up to accompany you. And who would
bring you back if Nancy had to take this young lad to another part of
town? Besides which, we'll be closing in just over an hour and I'll need
your help to shut up shop and cash up.'

'Don't worry,' Gideon interrupted. 'I'll find my way easy enough with
that map of yours.' He pulled it out and gave it a glance. 'That's providing
I don't come across any of the witches, goblins or rabbits. Don't you worry,
Mrs Clough, I can look after myself.'

107

'That may well be, but don't linger down that street. They're a rough, nasty lot down there.'

With a cheery wave, he was off down the aisle to the main doors, skipping down the steps and turning left along Kirkgate. On his arrival in Bradford he had had little time to look around. He had been intent on finding the market and his hoped-for freedom, but now it was different. There was an air of expectation in his heart and a jaunty spring in his step as he gazed around at the shops and offices. It wasn't as impressive as Leeds, with its wide, majestic Headrow and its fine public buildings. Gideon turned left at the end of the street, then found the opening for Silsbridge Lane. The area was no better nor any worse than those he had seen in the slums of Leeds. He stopped by a shop window and took out the bag of sweets to pop one in his mouth, not noticing three pairs of eyes watching him from a recessed doorway. The boy put the bag back in his pocket and sauntered on down the uneven cobblestones.

'Where you from, Blondy?'

The accent was not from Yorkshire. Gideon looked round warily. The two boys in front were about his size and dressed in filthy, ragged clothes and large flat caps. Their faces were mean and unwashed. The one who had slunk up behind him was bigger than he was.

'We'll be havin' those sweets off yer,' the darker of the two demanded. 'That's the price you have to pay for comin' through our patch, that and the odd black eye and broken tooth to go with it.'

Gideon felt an arm around his neck and a knee pressed hard in his back. He was losing his balance, and a punch on his cheek sent him spinning to the ground. The cobbles hammered hard against his shoulder. Scarcely had he winced with the sharp pain, than he felt another as he was kicked hard in the back, and then the two boys in front were on top of him, one raining blows on his face and the other rifling his pockets for the sweets. He found the precious booty and with glee rolled off his victim, intent in having the first pick. The other two were not so easily distracted. Gideon felt another kick on his thigh and punches were still raining down, but now his arms were free and he could fend most of them off. At last he could move his right leg, and he sensed his chance. He kicked as hard as he could between the legs of the boy on top of him. Bull's eye! The attacker rolled off, groaning and clutching his groin.

'Be Jesus, the bastard's got me in the marbles,' he shouted. 'Give it to him as well.'

A well-honed instinct for survival immediately took over. This was not the first time Gideon had faced such a situation, and his reaction was quick and decisive. In that split-second he bounced up from the stone sets and was off, with the speed of a whippet, dodging to the right and making for a gap between his assailants and a low brick wall. The boy with the sweets had anticipated his move and skipped quickly to his left to block his path. The street was narrow, but Gideon judged it was just wide enough. The cobbles were slimy, and the gutters were covered in manure and weeds. He swerved back to his left, and the boy tried his best to keep his feet on the treacherous surface – but he was deceived. It was a feint. Gideon's side-step to the right left his opponent floundering, and it only took the lightest brush of the shoulder to send him tumbling to the ground. It was achieved with a finesse that would have brought cheer to a crowd watching Bradford in a Saturday afternoon rugby match. Gideon had never known where or from whom he had got this instinctive ability to run and dodge at full speed, but it was effortless and it had served him well many times before.

He was off down the lane, and after a few yards his pursuers gave up hope and turned back to reclaim their prize. It was in vain. The remaining humbugs lay scattered around in the mud and horse muck. Three hundred yards down the lane, Gideon slowed and began to look around. The adrenalin had left his body, and he was beginning to feel the pain of the encounter. He saw the sign for Silsbridge Lane Mission Church and dived through the gate, stopping for breath when he reached the half-open door. He peered through. Some girls were polishing and dusting the hall. Nancy was doing the same, and trying to direct the unwilling workers as well. He walked in, unaware of how bruised and bloodstained he was. The girls stared at him in disbelief.

'What ever happened?' asked Nancy, putting down her duster.

'These lads attacked me, miss, and took my sweets.'

'Sit down on this bench. Rebecca, fetch a bowl of water. Deborah, bring me a towel from the washroom.' Nancy returned a minute later with a small bottle. The label read 'Tincture of Iodine'.

This may hurt a bit, but it'll clean the wounds and stop any infection.'

'That's all right, miss. Can't be any more painful than what those lads gave me.'

Nancy held the bowl in her hand and began to gently clean the wounds with a small cotton cloth. As each one was washed she applied a dab of the odious purple solution. The other girls stopped their work and gathered round to watch. 'There, there, Peter,' she said, as he winced in pain at her touch on his cheek.

He looked up to give her a long, loving smile. Something stirred deep inside at that smile, a long-forgotten memory from the distant past. She returned it willingly and gladly.

'That's not Peter,' exclaimed Deborah, who had just arrived with the towel. 'That's Gideon, from the orphanage in Leeds. Hello, Gideon. What are you doing here in Bradford?'

Nancy stared into the boy's eyes, her pale face etched with a look of fearful recognition. The bowl of water fell from her hands and smashed into a hundred pieces on the floor. The girls stood in silent amazement. They had never seen such a look of shock and bewilderment on the face of the normally calm, confident and controlled Miss Nancy. After staring for over a minute into the void in front of her, she collapsed on to a chair and began to sob.

* * *

There was plain white everywhere, not a flower or colour to be seen. Was she in a dream? There was a smell of chemicals, soap, something familiar. Her head was spinning. It ached inside and out. She couldn't make out any details at first, what the room was like or if she was alone. But she could sense there was someone close by.

'There, there, my dear, stay still and rest. You've had a very nasty fall.'

She moved her hands around her face as if to confirm it was her, and that she was still alive and not in some other world. She touched a swelling on the side of her head, and winced. Gradually the room came into focus. It was quite small and there were no windows. A bed next to hers was empty. Walter wasn't lying there: a dark blue blanket and white sheet were wrapped tightly around it. There was something else as well: a deep, slow, gentle throbbing that seemed to make the whole room vibrate.

'Walter! Walter!' Eliza cried.

'He came to see you yesterday,' the nurse whispered. 'He was worried after you had your fall, but you were still very drowsy. He said you'd mistaken him for someone else.'

'Where am I? This isn't our cabin.'

'You're in the ship's infirmary, madam. You've had a nasty fall, but you seem to be getting a little better. Perhaps before we reach New York we can let you go back into your own cabin.'

The face before her gradually came into focus. It was pale and square with large grey-blue eyes. On her head the nurse wore a white, tight-fitting bonnet, almost like a cap. Behind it was a mass of light brown hair, wound into a tight bun. The plain blue dress was overpinned with an immaculate white apron. The nurse smiled, and bent down to bathe Eliza's head with cool water.

'I've got to get off the ship and go back to Liverpool. I must see my husband. He's missed the boat. Ask the captain to put me off at Holyhead or Cork or somewhere.'

'I'm sorry, my dear, we can't do that. We're out in the Atlantic. We saw the lights of Cape Clear last night. All the Irish passengers were out on deck, waving, cheering and crying. It's the last bit of land we'll see for over a week. The next will be New York.'

* * *

'You're deceitful and wicked. You've contrived to bring unhappiness and shame by your actions. You've lied and deceived everyone for your own ends.'

Hannah stood in the drawing room in front of her three accusers, her mother the most outspoken. Tears streamed down her cheeks. Nancy looked pale, and was withdrawn and quiet. Annie was at her angriest – and she could be very angry when she tried.

Only her uncle seemed calm. James stared at his niece. 'Why did you do it?'

'What's happened to Gideon?' Hannah sobbed.

'He's been taken back to the orphanage in Leeds,' James said. 'The police had to be called.'

Hannah burst into tears. Nancy turned away. Tears filled her eyes too, but she could not let the others see.

'I only wanted everyone to be happy,' Hannah said. 'It seemed the right thing to do.'

'But you're only a child,' James whispered. 'At your age you can't always see what's the right way. What seems so obvious to you could lead to far worse things. The Mission couldn't be implicated in helping a runaway to abscond, to escape from a place that's lawfully his home. Can't you see that?'

'What I want to know is how you found out about all this,' interrupted Annie. 'It can't have been by proper or honest means. Now come on, young lady, let's have the truth. I've never laid a hand on you but, by God, if you don't start telling the truth I'll be severely tempted.'

'Let's start at the beginning, Hannah,' James said in a stern but soft voice. 'We're not going to let up until we find out how you came to do this. Of that you can be sure. You might as well make a clean breast of it all.'

Hannah's tears slowly subsided, and James passed her a handkerchief. She wiped her eyes and looked at all three of them. Grandma Ackroyd wasn't there: she couldn't understand why, but silently thanked God she wasn't. She didn't normally pass up an opportunity to accuse or malign her grandchildren, and her carping would have been the last straw. Hannah could put up with her mother's anger, and her dear aunt was too upset to join in. She turned towards Uncle James. Although he was insistent and persuasive, he alone might understand her motives. 'I overheard you and Grandma Ackroyd talking. I didn't mean to listen. I just heard everything that was said in this room.'

'The cupboard!' interrupted James. 'Do you recall, Annie? We used to overhear things from there. You remember how we . . .'

Annie blushed. 'That's the last time you'll be allowed in there, my girl. There'll be a lock on it from tomorrow.'

'I didn't mean to listen,' protested Hannah. 'We were playing hide and seek and it was the perfect place to hide. You had gone out, Mummy. Grandma Ackroyd was talking to Uncle and saying some nasty things about Daddy, how you shouldn't have married him, how he caused trouble to the family and how it was Daddy's cousin who . . .' She hesitated, not daring to say the words.

'Yes, Hannah?' her mother asked.

'That Aunt Nancy had a baby boy. She called him Gideon and she had to give him away,' she gabbled as fast as she could.

There was silence for a few seconds. Nancy was looking at her niece, but it wasn't in anger. Her expression had changed to one of earnest curiosity.

'Is this true, James?' asked Annie

It was James's turn to blush. 'I'm afraid so.'

'Uncle didn't say any nasty things,' said Hannah. 'He argued with Grandma, and wouldn't have it that it was Daddy's fault.'

Even Annie was too stunned to rebuke her daughter.

Nancy put on a brave face and turned towards her niece. Her voice was quiet and restrained. The others seemed too afraid to interrupt her questioning. 'I suppose Deborah told you about a boy called Gideon.'

'Yes. She told me about the home and what a terrible place it was. I guessed it might be him, but it was only when I got his letter that I knew for sure.'

'But my baby was given to a good, kind, Christian couple who had no child of their own.'

'Gideon was, Auntie, and he was happy with them. But they died, and because he wasn't their own no one would look after him, and he had to go to the orphanage.'

'But why did you write to him?'

Tears came to Hannah's eyes again. She found it hard to look Nancy in the face. 'I knew you must have loved him when he was a baby and I thought that if you found he was in such a terrible place you could find it in your heart to love him again. I thought you would never allow him to be so sad, and you might have him back and be happy yourself.'

Nancy got up and moved to the window, not daring to look at her brother and sister.

'It isn't as easy as that, Hannah,' said James. 'It's better that . . . it's better that he's brought up in a family with a mummy and a daddy, and if not, in a home that looks after orphans. Nancy couldn't look after him by herself. People wouldn't think that right. They wouldn't like that.'

'But does it matter what people think?' protested Hannah. 'Mummy looks after us now that Daddy's not here, and no-one says anything about that.'

'That's different,' answered her mother. 'It's my duty. It's the right thing to do.' She was trying to sound convincing. Silence fell. When Annie spoke again it was in a softer, gentler voice. 'Hannah, you must stay confined to your room for two days. I feel that's a right punishment for the distress and trouble you've caused. You may draw, read or write, but I also want you to think about your actions and the consequences. You must not speak a word about any of this to anyone. Do you understand?'

'I never told anyone about this, Mummy. You can be sure. Deborah and Gideon don't know why I did it either.'

'Thank God for that!' said James.

Hannah left the room, her head bowed. Her footsteps trod softly on the stairs.

'We mustn't let Mother know about this,' said Annie. 'That tongue of hers has caused enough trouble already.'

'Most definitely. And you must remember that I never subscribed to her view of Walter. You've always known I thought he was a very decent chap.'

Nancy nodded in agreement but stayed silent. She was thinking of everything that had happened, and the decisions she had taken. She was beginning to realise that her life of probity and respectability might now be tainted, not just because of her own secret but also thanks to her knowledge of Walter's affair, which she had kept so carefully hidden from her sister.

* * *

Hannah lay face down on her bed. She didn't want to think about them, but the events of the last two days revolved round and round her head. The door opened with a slight creak. She buried her head even further. More reproof from her mother she could take, but facing anyone else would be beyond suffering.

'What's the matter, Hannah?' asked a small voice. Tom stood in the doorway. His fair hair and sweet round face were lit up by a narrow shaft of sunlight that slipped between the curtains. In her hurry to find the safety and comfort of her pillow, and to shut out the outside world, Hannah had failed to close them fully.

She turned her head to glance at him, her face half hidden in the pillow. He looked like an angel framed in the doorway. And she was the sinner, according to her mother, almost the devil incarnate. Yet she had acted for good: to rescue a lost soul, to right a wrong, to bring a family closer in its hour of need.

'Why are you in trouble? Why is Mummy so cross with you? What have you done?'

'I can't tell you, Tom. Please leave me alone.'

'Please don't be sad, Hannah,' he whispered, almost beginning to cry himself. 'Come and play with me and Rosie.'

'I can't. I've got to stay in my room.'

Tom tiptoed away, closing the door behind him. The silence was only broken by the occasional rumble of wheels or the fast trip-trap of shoes on the pavement. Sparrows chattered on the roof, basking in the bright summer sunshine, but Hannah's prison lay still and dark.

Almost imperceptibly the door creaked. Soft footsteps crossed the floor and the bed gently heaved as a small, light body sat down beside her. There was no further movement except for a gentle touch that stroked her hair. No word was spoken for a full five minutes. Hannah eventually lifted her head and turned round to look into Rosie's dark eyes, which were also filled with tears.

'There, there,' she whispered. I'll always be your friend as well as your little sister.'

'Not my little sister. My grown-up little sister.'

A brief smile crossed Rosie's face. Even Hannah had to admit that Rosie was the most beautiful of the three girls, with her jet-black hair, round face, small button mouth, pale, perfect complexion and those eyes, big, round and deep brown.

'You can tell me,' Rosie said. 'I can share a secret. I'll never tell. A trouble shared is a trouble halved, that's what they say.'

'No. I can't. I promised Mummy and Aunt Nancy and Uncle James never to tell. So that's it.'

'It must have been an awful wicked thing that you did for them to be so angry, and for you to have to stay in your room for two days.'

'No, it wasn't that. I was trying to make things better for all of us, but it just turned out all wrong.'

'So why is everybody so angry and upset? It doesn't seem fair.'

'I can't tell you. If you knew you'd understand I haven't been wicked. All I did was find out a secret.'

Rosie looked perplexed. 'What secret?'

'I can't tell you. You wouldn't understand anyway.'

'Yes I would. It's a secret to do with the cupboard in the parlour, isn't it?'

'How do you know that?'

'Uncle James was putting a bolt on it, high up where we can't reach it. When I asked him, he was ever so strange, not his usual jolly self. Said we were never to go in there again. When I asked him why, he said it was dangerous.'

Hannah bit her lip. She tried so hard not let her face show any reaction, but it was no use. Rosie, who had been her sister for eleven years, had slept in the same bed, knew every expression, her thoughts, even, detected the faint grimace that crossed Hannah's face.

'It's that cupboard. You found out a secret when you were in there. That's where you hide from us when we play hide and seek. You hide behind the rugs and boxes and cases. There's a secret you found in there. What is it?'

Hannah shook her head. Her eyes were closed: she couldn't even look at her sister.

'Is it a secret passage down to the cellars, or a body?'

'Don't be so silly, Rosie.'

'You're right. That is silly. That's my imagination running away with me. But it's got to be something. Something you found out to do with somebody, Grandma Ackroyd perhaps, or Aunt Nancy?'

'No, no! Can't you see? I can't tell you. All I wanted to do was make everything better for us, for – oh! What's the use of it all? Go away, Rosie. I can't stand it any more.'

Rosie jumped down to the floor and walked a few steps across the room. Hannah buried her face again, soaking the pillowcase with her tears. 'I'll go away now, if that's what you want. Don't worry, whatever it is, it'll all work out in the end.' She rushed back and flung herself on her sister, giving her the biggest hug she could, then tiptoed out again, leaving Hannah alone in her prison.

Chapter Sixteen

The cell door clanged shut. Walter was alone – but it was what he wanted after the humiliation of the initiation to prison life. To him, a man who had treated people as individuals, valued their contribution to society, whether shopkeeper, fisherman, preacher or artisan, it had come as a shock to find himself just a number chalked on a prison door. He was a human animal who was being processed in an impersonal, degrading and soulless system. He had not been prepared for it, and it had come as a terrible shock.

After arriving inside the prison gates, Walter was marched between two guards into a stark, featureless office. The prison officers in their dowdy blue uniforms treated him with contempt. In front of a trestle table, the admissions officer had made him strip naked and put his clothes and possessions before him. His body was checked for identifying marks, and these together with a general description were written down on a blue admissions form. His face was photographed and his fingerprints were taken. Another prisoner waited behind him. He was an old lag who had passed through this ceremony many times before, and seemed to regard it with total indifference. But when the officer recited Walter's possessions he took careful note: they included a solid gold pocket watch. As the older man reached the table he slyly leaned over to inspect it.

Walter was led to an adjoining room, where he was ordered to take a bath. The water was cold and scummy, and had obviously been used by others before him. He was left alone a few minutes in the company of the old lag, while the presiding guard, having locked the door, went to find some prison clothes that would fit Walter's taller frame.

The other prisoner noticed Walter's disgust at the state of the water. 'This ain't nuthin', young feller. You ought to have seen the baths over in old Kirkdale. They was like beef broth, they was so foul. How long you in for?'

'Three months.'

'This your first time in, ain't it?'

'Yes.'

'That was a nice suit you came in. You won't like it when you get it back. After they've fumigated it you'll smell like you worked in a match factory. Now the trick is to come in the most stinkin' filthy clothes you can find. They'll burn 'em, and give you a new set of liberty clothes when you're set free.'

The bolt slid in the lock and the guard returned, carrying a bundle of grey clothes. He was accompanied by another prison officer who wore a dirty white apron and carried scissors and a bowl of water. Walter was ordered to sit down, and his hair was cropped to the scalp. He was then told to dress. The underclothes were coarse and itchy. The jacket and trousers, although the right length, were meant for a man of much greater girth, and hung limply around him. The boots were like heavy stones attached to his feet. He was marched back to the desk, where he signed a form acknowledging the items of clothing and possessions that he had handed over, and then a long list of prison regulations was read. 'Do you understand these?'

Walter nodded.

'You do not nod to a prison officer. You're not a donkey. I say again, do you understand these regulations?'

'Yes I do. Sir.'

That was it. He had answered as required. He had been transformed, brainwashed, institutionalised, depersonalised. He was prisoner 8577, not Walter Adams, not Walter Clough, not even Walter Adams Clough. His new life had begun.

Now he was alone with his thoughts. But he didn't want to think any. He wanted to keep his mind blank for the next three months. Walter lay on his plank bed listening to the clicks and taps on the pipework, and wondered what they might be. They continued for a while, then there were footsteps and a voice barked, 'Silence along this landing.' There was the sound of spy holes being opened and closed along the corridor. His turn came. Clink! Metal slid along metal, a pair of eyes was just discernible, then the slit closed again. Tea came half an hour later: a thin gruel sweetened with molasses and a hunk of dark doughy stuff that passed for bread.

As night fell, Walter settled himself on the plank bed. The cell was stuffy, but lying on the blanket made the night's endless hours just about bearable. How was he going to survive the next ninety days? He was scared and lonely. He would have given anything for a trek across the open sands of Morecambe Bay in any weather, facing any dangers. And who was going to help him now?

The routine had begun; each day the same as the one before and the same as the next. That first night in prison Walter had hardly slept, partly because of the plank bed but also because of the incessant chatter from the pipes, which kept on until the early hours. For a time he had tried to recall the Morse code alphabet and make a vain attempt at deciphering the sounds, but it was useless. It was a language he could not fathom, a secret language known only to the senders and receivers, men who had spent years in prison learning and perfecting their art. The prison rule of an isolated, silent regime was a mockery, except for him. He was alone, unable to speak to anyone.

Breakfast, consisting of a mug of cocoa sweetened with a dollop of the inevitable molasses, was at eight o'clock. This was followed by slopping out and what seemed like another interminable wait, alone in his cell again. It drove Walter to an act of defiance, his first breaking of a prison rule. He listened with his ear to the door, and having satisfied himself that there were no footsteps along the corridor he climbed on his stool and peered through the bars of the window. Having sensed that he was on the top floor of the prison, he wondered if he might be rewarded with a good view. He was: the windows of the wing opposite, rooftops, a stretch of wall, streets and houses beyond, and above it all a small piece of sky. This insignificant scenery seemed to dampen his spirits rather than raise them. He caught the sound of footsteps and clanging doors, and immediately jumped down. A few seconds later his door flew open and a voice roared, 'Prisoner get ready for exercise!'

Walter stepped out on to the corridor along with about thirty others from his landing, and a similar number on the landing opposite. Like a silent army they all turned to the right and marched down the corridor, through a barred door and down a flight of stairs, whereupon the silence was broken by the deafening noise of numberless pairs of boots on iron steps. Prison officers stood watching at the top and bottom of the staircase, but could not stop a wave of chatter that was hidden by the din.

Walter was over half-way down when a strong hand grabbed him by the collar and forced his head against the side of the caged stairwell. He sensed a face close to his and foul breath in his nostrils, almost as unpleasant as the pain of flesh on the metal mesh.

'The name's Seamus Mooney, and if you want to get out of this place in one piece you'll be handing over that gold pocket watch to my friends when you get free after yer three months. They'll be waitin' fer you when you comes out.' Walter's head was banged against the caging in time to the word 'Un-der-stand?'.

It was an evil face, large, round and flat, with a stub nose and a slightly deformed lip. Small piggy eyes stared into his. To Walter this was the ultimate degradation and terror. He had made an enemy, though why he could not understand; one who threatened to make his miserable life even more unbearable. His ear grated and bled against the wire, and he felt himself choking from the shirt twisted tight around his throat. For a second he wished he was dead.

The grip suddenly loosened, and he felt himself falling uncontrollably forward. His torturer was being propelled even faster into the void. Walter felt his shirt grabbed from behind, and he was pulled back until he felt the firm ground of the staircase beneath him. His assailant did not stop: he went tumbling through the other prisoners, his body bouncing on the iron steps until it came to rest in a heap.

By the time Walter had reached the bottom of the stairs a thin, weasel-faced prison officer had arrived. 'You two help that man up and bring him here.' He pointed to Walter and the giant of a man just behind him. They bent down to pick up the bulky, motionless form. To Walter it was a dead weight; to his large, muscular companion it was nothing. Gripping Seamus under the arms and raising him up, Walter's face came close to both his attacker's and that of the other prisoner. Walter had not recognised him clean shaven and without his mass of long, black hair: he was staring into the grinning face of Caleb Stone, the prisoner from the black maria.

'Allow me, Seamus, to introduce you to my friend Walter,' Caleb whispered into the assailant's ear. 'My very good friend Walter.'

The grey piggy eyes, which a few seconds ago had been so cruel and all powerful, showed only terror and agonising pain. This pain grew worse, as Caleb was none too gentle with his charge and pressed hard into his ribs, causing him to give a scream of agony.

'Beg pardon, Mr Woodward, sir,' said Caleb to the thin-faced warder. 'I think he may have broken a rib or two in that fall.'

'Right then, you two take him down to the prison doctor.' He turned to the prison officer who stood further down the corridor. 'Mr O'Malley, you accompany them. Tell the doctor what happened. Get rid of those old lags shirking in the medical queue and have them sent back out to the exercise yard. This one could be serious; probably prison hospital.'

They followed the warder down a long central corridor below a magnificent vaulted glass roof. A guard unlocked a door, let the party pass through, then locked it behind them. They were in the centre of the prison, in a large pentagonal office which served as its hub. Glancing round, Walter could see four other corridors splayed out from the centre. It was as if they were in the centre of a giant five-leafed clover. Even amid the shock and turmoil of his predicament, Walter looked around in wonder: the awesome geometric architecture took his breath away. An iron door was unlocked, and all three were taken across a small yard. The weight of Seamus Mooney seemed to grow heavier but Walter didn't mind: he had some fresh air in his lungs, he could see blue sky again and he had a friend to help him through his troubles. He grabbed Seamus more tightly, taking his cue from Caleb. Seamus winced and then groaned with pain.

They deposited their charge on a bench, and for a short time were locked alone in a small room while the prison officer spoke to the doctor. The order had been 'Silence!' but as soon as they were on their own Caleb began to whisper. 'Now, Walter, it's church tomorrow.'

Walter was surprised to find this was the subject of conversation. 'Yes. I'll be attending the service at ten.'

'No!'

'Why not?'

'From now on you're a Methodist. Go to t'non-conformist service at eleven. Pretend you made a mistake on t'admission form. They won't stand between a man and his religion. They takes that kind o' thing very seriously.'

'But why?'

'It's not as crowded as t'others. Catholic and C. of E. is normally full up. Mr O'Malley's on duty and I can wangle a seat next to you.'

'We can't speak to each other, surely.'

'You leave all that to me. Hymns are a lot longer and noisier than t'others. So are the sermons, mind you. They'll put you to sleep if nowt will.'

'So what's going on?'

'You'll understand tomorrow. We'll have missed exercise this morning but that don't matter. Shot carrying's a bit hard but you'll get used to it after a bit. By three months you'll be carrying cannon balls around like a loaf o' bread. Not prison bread, like. I bet you've found it's just as 'ard . . .' His laugh was cut short by the sound of a key turning in the lock. They stood silently to attention, and were soon escorted back to their cells by Mr O'Malley and another warder. O'Malley kept looking at Caleb, and just once Walter thought he detected a wry smile from the corner of his lip.

Walter's spirits were reviving. He *was* going to get through the next three months. Caleb would see to that.

It was unlike any church or chapel he had ever been in. It was more like a theatre, with the tiers of wooden pews sloping steeply down to the front, where there was an enormous pulpit raised high above the floor. To each side was attached a small wooden dock, in each of which sat a prison officer, keeping watch on the congregation of sinners. The organ was at the back of the central aisle, its tall pipes almost touching the panelled ceiling. Prisoners filed into the pews, each one like a tiny wooden cell, the sides high enough to prevent the occupant seeing or talking to his neighbour. The only view was of the pulpit, the ceiling and the prison guards. Walter was directed to an empty row, but when he got to the end he found the compartment by the wall already occupied.

The service began with a recitation of the rules for attendance at worship: 'No communication with your neighbour. No calling out or any untoward noise. No sleeping in the pew. No lewd or provocative act or gesture. Everyone sings the hymns and responses.'

They rose to sing the first hymn, which was 'Onward Christian Soldiers'. From the corner of his eye Walter saw Caleb next to him. As both were tall, their heads and shoulders rose above the partition.

'Onward Christian Soldiers – Mornin' Walter Adams.

With the cross of Jesus – Got a surprise for you.'

The first half of each line was sung loudly, the communication with a softer voice, but with mouth open and as if in song. Caleb continued for the rest of the verse.

'Like a mighty army – you're on a working party.

Brothers we are treading – first thing Monday morning.'

The chorus was sung to the hymn's original words, and in the second verse Walter took up his cue.

'At the sign of triumph – How did you do that?

On then Christian soldiers – I'm down to pick oakum.

Hell's foundation's quiver – Will it be hard work?

Brothers lift your voices – Thanks again, Caleb.'

Walter noticed that during the verses some of the other prisoners' lips didn't seem to match the words. There seemed to be an innate understanding among them: some sang the real words, while others continued a conversation. Amused, Walter realised that no matter how tough the rules were in prison, the prisoners seemed to be able to break them with impunity. He had already noticed a code of hand signals, gestures and innocuous expressions that seemed to convey a plethora of hidden meanings. His quick brain had already learnt a few, including the touching of the nose for 'snout' or tobacco, and a screwing gesture for 'screw' or prison warder.

In the third verse Caleb resumed his conversation.

'Like a mighty army – Mr O'Malley's a friend of mine.

Brothers we are treading – My Jenny gets him snout.

We are not divided – Likes a rough shag for his pipe.

One in hope and doctrine – Work party's all right you'll see.'

Caleb did not talk during the other hymns but left others to communicate. Despite the rule, some prisoners dozed during the interminable sermon, and the warders seemed to do little about it as long as the prisoner behind the sleeper tapped him on the back of the head when it finished. The officers seemed to let some things go for the sake of a quiet life. Walter sensed a code of unwritten rules between the prisoners and their guards. If the former caused no trouble, rules were relaxed and minor indulgences allowed, unless there were inspections or there were certain senior officers on duty – those who stuck to the official code with a messianic zeal.

Walter awoke that second morning more refreshed. The cocoa was the same, the bread just as foul, but there was the working party to look forward to, instead of being cooped up in a tiny space for hours. He was ordered out of his cell at eight o'clock and taken down to the front gate. Caleb was there with another four prisoners, mostly older men, waiting by a cart loaded with crushed stone. Shovels and a pick were piled on top. There was no horse waiting between the shafts: the prisoners had to manhandle it themselves. This was where the sheer strength of Caleb and another large prisoner came into its own. They took the shafts, and Walter and the others pushed from behind. Walter had not done such heavy work since he had helped Reuben collect mussels off the skears on Morecambe Bay some three years before.

On reaching the work site, a wide path that was under the process of construction, Mr O'Malley ordered ten minutes' rest. One prisoner was posted as watch, while the warder lit an enormous briar pipe and his companion a cigarette. The rules of solitude and silence were immediately broken. Caleb came over to sit next to Walter.

'How did you manage this?' whispered Walter.

'Ah, I'm a ticket-of-leave man, Walt. With my contacts at the canal wharf at Stanley Dock I can organise all kinds of stuff to go into the prison. My Jenny runs it at t'other end and everyone's happy. They're glad to see me back again. An' it were easy getting you on this. A first-timer with only three months to serve ain't goin' to run away. If he's any sense, that is.'

'It's hard work. I'm aching already.'

'You'll get used to it. An' it's better than pickin' oakum in your cell, ain't it? You've got fresh air, a bit of company an' a nice surprise later. But tell me, Walt, how did a good chap like you come to find thysen in jail?'

Walter told him the whole story: his disappearance on the sands, Eliza, baby Martha, the planned voyage to America, the blackmail letter, the arrest. He spared no detail.

'And you blame it all on that Lem, then?'

'I do. It could only have been him that organised the blackmail. And I saw the envelope. It had a Bradford postmark. Wasn't his writing, though. Someone else must have done his dirty work.'

'He'd better not cross my path,' muttered Caleb. 'There wouldn't be much left of him if he did.'

'No, not revenge. That would solve nothing. He can't help being the way he is. He got me that job in the first place, after all. And my Eliza, well, she did let slip about his affair. It must have caused him a hell of a lot of trouble, especially if his wife found out. And what about Ledger's office and shop? It must have caused more entertainment than they've had in a month of Sundays! Big fat Lem having a to-and-fro with that little spinster Madge Dobson . . .'

'Hey, you two over there, break's over. Get your spades and get working!'

The call came from the younger prison guard. Walter picked up a shovel and Caleb grabbed the pickaxe which had been left for him. His large hands swung it with a dexterity no other man could match. The ground tore up before his feet, and the others shovelled out the dirt, scarcely able to keep up with him. It seemed in no time at all that the earth was loaded on the cart and the crushed stone had been laid and levelled for another forty yards. As they were ahead of schedule and dinner time was approaching, O'Malley signalled a break. The great black pipe was soon belching forth like a mill chimney, and the prisoners settled down in the shade of a hedge. Another prisoner was posted on watch, and on the nod from the prison officer another one collected a few coppers from him and disappeared down the lane. He returned a few minutes later with a giant dish containing a steaming hot meat pudding. The aroma hit them from almost ten yards away. They wiped their hands on their prison uniform, and each proceeded to grab a piece and eat it with their bare hands. Never had a humble pudding tasted so wonderful to Walter. Not since he was a boy had he eaten with such bestial table manners, but it was the most wonderful meal he had ever had. One piece of pudding was left for the watch, who changed over in five minutes. It was also his privilege, according to the ritual, after finishing his piece to lick the dish clean. This he performed with admirable efficiency.

They returned with the cart, first dumping the earth further down the edge of the lane and spreading it so that the spoil was not too obvious.

The boiled meat and potatoes awaiting the prisoners for dinner seemed foul and tasteless, but on Caleb's advice Walter did not leave them. To do so might cause suspicion, and every scrap of food was precious in keeping up your health and spirits. Treats such as those they had relished with the working party were not to be had every day. You had to learn to enjoy them to the full amid the wretched, monotonous prison life.

Walter stretched out on his bed that night tired and aching in every muscle. But he was calmer and happier than he had been two days earlier. Life was taking on a new meaning. He was starting to see it through a different pair of eyes, and learning to appreciate its small pleasures.

Chapter Seventeen

The small iron door clanged shut behind him. The weather was cloudy and a soft drizzle off the Irish Sea filled the air, soaking everything in a fine mist. But he didn't care. He was free again, and there before him was the woman he loved, come to welcome him back to the outside world. He took her in his arms and there, out in the street, before the tall and forbidding prison walls, they kissed. It was an act of love but also one of defiance, to show the world what mattered.

When at last his large muscular body released her tiny frame she spoke. 'Caleb, I got some beef stew ready to cook in the pot, just for you. Sarah from the next boat, you remember, that nice grey-haired woman from round Wigan way, she's looking after the kids for me this mornin', and the wharf manager he's got a load of potash needs shiftin to Leeds, an' he says we can 'ave it. Now ain't that all nice?'

'We'll slip off on the way fer a drink, though, lass, to celebrate. Then we'll load up an' be on our way early in the mornin' before anyone's awake. We'll get to the Stanley locks first thing afore anyone else is there.'

'Won't you want a lie-in, Caleb, first mornin' back?' she whispered in a low voice.

'Na. If we call in at t'Albion Hotel, t'landlord'll let us 'ave an upstairs room for an hour. No need to wait for tomorrow morning.' He kissed her again. 'Horse all right?' he enquired.

'Yes, Bessie's fine. She's been at some stables ten minutes away. Bloke was lookin' after her for free. Said it was an arrangement you made.

Anyway, she's ready for the long pull. Put on a bit of weight, she 'as. Not like you.'

She held him again. 'That prison food ain't to your taste, is it?' she said, looking up into his eyes.

He took her in his arms and gently, so gently, hugged her. 'There ain't nothin' in there to my taste, not compared to what you can give me, Jenny. And if we find that that nice spot, up beyond Gargrave, out in the country and away from the factories and wharves and coal tips, then we can moor t'boat up an afternoon. We can take along a picnic of ham 'n' cheese 'n' fresh bread. Kids can run around in t'woods and me and thee can stretch out together and enjoy t'sunshine. Bessie can feed on fresh grass, Thunder can guard t'boat an' all will be right with the world again.'

* * *

My dearest, darling Eliza,
Why oh why have you not replied to my letters? Why have you left me so alone, rotting in this jail for over two months and never visited me? I only took that money from the firm for our sakes so that it would see us through the first months of our new life together in America. I did intend to pay it all back. That is the truth. I swear to you.

I forgive you, so please forgive me. I found the blackmail letter and I now see that what you did you did for love, our love. I realise now that you took the money from the clock to pay the blackmailer. And that blackmailer was Lem Metcalf, I'm sure of it. It was his attempt to get even with us, and it succeeded. I know the letter wasn't in his handwriting, but he was behind it I'm sure.

I can only assume that if I get no reply you feel everything is over between us, and that you have already abandoned me and gone back to Bradford, in which case this letter is futile. I would never go back to Bradford, so it would mean that it's all over. But I will never forget you, and wherever I go and whatever I do I will always love you.

Your dearest Walter xxxxx

Walter read over the letter. His stomach hurt again, as it had for the last two nights. Eventually he had gone to sleep and in the morning the pain had gone. He would go to sick parade the following morning and ask the doctor for some bismuth. The discomfort was probably caused by the prison food, but in just over a week's time he would be free, and with a good diet and fresh air he would feel better.

He turned his thoughts to his release. What would he do now? There would be no chance of getting a salesman's job with any reputable firm, he knew that. But there might be other things he could do using his experience and his innate gift of salesmanship: the charm, the patter, the bonhomie and the acting of many roles. But he would need capital – that was the key.

The chatter of the pipes interrupted Walter's reverie. It was as ceaseless as the wind in the trees, the sparrows on the rooftops. It stopped when the warder did his rounds along the landing, but immediately resumed when his footsteps were gone. Walter put his stool against the outside wall and climbed up to gaze out of the window at the sky. He caught a glimpse of the Pole Star, which he could always see on a clear night from his north-facing window. The cell's aspect made it cool in the heat of summer, not like those on the other side of the landing, which fried throughout July and August. It would be different in the winter, but he would not be here then to shiver on the hard planks and wrap his blankets tightly around him. Walter traced the line of the Plough and the specks of the Great Bear. He thought of Caleb, whose barge would be tied up by green fields, after he had wended his way over locks, through tunnels and past the interminable factories, spoil-heaps and industrial detritus.

* * *

Caleb didn't know that the stars around Polaris constituted the Great Bear, but he enjoyed looking at them all the same. Someone had told him once that the nearest one was so far away that it would take two lifetimes of travel on a canal boat to get there. Thunder, his big black lurcher, lay beside him, head resting against his master's foot. He too was glad to have Caleb back, as were Jenny and the four children. The boat was moored near Gathurst, in a small stretch of serene countryside between the towns and factories. The only sound was from the occasional call of an owl or Bessie stirring in her sleep, giving a little whinny at a passing dormouse or another night creature. Caleb had worked her hard that day, a full thirteen hours, and after the months of idleness she had seemed reluctant to get back into harness again. But this was compensated for by life in the open air and the chance to feed on fresh grass.

Caleb lit his pipe, not unlike the enormous briar that Mr O'Malley sported. Puffs of smoke warded off a small cloud of midges that had been attracted by the glistening sweat on his neck and arms. Thunder was grateful for this too. It seemed as if all was at peace – but it wasn't. Caleb was anxious. He knew that in a few days he would reach Shipley, back in his beloved Yorkshire. It was no more than two miles from Bradford, a town he knew quite well. And living in that town was a man who had done his friend a great deal of harm; destroyed his life, in fact. And while Walter would walk free from jail in a few days, he would be a ruined man: no job, almost penniless, his woman gone. But his tormentor would be prospering and enjoying the fruits of a rich life, with plenty to eat, lots to drink, fine clothes, a comfortable home and even a mistress, his fancy woman, to keep him entertained. It didn't seem right. And yet Walter was set against revenge. It didn't seem right to Caleb, who sat gazing up at the mocking, twinkling stars.

* * *

'Just one more time.'

'No, I don't think so.'

Like two lovers in a secret tryst they stood together behind a wide oak tree. It shook its branches towards a clear starlit sky.

'Then after that we'll give it up, leave it for good.'

'It's too much of a risk, Lem.'

'You didn't say that when you had the money off me for that dress. And I'll say this, Madge, it looks reyt grand on thee.'

She was not her usual self that evening. For once they weren't meeting in a busy restaurant or in the middle of a distant town, and crowds of strangers always seemed to give them more anonymity in her eyes. But in late evening, far from Lister Park's main paths or the magnificent bandstand, even Madge realised she would be unlikely to bump into anyone she knew. Lem was more uncomfortable: he knew too many people in Bradford from all walks of life, and he knew he had made a few enemies in his time. It was he who was nervous of meeting in this spot.

'That second letter you made me send went unanswered. Either they're not at that address or they won't give any more. I think it's time to call it a day.'

'I'll get that detective on to it again. We needn't pay him too much this time. After all, he's got a thread to follow, an old address to work on. We'll try one last time before that trip to America; that is, if they really were going there. It may have been a ruse, Madge. He's a crafty blighter that Walter Clough, or Adams as he calls himself now. He might have said it to put anyone off the scent or scarper without paying rent. I wouldn't put owt past him.'

'No, Lem. No more *blackmail*.' She moved closer to him and whispered, so that not even the flowers around might hear. 'If it ever came out we'd be in trouble. We've got what we want, a little revenge. Let's leave it at that.'

Lem felt uncomfortable for once. There was a determination in her eyes that he could not shift. 'Oh all right, Madge, you win. No more demands for money. Perhaps they've gone over to America after all. I'll put out some feelers. Start spreading a few rumours. Let the Ackroyds know what really happened. Even drop a hint to the papers.' She was still staring at him, a look of disquiet and censure in her eyes. 'Don't worry, Madge, I'll cover my tracks. They won't know where it's come from. You can rest assured on that count. There'll be no path back to us.'

'No, Lem.' She moved closer and looked him straight in the eyes.

'But it's what we agreed.'

'No. Leave it as it is. No revelations. No upsetting his family. That wife and kids of his must have gone through hell these past few months. They've had enough to put up with. If they ever find out on their own account then so be it. Perhaps they have a right to know, but not that way.'

'Come on, Madge, there's more to it than that. What's up? What are you thinking? Why have you changed your mind?'

She stretched out and took his hands in hers. The gesture took him by surprise. 'Please, please Lem, let it rest. We thought they were having a fling, a bit of fun, an affair. But it's turned out more than that. They've been prepared to risk everything, and even start a new life together far away. Let them be. Let their families grieve. Do it for my sake, Lem.'

'You've been thinking about it, lass.'

'Yes I have. You know, it's so hard to find happiness. Life's full of wrong choices, things that might have been. If you get one little bit of bliss once in a while then it's all you can ask. And them losing that baby set me thinking. They've had enough to suffer for their love, despite the misery they've caused.'

'All right, all right. I won't do owt if that's the way you really feel.' Madge gave his hands a gentle squeeze, and to his surprise he found himself reciprocating. 'Now come on, lass, we'll have a turn next week round the best shops in Leeds. We'll have tea at the Grand, nothing more I promise you, unless you want it . . . I'll buy you one more nice dress and this time I'll choose it for thee, cos it'll be out of my own pocket.'

Madge gave him a peck on the cheek and slipped away down the path towards the east gate.

* * *

129

The alleyway was dark and forbidding at the best of times, but in the middle of a grey, drear, rainy afternoon, it took on a menace all of its own. Blackened stone walls rose sheer on each side for three storeys. A high wall at the back offered no escape, being surmounted by iron spikes. A rusty iron staircase dripped water on to the mossy cobbles, rising above Caleb to the door on the first floor. He waited patiently, using the door below, at the back of the ironmonger's shop, for both cover and shelter.

He wondered if he had set up his plan well enough. Would it work? He wondered if he should be doing it at all. Everything had seemed so easy yesterday afternoon. He had left the boat moored along the wharf at Saltaire, then walked the two miles along the Bradford arm to the Victoria in the city centre. There he met a few old friends, asked around and was introduced to Jonas Crabtree, a wagoner who worked for Ephraim Smith. He had heard of Lem: in fact he told Caleb that a Lem Metcalf had been asking around, and had used a private detective called George Sugden to trace Ephraim Smith's daughter and a man called Walter.

Encouraged by the success of his enquiries, Caleb had paid George Sugden a visit, catching him just before he finished for the afternoon. The detective had been reluctant at first to give him any information, but a smashed chair and threats of personal violence had encouraged him to come round to his visitor's point of view. After further persuasion, Caleb pointing out to him that it would be difficult to write his case notes with a broken arm, he agreed to lure Lem to the office by sending an urgent message: the bait of further revelations about Walter and Eliza, which might be to his advantage, would do the trick. The time was arranged for late the following afternoon.

And here he was, a man exactly fitting Sugden's description rolling down the alleyway, a portly middle-aged man smoking a fat cigar. The sweet odour of best Havana drifted down the narrow path, reaching the watchful Caleb a second or two before Lemuel Metcalf drew level with him. Caleb stepped out in front of him.

'Excuse me, sir, I wondered if we might have a word.'

Lem eyed the large man up and down. He was apprehensive but didn't feel threatened. After all, he had been approached politely. But he could tell the giant wasn't a policeman or another private detective, because of his workmen's trousers, heavy waistcoat and working boots.

'I'm sorry but I've urgent business.'

'Not so urgent if it concerns a mutual friend of ours.'

'What mutual friend? I'm sure we have no friends in common. Now if you will excuse me, I'd be much obliged if you would let me get on with my business.'

'It's a very good friend of mine. He goes by the name of Walter. It seems you haven't been too nice to him recently.'

Lem stopped dead in his tracks. He took the cigar from his mouth, and felt the acid in his stomach rising up in his throat. His heart was pounding in his chest. He knew he could not outrun his burly adversary, and fighting was out of the question: he would have to talk his way out. 'I think you've got the wrong end of the stick, my friend,' he squirmed. 'I knew him once, long, long ago. He was an employee of mine at Ledger's, but that was years ago. I even got him his job there, you know.'

'And sacked him.'

'Yes, well, I had to, you see. And that was over three years ago. I haven't seen him since.'

'My, my. For a man in a good job you've got a bad memory. What about the Adelphi in Liverpool, and Bradford station eighteen months ago?'

Damn! The man knew too much. 'I know, but it was an empty threat. After all, he spread a malicious and untrue rumour about me. It could have caused me a lot of trouble, lost me my job even. But I didn't tell his family.'

Caleb took hold of his lapels and held him against the wall. 'No. You decided to blackmail him instead.'

'No, no, you've got it wrong,' Lem gabbled. 'I didn't write that letter. I had nothing to do with it. It was someone else. I admit it was me who hired the detective and found out about Walter's disappearance, but I wasn't in favour of the blackmail. After all, it's criminal, isn't it? I tried to persuade them not to do that.'

Caleb looked down at the blubbering, quivering jelly in his grasp. He could have beaten Lem senseless with a couple of blows and extracted the blackmail sum from him with impunity, but it wasn't worth it; not from a hopeless excuse for a man like this. He remembered Walter's plea: 'No revenge. It's not worth it.' A strange calmness overcame him, and he felt nothing but contempt for the pathetic, pleading figure in his grasp. Caleb let him down and looked him straight in the eye. Lem seemed to realise that no revenge would be exacted. He stared into his assailant's face and dropped his gaze in utter shame. Caleb shook his head and walked off down the alley.

What was Lem to do? He decided not to follow the man back into the street. After all, he might change his mind and still beat him to a pulp. Better to seek the sanctuary of the detective's office up the iron staircase. He started to climb the steps slowly, one at a time. His heart was still pounding. By the time he reached the fourth step a pain was searing through his body, across his chest and down his arms. Despite the cool, rainy day, he was sweating. The effort was too great. He felt dizzy. The pain reached his legs, and each step was agony. Then it became too much. He could not feel the solid iron under his feet. He was falling backwards through the air. Then he felt the jarring crunch in his back. His body found it again . . . then another step . . . then another.

It was as if he couldn't feel, or see, or hear anything, at least for a time; how long he could not tell. When he came to there was a face looking at him. He was being cradled in arms, in soft arms, and he felt the hint of a bosom against the side of his face.

'Madge, oh Madge, love, I knew you'd come back to me. We always made a reyt good pair.'

'Oh Lem, I got your message and I wanted to stop you, but it's too late.' She bent down to kiss him. For once she didn't mind if the long, luxuriant moustache tickled her top lip. 'Oh Lem, oh Lem.'

He pursed his lips to kiss her. He closed his eyes. It was perfect. He didn't feel the need to open them again.

Chapter Eighteen

Eliza had come up from her cabin to view the stars on the fine, warm night. It was not a comfortable cabin but a small space, deep in the bowels of the ship. It was not even a passenger liner like the *Oceanic* on which she had made her fateful lone journey to America, but a smaller mixed passenger and freight ship, which rocked and pitched its way across the Grand Banks in a heavy swell. Now well into the middle of the Atlantic, it had reached the peace and calm of a massive late summer anticyclone, which stretched from Shetland in the north all the way down to the Azores. She too could see Polaris and its myriad of accompanying stars.

As she gazed at the constellation she thought of all that had happened: the awful shock of finding Walter gone, and her struggle in America to keep body and soul together for two months. She remembered her desperate search for employment and her lucky break, when she got a bookkeeping job with the comfort of a few dollars and savings for her return journey. She remembered the lecherous boss who had promised her more money and a comfortable existence if she shared his bed as well as his office; the assault he had made on her, and her desperate struggle and violent rebuff. Thank God for that inkstand, that heavy inkstand which had left him without three of his front teeth. But then there were the threats of arrest and jail . . . In desperation she had fled with her few possessions and savings to that seedy waterfront hotel, with its equally seedy proprietor and its assortment of dubious characters.

But she had got out, and just in time too. The cabin on the *Oric* was the last one free, but it was going back to England. It had a charming

133

second officer who had been solicitous, and was most concerned that she had to put up with the cramped and miserable conditions – so concerned that he offered to share his spacious cabin with her! Were all American men like this, so forward, so brazen? Or did she appear so vulnerable that men thought she was easy prey?

Eliza leaned over the rail to watch the rush of white water under the bow. It was the only thing visible in the darkness below. She sighed. Why had he left her and run away? She was so sure that he had loved her. It had puzzled her, no, tortured her on the *Oceanic*, in New York and now on her journey home. Had he planned deliberately to leave her alone on the ship? Perhaps the pull of his family and the love for his children had been greater than she had ever thought, especially since the death of their own dear Martha. Did he think that she might not bear him any more children? Or had something happened on that journey back – an accident, a chance meeting . . . Perhaps something when he arrived back at their house, to search for the letter. That was it! Why had she not thought of it before? She gripped the rusty rail and drew a sharp breath. Perhaps he had found the letter . . . but had also found the blackmail letter. The one she had mislaid. Had he discovered it, and all her secrets? Did he think that their love had been based on deceit? Had he discovered not only the secret of the blackmail and the missing money but also realised that she had used Lem Metcalf's threats to make him choose between her and his family. Had she, the deceiver, now been deceived?

* * *

Eliza waited patiently at the door. The whole of Albion Street was quiet. There wasn't a soul to be seen, but curtains twitched and eyes watched her every move. No welcoming neighbour came out to greet her. There was no friendly wave, no cheery call of 'Afternoon, Eliza,' as there had been in times past.

After all, it had been the biggest scandal to hit the street since it had been built. The police had been at the front door and round the back guarding the entry. The man who lived there had been arrested and led out in handcuffs by Sergeant Butcher himself. Rumours had flown back and forth like the waves of an incoming tide, growing bigger with every surge. The fifty pounds stolen had rapidly become a hundred, even two hundred. And it turned out that they hadn't been married, and they had flitted without paying the rent. And there had been a baby who had been born out of wedlock. It was sad that it had died within a few hours – but it was God's judgement, to be sure! And there were tales of earlier crimes, of a previous wife whom they had murdered, perhaps. Then, with the police hot on their trail, they had tried to flee to America, and it was only by sheer good luck the police had caught him – while she got away scot free. Now here she was, back at the scene of the crime, knocking on her own front door, bold and brazen as you like. The shame of it!

'What do you'se want?' A sharp-featured woman with wire-rimmed spectacles, brown hair and wet hands was at the door.

'I wonder if you can help me. I'm trying to find out about a person who used to live here.'

The woman immediately became suspicious, and her reply was defensive. 'That depends on what youse might want to know.'

'My name is Eliza Adams.' The woman stepped back and put a hand over the door knob. 'I lived here a few months ago with my husband. I went on ahead to America and he had to stay here because of his business. I wonder if he left a forwarding address.'

The woman stared at her for a few seconds. No, but I know what he did leave: he left you in the lurch . . . So this is the hussy. Yes, very pretty. Would turn any fellow's head, to be sure. Looks like butter wouldn't melt in her mouth, never mind living with him as his wife and bearing his child out of wedlock. And I, Maggie Richards, know a lot more than that, from all those letters that arrive here from the jail. But it wouldn't do to admit you read other people's letters, even if they were from a criminal. You had to show your neighbours you could act like a lady, now you lived over the water in Wallasey. 'Sorry, luv, don't know where he's gone. Didn't leave no forwardin' address.'

With that she slammed the door, and Eliza turned to walk back to the promenade. Half a dozen curtains twitched again, and three or four women made plans to call in on number fifteen for a chat, or invite their new neighbour round for a cup of tea. At the corner Eliza passed the postman doing his round. Among his wad of letters was one from the jail. It would be read, its contents digested, and would then be confined to the flames.

Twenty minutes later Eliza reached the Egremont ferry. Across the water she would take a cab to Lime Street station, pick up her small amount of luggage, take a train to Manchester and then another to Bradford. She did all this like an automaton, without thought, feeling or hope. She picked up a sixpenny book from the stall at the station, hoping that by filling her thoughts with its contents she might stop thinking about the last three years of her life, and the man who had occupied them.

* * *

Eliza's first thought on reaching the door was to turn and run back. She had told the cab driver to wait a short way down the street, why she was not sure. Was it because she knew that at the last moment she might lose her nerve and the cab would be a ready means of escape? She had even instructed him to leave the luggage on board. Eliza could just see him from the doorway, his black horse motionless, munching its bag of oats.

The cab driver leaned back in his seat observing the grand houses of the wealthy folk of Bradford. So this is where she lived, he thought. Or did she? Why had she instructed him to leave the valise and that damned heavy trunk on the cab? Why was she dressed like she was, in a dowdy black dress with no frills or ribbons? Still, it couldn't hide her trim figure. And you couldn't hide those dark eyes, the long dark hair, that regular face, immaculate complexion and lovely mouth with full red lips. She was a beauty, to be sure, but she dressed as if to hide it all. Very strange indeed!

Eliza tugged the bell-pull and stepped back to await footsteps down the hall. The door opened, but the face framed in the doorway was not one she knew: it was a new maid. Had she been away for so long? The young girl had reddish-brown hair, a small retroussé nose and delicate ears that peeked out from beneath her cap. 'Good morning, madam. Who shall I say it is?'

This was the moment she had dreaded. How would she be able to explain what had happened? How would her mother feel, with the shame of it all? Her fear and uncertainty took over. 'I'm Mrs, er, Adams, an acquaintance of Mrs Smith. We haven't seen each other for a long time. Do you think she would mind if I called in for a couple of minutes?'

Eliza's lip quivered. She wanted to turn and hurry away.

The young girl caught something, perhaps a look or a mannerism she had seen in her mistress, and interrupted before Eliza could depart. 'Of course, madam. Please, please step inside. I'll bring the mistress straight away.' She smiled and reached out to help Eliza step over the threshold. She smiled again at the petrified visitor, closed the door behind her, then hurried off down the hall.

There was the sound of voices, a familiar voice, then raised voices again. 'Why should I come and see this lady? I don't know anyone called Mrs Adams.'

'Ma'am, I think you should. You *must* come.'

Jane Smith was half-way down the hall when she caught sight of Eliza. She stopped for a second and stared in disbelief. They met five steps from the front door, rushing into each other's arms. The young maid stared at them before bursting into tears.

'Oh, Eliza, it's wonderful, just wonderful to have you back.'

'I'm so sorry, Mum. I've made such a mess of my life.'

'Hush, my child. All that matters is that you're back.' She eventually looked up from her embrace. 'Sally, tell the cab man to bring in the luggage. Here's a shilling. Take the cab down to the yard and tell Mr Smith to come home at once. Tell him . . .'

'I know, ma'am. I guessed who it was,' the young girl burst out. 'I've got to tell him that Miss Eliza's returned.' She rushed out of the door, and was soon eagerly helping the cab driver deposit the trunk and valises inside. They were off in the cab within a minute, and even the black horse seemed to realise the urgency of their mission. They trotted off at some pace in the direction of the city.

Despite the love a daughter may have for her father, and the delight a daughter may give to her father, there are some things only a mother and daughter can share. After an afternoon and evening of many tears and smiles with her parents, it was on the morrow, when Ephraim had returned to his business, that Jane took her daughter aside and bade her sit down with her in the quiet of the sitting room.

Jane Smith had originally come from the mean streets in the centre of the city. On marriage she had moved into a better house, though it was still small, on Manningham Lane. Lately she had moved again, with the success of Ephraim Smith's business ventures, into the secluded and prosperous streets of Cottingley, far away from the grime and misery of Bradford itself. But she had never forgotten her childhood and family, and was generous with them to a fault. Neither did she insulate herself from the miseries and conditions that existed in the city: she did not despise it as many ladies in her street did. She understood what life could be like, and the evils and tragedies that could affect any family. She was never one to judge others for the circumstances they might find themselves in.

She spent the whole morning with Eliza, listening to her story and comforting her when painful memories brought her daughter's words to an abrupt halt amid floods of tears.

'What am I to do now, Mum?' Eliza asked.

'For now, my dear, do nothing. There are too many things spinning around in your head at the moment. You need to rest, clear your mind and think about them one at a time, then you'll be able to think more clearly. Just remember – I'll be here to comfort you and give you advice, but only if you ask.'

'But what about Walter? What can have happened to him?'

'If you like, your father can pay for a private detective to make enquiries.'

'Yes, please do that.'

'Do you want him back if he'll come?'

'I don't know, Mum.'

'Will you live in sin with him if he wants to come back to you?' Eliza stayed silent. She could sense her mother's disapproval, although she hadn't voiced it. 'Perhaps if he wants you he'll seek a divorce. Then you could marry. But it will take time, a long time.' Eliza looked bewildered and tears filled her eyes. Her mother could see she was upset and went over to comfort her. 'There, there! I know it's not easy, especially as he's the man you love above everyone and everything.'

'It's easy for you to say those words.'

'You're right. I was lucky. I married the man I loved. But if he were still that one cart haulier and we were still struggling to survive in that cramped little house in Manningham Lane, I'd still be at his side, tripping over the piles of books he brought home, grumbling – but still loving him.' The memory of the chaotic household of her childhood brought a smile to Eliza's face. 'You must know that all this, the lovely house, servants to do the work I once had to do, all means nothing compared with the man I love. I'd put up with anything to always be with him. I do understand how you feel, love. I'm not condemning you for what you've done.' She held her daughter close to her as their tears ran down each other's face. 'I'll say no more. Let's find out what's happened to Walter first. I'll have a word with your dad tonight. He'll know how to get things going.'

'Thanks, Mummy.' Eliza was her mother's child again. She hadn't called her 'Mummy' since she was a little girl. It brought another tear to Jane's eye. 'There's one more thing I've got to ask you. Should I try to contact Walter's family, to let them know he's still alive?'

'That's difficult. It would be cruel to keep them in ignorance, yet the shock could harm his wife and children. Let's wait until we find out what's happened to him before you decide. He could . . . he could have . . .'

'He could already have gone back to them, and it might be over between us.'

'Yes, I'm afraid so. It's a possibility.'

'I suppose you're right. He never forgot his family, despite all the difficulties in his marriage. I knew he could never forget them. He always loved them. It seemed to come between us at times, when he had his silent moods. But if he hasn't gone back then they've got to know eventually.' Eliza sat in the welcoming velvet-covered armchair and stared for a minute into the fire. 'I suppose that's what I've got to face next. I've made this mess and I've got to try to undo it.'

'I know, but let's take things one at a time, my dear. Wait until your papa's engaged a detective and we've found out what really happened.' Jane took her daughter's hand, and they sat staring into the fire, each with her own thoughts.

Chapter Nineteen

The heavy iron door swung open and the solitary prisoner stepped outside into the grey, misty morning. He turned round to have one last look at the impressive gateway that loomed above him like the entrance to some medieval castle. Through the mist he caught sight of the prison blocks themselves, with their thin corner towers and castellated crowns. It was like a magnificent, elaborate folly built by a rich man. That was the exact description, Walter surmised: an enormous folly.

He was free at last, but no birds were singing to welcome him back to the life outside. No sun shone to warm his pale, drawn face. He had seen scenes like this a thousand times, but today it seemed different. It had a strangeness, an unfamiliarity, and it seemed, yes, it seemed threatening. His clothes hung off his body and, as promised by the old lag he had met on his first day, they stank of something akin to matches.

'They'll all know you've come out of clink,' he had said. 'They'll say you'se been workin' in the match fact'ry, wack, but they'll know where you'se been all right.'

Walter came out with the same belongings as he had gone in with: his wallet containing a five pound note, a few extra clothes in a small bag, some small change, some letters, a handkerchief and his gold pocket watch, his pride and joy. It was a possession that would, he hoped, help him to make his way for the next couple of months. He also carried out something else: it was his secret, and he knew it would change his life.

He trudged down the road in the general direction of the docks, eventually coming to a small market - a name that the gathering scarcely merited. The one or two wooden stalls displayed the poorest and cheapest wares you could ever find. For the rest, it was a collection of people with baskets, boxes and small barrels who had congregated in a clearing at the end of a street to display their few wares. Groups of ragged women, shawls wrapped tight around them, sat on walls and huddled on doorsteps, ignoring the cold and misty drizzle. They chatted and called out to passers-by, selling vegetables from wide baskets. 'Fresh this mornin', luv, picked em myself, I did.' This seemed to fool no-one. One woman shouted, as he passed close by, 'Oi, you've come from a shift out o' the match factory.'

An older woman next to her added, 'Aye, a six month shift to be sure.'

Walter smiled and walked on past the sellers of white crockery and then the poorest and most pathetic, those who sold piles of second-hand clothes, which gave off a distinctive aroma of sweat, filth and damp mustiness. He remembered that the Scouse prisoners had called Liverpool 'the city of second-hand roses', as so many sought to earn a crust from this noxious trade. He stared down into the eyes of a young girl, no taller than his own Hannah and scarcely looking a year or two older. The stained brown dress hung from her bony shoulders like a sack, and within her shawl lay a small infant. She squatted on the cobbles, unmindful of the cold, damp ground. A pair of spindly legs and mud-spattered feet poked out from the bottom of the skirt. Walter stopped to look down at her. She had a fresh, round, once innocent face and a mass of light brown curls tight around her head. She was as pretty a young girl as you would ever find in any city, on any street, and in this hellish place, he thought, she was too pretty for her own good.

'Want to buy any fine clothes, sir?' she enquired, pleading with her large grey eyes. For the most part her 'fine clothes' were just a pile of stinking rags, but one item had caught his eye: a black suit hanging from the railings behind her. He went over to inspect it. It had obviously been made for a tall and very thin man. It would never have fitted him before his stay in jail, but now it might do the trick. And it looked new, or nearly new.

'That's my Uncle Joe's,' she piped up. 'Or at least it was. Died of consumption, he did, last month. Only had a chance to wear it once. Smart man he was, sir, as you'se can see, a big tall skinny bloke. It was his Sunday best, honest, mister.' But it don't fit anyone round 'ere.'

There was a slight musty odour to the garment, but compared with the stench from the other clothes she sold it wasn't too bad. And it certainly didn't smell of *matches*.

'I'll try the jacket on, miss,' Walter said with overt politeness. It fitted his lean figure perfectly. He held the trousers to his waist: they were the right length too.

'Can't show you a mirror, mister, like in all the posh shops. But I'm tellin' you, with a nice black suit like that you looks a treat, a real toff.'

Walter removed the jacket and rolled it up with the trousers. 'All right then. How much?'

'Three shillin'. But to a nice bloke like you, who suits it so swell, two shillin'.'

Walter knew the custom was to haggle. He was sure he could talk her down to a shilling, but he hadn't the heart. He smiled. 'All right. Two shilling it is, young lady, and make sure you spend some of it on that baby of yours.'

Her eyes were a mixture of pure delight and sadness. They shone brightly, but he could also see tears welling up. Walter guessed she rarely received a kindness or even a smile from any man. 'Thank you, sir. You're a gent, too good to 'ave spent time in the Gurk. Whatever was it for?'

For once Walter was embarrassed. He handed over the two shillings, the last coins in his pocket, then he hurried on down the street with his bundle in the direction of the pawnbrokers.

Rafferty's had by far the largest frontage of any shop along Badger Street. There were two entrances, marked 'Clothes' on the left and 'Other Valuables' on the right. Walter entered the right-hand door, and as he approached the long counter he removed his pocket watch. The aroma of second-hand clothes from behind the counter to his left was overpowering. The shop was empty apart from a woman on the other side delivering a dress and coat to the counter and a young man facing Walter, who frowned when he saw the bundle under his arm.

'You'se come to the wrong side, wack. Clothes is over there on the other side.'

'I've not come to pawn clothes,' Walter replied, putting down the black suit. 'It's this I think you might be interested in.' He placed his pocket watch on the counter.

'One gent's pocket watch – two quid,' the young man said, as if reciting a chant.

'I don't think you've looked at it closely. It's solid gold, not gold plated or brass.'

The assistant eyed him up and down. He must have caught the aroma of the clothes Walter was wearing and realised where he had just come from. 'I think I'll ask Mr Rafferty senior to deal with this one. He can assess the value of these things better.'

He hurried off to the office at the back, and after a minute an older, bald-headed man appeared. Unlike the other staff, who removed their jackets for handling clothes and other goods and wore a regulation black waistcoat, he was immaculately tailored in a brown three-piece suit. He walked purposefully over to the counter, picked up the pocket watch and was clearly surprised by its weight and quality. 'Yes, erm, fifteen pounds, I think,' he whispered.

'You've got a similar one in the window at thirty pounds.'

'Can you prove this is yours? This is a respectable establishment, and we do get visits from the bizzies to check on our more valuable items, you understand.'

His smooth, urbane manner did not deceive Walter. No doubt there were many pieces of contraband and items burgled from the homes of Liverpool's more wealthy citizens hidden among his wares, but he had to be careful that the police could not identify anything. 'It has my name engraved on the inside and, yes, before you mention it, I've been discharged from prison today. Here's the discharge paper with my name on it. As you can see, the watch is definitely mine.'

The old man nodded. 'I see, I see.'

'And I want twenty-five pounds for it. I won't want to reclaim it. It's yours to sell.'

Old man Rafferty looked up at him. This was definitely no run-of-the-mill prisoner: he was tall, smart, with a distinctive, educated voice, but not from within thirty miles of the Mersey. The suit he wore, although ill fitting and smelling of sulphur, was of good quality. He wondered why he had been in prison. A list of crimes and misdemeanours flitted through his mind.

'Twenty pounds, and that's my last offer.'

'All right. But I'll have one of your gilt pocket watches as well.'

'A metal-cased one.'

'No, a gilt one. It's got to look good even if it's worthless.'

Rafferty smiled. 'Agreed. But if I were you I wouldn't go about doing any business in a suit that smells like that. I'll have it off you into the bargain. There's some round here that'll buy it despite the smell. After a month or so the habits of some round here will make it smell far worse than any match factory.' Walter laughed. 'I see you worked that out already,' Rafferty continued, winking and pointing at the black suit Walter had laid on the counter.

'You can have it, then. But I'll have a small case for it in exchange. Cardboard or leather board, I don't mind which, as long as it's got a lock and key.'

'I'll leave that to my assistant. You can change behind that screen over there. Most people who come to this establishment don't bother. You should see some of the sights here on a Saturday night when they come to redeem their best clothes and can't wait to get dragged up. Change right here in the shop some do, in front of the staff and other clients. Modesty is not a virtue valued by many round here. And I'll tell you now, for the most part it's definitely not a pretty sight.' Walter smiled at the jocular Irishman and shook his hand. 'A pleasure to do business with you, *Mr Clough,*' Rafferty said, with a grin.

Walter stopped in his tracks. For a moment he was confused. How did the Irishman know his real name? Then the penny dropped. Here he was passing himself off as Walter Adams to his former employers, the police, the magistrates' court and the prison authorities, but his old name had been there for anyone to see if only they had bothered to look inside his watch. He burst out laughing. The old man joined in the joke and waved him goodbye, wandering back to his little office, chuckling to himself.

At the bidding of his boss the young assistant returned with a couple of cases for Walter to inspect. He chose a cardboard one – of poorer quality than the leather board one but newer and smarter. He changed behind the screen and gave the old suit to the young man, who passed it over to the other counter. Walter's new suit fitted well. He walked out on to the street, suitcase in hand, twenty-five pounds in his wallet and a gilt pocket watch in his waistcoat. Now he was a new man, untainted by prison, and he knew what he had to do to make a living, at least for the next couple of months.

* * *

The face of the clock opposite Stanley Dock was showing twenty past seven that summer evening. So did the other five faces, but from his viewpoint opposite the giant five-storey tobacco warehouse Walter couldn't see them. The Dockers' Pocket Watch was a curious piece of architecture, set down in the middle of the docks like a giant chess piece or a fortified tower, set there to guard the dockers and their cargoes from bands of marauding pirates. Walter had had time to study it in detail, as he had waited patiently for over an hour.

Suddenly he noticed activity over to his right at the small lock entrance between the giant warehouses. Water was pouring into the basin and the lock from the canal was emptying. After a few minutes the torrent stopped, the wooden gates swung open and a barge nosed out of the lock. It was the *Bluebell.* The barge glided across the corner of the dock under the momentum of the escaping water. Walter grinned. He could see a horse being led round the corner of the rectangular basin by a young girl, while in the back the figure of Caleb held the tiller. The barge came to rest no more than thirty yards from where Walter was sitting.

Caleb lay back. His hand released the tiller. 'Why, Walt, nice to see you, lad! My, you does look smart in that natty suit. And what you got in that case?'

Walter got up, wandered over to Caleb and shook his hand. His was like a child's hand clasped in a giant's. 'Good to see you, Caleb. I was wondering if I might ask you a favour.'

'Certainly, Walt, you've only got to ask.'

'I was wondering if you might give me a ride on your boat up to North Lancashire – around Burnley or Colne, say.'

'Of course, Walt.'

'I'll pay my fare, of course. I'm going to try my hand at a bit of selling, door to door, markets, inns. I've got a nice lot of haberdashery in the case: small bulk, high value stuff. I didn't steal it,' Walter grinned. 'I know a wholesaler down behind the docks. Told him I was going into business on my own.'

'Well we'll have some off you as well, Walt. My Jenny is a dab hand with curtains and lace. Makes our little cabin into a right palace, she does. Some of your bits and bobs will come in handy. Now we've got to load up in Salisbury Dock. I'll pick you up from here t'day after tomorrow round about midday. If you wants you can leave t'case on board.'

'Will it be safe?'

'Aye, unless there's any that wants to chance their arm or any other part of their body with Thunder.' He pointed to the big black dog lying on top of the cabin, half asleep but watching the newcomer out of the corner of his eye. 'And if they gets past him there'll be Jenny to deal with; just as fierce an' twice as dangerous.' He winked an eye in the direction of the cabin. As he spoke a slight woman dressed in a white laced cap and matching apron emerged from inside the cabin and climbed up on to the stern. 'This is Walter, my love.'

'Nice to meet you, Walter. I heard what a good friend you was to my Caleb when you was in prison.'

'It was more the other way round. I don't know how I'd have survived if it wasn't for your husband's help.' There was an embarrassed silence.

'Ah well, that's it, Walt,' muttered Caleb. A look passed between him and the slim figure at his side. 'Though we gone through a kind of ceremony some years ago, the kind that we boat people have sometimes, we ain't exactly married in the sight of God; not proper like.'

'Aye, and I been thinkin' it's about time you made an honest woman of me, Caleb Stone, for my sake as much as those of your children. And as we're passing that boat people's mission in Burnley you can do it this time. They can get you a special licence there, real quick, and after that we'll 'ave t'kiddies baptised proper like, by the pastor. You'll not even have the excuse of not having a best man. I'm sure Walter here will be glad to help.'

Walter looked from one to the other, wondering whose side to take. He could see a slight smile on the face of his friend. They had both been trapped by the sweetly smiling woman before them. 'I'd be delighted to serve as your best man, if the opportunity arises,' he said, sensing the way the wind was blowing.

'Aye, all right, lass, you win at last. As you always does!' Caleb grinned. 'And as Walter's comin' on board for a few days it will be as good a time as any. Don't worry, I'll make an honest woman of thee and we'll have a reyt celebration after, at the Boatman's Arms in Brierfield. You'll find out how boat folks really enjoy themselves, Walter. But I'm afraid there ain't no room in our little cabin of a night: you'll have to sleep out under the tarpaulin. It's all right while it's still summer. Jenny can fix you up with a blanket if needs be.'

'Nonsense, Caleb,' his wife interrupted. ''E's our guest and I'll make him a bed in t'second cabin, where John sleeps. We're lending him out to my cousin as his first mate from tomorrow. Didn't I tell you?'

'No you didn't, love. But if John doesn't mind . . .'

'Of course he doesn't, you big lump. Our Rob's got no company on his journey back to Leeds, and John thinks the world of him. He can do owt that's needed on a barge. He's really come along while you been wasting those three months away.'

'Where's Rob's wife and family then?'

'Don't you listen to owt I say? I told you two days ago. They're going to her sister's. Her sister's husband's got t'job of lock-keeper at Dobson Locks, just past Shipley, and it comes with a nice little house in the country. He says he's getting too old for the life on t'water now.'

Walter could see that Caleb was completely under the spell of this small, chatty and friendly woman. Captain of the *Bluebell* he may have been in name, but he had happily surrendered everything to the woman he loved.

A day later Walter was welcomed aboard for the journey north. He was surprised when he entered the cabin that so much could be fitted into such a small space. Tables folded into beds, cupboards folded into beds and floorboards lifted to become cupboards. White lace-edged plates hung from the walls together with pans, jugs and bowls, each one decorated with a delicate pattern of bluebells that matched the painting on the outside of the boat. Everything had its place in an immaculate little 'house' no more than twelve feet long and seven feet wide. And everything was as neat, tidy and clean as a new pin. Decorated cotton lace abounded, as curtains, table-cloths, door hangings and shelf covers, each one with a distinctive, intricate pattern crafted by Jenny.

As they left the Stanley lock, and the warehouses grew smaller and smaller behind them, Caleb posted himself on the top of the cabin with Thunder to deter the stone throwers who were a nuisance to boat people in those parts. Within an hour they were out in the country. Jenny took her turn leading the horse, while Leah, their eight-year-old daughter, walked behind her, checking the hundred foot rope for any snagging. Caleb sat back, his foot on the tiller, puffing on his pipe and chatting to Walter as the fields, trees and bridges glided by.

Chapter Twenty

Eliza stared down at the piece of paper in horror. It was brief and to the point. Her answer was there in front of her. The Liverpool detective agency had done its work.

Dear Mr Smith,

With reference to your enquiry concerning the whereabouts of Walter Adams/Walter Clough/Walter Adams Clough. Following our enquiries over the last three days we have found the following:- The said person no longer resides at 15 Albion Street, Wallasey. The said person was arrested for theft of monies from his employers Field Brothers of Liverpool on 7th June 1900. The said person was convicted and sentenced to three months in jail. He was in Walton Jail from 9th June to 9th September 1900. The said person has probably left the Liverpool area. Rumour has it he may still be in the Lancashire area working as a door-to-door salesman or market trader in haberdashery. We must emphasise that the last piece of information is only based on hearsay and rumour.

We remain your faithful servants.

J. Parsons

CHAPTER TWENTY

Bentley and Soames – Detective Enquiry Agency, Liverpool

'Well, my dear, there you have it. What are you going to do now?' Jane Smith put her arm around her daughter's shoulder and read the letter again. She put her spectacles down on the table. 'Do you want your father to ask them to make further enquiries? They seem very capable. Mind you, they're not cheap.'

'I'm not sure, Mum. I don't know what to do. I do know that what we did was wrong and that it hurt a lot of innocent people, but . . . we were in love, you must believe that!'

'Love can make us do the strangest and most foolish things, my darling. I know that, even though your father and I have been happily married these past twenty-five years. But it was never based on deceit and secrets, Eliza. If you want to spend your lives together, my love, you've got to be open and truthful.'

Eliza was silent for a moment, then took the paper to the fire and threw it in the flames. 'It also means I've got to be truthful with others as well. And that includes his wife and children.'

'How are you going to do it? You must be careful – gentle. Confronting them with the truth could be embarrassing . . . distasteful . . . harmful, even.'

'I know, Mum, but there must be a way.' Eliza rose from the chair and wandered round the room, stopping in front of the window and gazing out into the street. 'I know. I could speak to his wife's sister, the one who works for that little mission church down in the slums.'

'I've heard of that lady preacher. She does a grand job rescuing all those runaway girls. Our ladies' circle has raised quite a sum to help them.'

'It's not only that. She knew about our affair in the beginning and didn't tell Walter's wife, because we ended it there and then. She seemed sensible, and she was careful not to upset her sister and the family. I'm sure she might listen and find a way of telling them.

Jane nodded and looked her daughter in the eye. 'That's a good idea, Eliza. I think you're starting to think straight at last.'

* * *

With her stomach churning, Eliza walked from the elegant shops of Westgate, where she had shopped so often and extravagantly in the past, down the narrow, twisting street that was Silsbridge Lane. She had to take extra care on the rough slippery cobbles. The cab driver had declined to take her all the way down, claiming the winding and treacherous surface was too dangerous for his horse and cab on a wet day. She wondered whether that was the only reason for his reluctance. Was it because he didn't want to be stoned by the numerous urchins, abused by the hostile drunkards or even robbed for his fare? She felt the eyes watching her, some leering, others staring in surprise, and heard a few whistles and cat calls. It was with relief that she saw the little church, opened the gate and mounted the shallow steps. Even now part of her wanted to turn back and run all the way to Westgate, then take a cab home, but she pressed on. At the door she thought of knocking, but didn't. She slowly turned the handle and stepped inside.

Eliza was noticed by four people, an older gentleman in grey clerical garb, a round-faced and white-haired lady who hummed as she worked, a young girl who left her task once in a while to pick up a book, and a woman she knew. After the first casual glances one pair of eyes appeared more intense than the others. They were the dark, piercing eyes of Nancy, the same look she had directed at Walter and Eliza all those years ago in Blackpool. Instinctively Eliza turned her gaze away and looked around, anything to avoid those eyes. The other people in the room resumed their work, cleaning and laying out the chairs.

The woman she knew stepped forward. Her hard, surprised stare subsided into a kind of sympathetic recognition. After what seemed an age she spoke. 'I know who you are,' she whispered. 'It's about Walter, isn't it?'

'Er . . . yes it is. How did you know?'

'We can't talk together now. I imagine that what you want to say will take some time. There are too many people around at the moment, and I've got to help to get the church ready for a Bible rally here this evening. Pastor Robinson will be leading the service.' Nancy looked in the direction of the older man, who was looking curiously at the two women. 'We've got a special preacher as well, coming all the way from Leeds.' She stopped, looked back to the pastor and then to Eliza. For once she was lost for words.

'I do see. It's inconvenient.'

'Could you come up to the house in Wakefield Road this afternoon?'

'Your family house? Oh I couldn't possibly speak about this to the others in your family, your brothers, your mother and . . . Walter's wife.'

If Nancy recognised the importance of Eliza's words, it hardly registered on her face. There was just a slight pause before she spoke again. 'My mother will be out, and Annie and her children, Walter's children, are going to a tea party at their other grandmother's. I'll be on my own and we can talk. You can say what you want to say, whatever it is. It will be all right. No-one else will hear, or even know, if that's what you want.'

'Yes, thank you,' muttered Eliza, surprised at the sympathy she was receiving. 'Will two o'clock be all right?'

'Half past two, just to make sure.'

'I'll be there at half past two.' Eliza gave a slight smile. Neither woman made an attempt to shake hands, but Nancy smiled again before turning away.

Eliza closed the door behind her and hurried back up the lane. The street was quieter now, and she only had to run the gauntlet of three or four drunks around the door of the Slaymaker's Arms. There was, however, the same chorus of whistles and catcalls that she had met on her way down Silsbridge Lane.

'My, you're a posh one to be workin' these streets, my lovely!'

'Bet you charge a lot more than Shillin' Gertie on the corner!'

* * *

Eliza noticed that the Minton tiles on the sides of the porch were the same as the ones in her own family's house at Cottingley, a dark leaf pattern interlaid with deep orange flowers with lily-like trumpets and deeper red throats and stamens. She waited a minute after knocking, but no-one came, so she knocked louder. Eventually she heard brisk footsteps coming to the door and Nancy was standing in front of her.

'I'm so sorry, Miss . . .'

'Smith, Eliza Smith.'

'Oh yes, I remember now. I'm so sorry, Miss Smith, but one of the children, Rosie, is ill. I crept upstairs to check. She's asleep but we'll have to be careful. Keep our voices down. I'm sure you understand.'

'Certainly.' They had reached the door of the sitting room.

'I'll bring some tea.'

'That would be nice. Thank you.'

'Please make yourself comfortable in the drawing room.'

Eliza perched on the edge of a large armchair and gazed through the window. For the first time doubts began to form in her mind. Nancy's footsteps retreated down the hallway in the direction of the kitchen.

Rosie was under strict instructions to stay in bed because of her nasty cold, which could easily turn into a bad chest, the last thing her mother wanted. Rosie was annoyed. The other three had gone off to Grandma Harriet's for tea, which would mean jelly, Grandma's lovely jam tarts and cakes and, as always, a small surprise present at the end. And the worst thing was that she had felt a bit better by the afternoon, so much so that she had got out of bed. She had seen the lady arrive. Such a beautiful lady, with such a nice dress. Then she had heard her aunt's footsteps, and had to dive between the covers and pretend she was asleep. Now she felt thirsty. There was no water left in her cup, so she had tiptoed downstairs to fill it up again. It would be all right: Aunt Nancy and the lady were in the front room.

Rosie had got to the kitchen and filled the cup when she heard her aunt coming down the hall. She slipped into the back parlour. Suppose Aunt Nancy wanted something from the dresser or looked round the door? She looked for a place to hide as the footsteps approached. She spotted her opportunity. The very place! She could hear Nancy in the kitchen, then in the back parlour taking cups from the dresser, then back in the kitchen and finally disappearing down the hall to the drawing room again. Rosie stayed perfectly still: she didn't want her aunt to hear her.

'You've come to tell me something very important, haven't you?' said Nancy. ' That Walter's not dead.'

'How do you know?' gasped Eliza.

'I don't *know*. I just, well, how can I put it? I just have a feeling. He was too clever to get caught on the sands after all the time he spent out there with those fishermen. The suitcase, the jacket: it was all a ruse so that you two could run away together, wasn't it?'

Eliza slowly nodded.

'He was good at deceiving people. That's the only thing I've never liked about him. He lied to me after I caught you two on that holiday together. He said he would leave you, but he never did, and I thought he had. And I thought I would never be deceived again, not by a man.'

'You weren't deceived.'

'How do you mean?'

'He did leave me, honestly. We didn't see each other for over two years. Then we met by chance in Bowling Park. He was with his wife and children and his new baby. It was me who engineered a second meeting. It wasn't Walter's fault – you've got to believe me!' Her voice rose in a crescendo.

Nancy jumped up and put a finger to her lips 'Please, please keep your voice down. We're not alone in the house. We don't want his child to hear any of this . . .' She had heard something. Was it a creak on the stair or a door closing? Nancy went to the drawing room door, opened it and listened intently. The house was silent, except perhaps for some coughing from the bedroom above. She closed the door and sat down again, facing Eliza. Neither teacup had been disturbed.

'What happened next? If you want me and perhaps my sister to know the whole truth of the matter, you'll have to tell me.'

Eliza's face was white and strained. She took a first sip, then placed her cup back in its saucer. 'He did come back to me. He did love me. The next year was wonderful.' Nancy scowled but passed no comment. 'We only met occasionally.'

'When he stayed over in Liverpool, you mean?'

'Yes. But something odd happened once. We bumped into Walter's old boss, Mr Metcalf, at the Adelphi Hotel in Liverpool, and the funny thing was . . .'

'What?'

'He was with his mistress too, a single lady from Ledger's office.'

'Such things may seem funny to you. They disgust me. Can't you see what harm you've done to his wife and family?'

'Yes, I do see. But please let me continue. That is, unless you don't want to hear any more.'

'I'm sorry,' sighed Nancy. 'If you're prepared to tell me everything it's the least I can do to hear you out. Please continue.'

'Then I discovered . . . that I was going to have . . .'

'You mean to say there's another child, Walter's?'

'I was desperate. I contrived a plan to make him choose his family or me. He chose me.'

'And the child?'

'Martha, yes.' Tears filled Eliza's eyes. 'She died a few hours after she was born. We were living together as man and wife in Wallasey. The firm he was working for didn't know anything. They thought we'd moved there from Bradford. He'd changed his sales area to Cheshire, you see.'

'You seem to have had everything well planned.'

'It wasn't like that. You must believe me. We *were* in love. I still love him even now, no matter where he is.'

'You mean you don't know?'

'No. I don't want to tell you all the details, but we were forced apart by circumstances. It was my fault he did what he did and ended up in jail.'

'In jail? Walter? What kind of a life did you lead him into?' Nancy stood up and her eyes flashed angrily.

'I did it all for love. I wanted us to be happy in a new life, but it didn't work out and he stole some money. We deceived each other. But we did it because we loved each other. You've got to believe me.' Eliza sank into the cushion, sobbing. Nancy bent down and offered her handkerchief. 'If you can tell me you've never loved a man so much that you'd do anything to have him, to keep him, then you can judge me for my wrongdoings.'

Nancy stayed silent. She reddened, and her head sank down to her chest. For a minute she was silent, lost in thought; the only sound in the room was the clock on the mantelpiece. 'Please don't be upset on my account. I'm sorry if I seemed harsh, but I know what harm and sorrow this has caused Annie and the children. You must understand that too.'

Eliza nodded. 'I do realise,' she said sadly. 'I'm sorry I can't tell you where Walter is now. The last we heard was that he might be in Lancashire somewhere, working as a door-to-door salesman. In time he may come back to Yorkshire. Who can say?'

151

Nancy shrugged her shoulders. They exchanged a resigned smile. When Eliza rose from her chair, Nancy showed her to the door. Before they parted she slowly shook her hand. 'Miss Smith, Eliza. If you do hear anything else you'll let us know, won't you?'

'Of course.'

"If you need to contact me I'm at the Mission most days. And if you ever wish to seek God's guidance, or have someone say a prayer with you, I'm there to help as well.'

'Thank you, Miss Ackroyd. I'll remember that.'

'I'll need to think about what you've told me before I say anything to my sister. I'll pray for guidance. I know this isn't easy, for either of us.'

They shook hands, and Nancy watched Eliza walk slowly down the street to the cab. They had too much to share, she thought: a lost lover, a lost child and a life torn apart by memories.

A small pair of reddened eyes also watched Eliza from the window above. Rosie climbed back into bed and tried to close her eyes to shut out the world, and pretend nothing had happened. But it had. She had heard, and try as she might she couldn't forget it. Sleep couldn't drive it away either. She lay there, her sobbing stopped for the present, but the pain still there.

* * *

Hannah was woken by the sound of Rosie crying, and she rolled over to face her sister.

'Are you poorly? Shall I get Mummy up?'

'No, no. It's not that. It's not that at all.'

'Then what in heaven's name is it?'

Rosie lifted herself up on the pillow. The half-opened curtains let in a shaft of moonlight that bathed her small, round, streaked face in a grey light. 'Oh, Hannah, I've found out your secret.'

'What secret?'

'The one about the cupboard.'

'How did you do that?'

'It was when you were at Grandma Harriet's. I'd been told to stay in bed, but I was thirsty so I went downstairs to the kitchen. It was when that lady was visiting Aunt Nancy.'

'What lady? No-one said anything about a visitor this afternoon.'

'She was a tall, dark-haired lady with large, sad, brown eyes. She was lovely, as beautiful as a princess. She had a nice pink dress and coat on. I heard her say that she'd once met us all in Bowling Park, but I can't remember.'

Hannah caught her breath. From somewhere she could picture her, even from Rosie's brief description. 'What happened then?'

'I heard Aunt Nancy coming back down the hall. The kettle was boiling and I realised she was coming to the kitchen to make tea. So I slipped into the parlour and hid in the cupboard.'

'It was open?'

'Yes. Someone had left the bolt undone. Oh, Hannah, I know about the cupboard now. It's not what's kept in there, it's what you can hear.'

'You listened?'

'I didn't mean to, Hannah. I'm sure you didn't either. But I found out your secret from what that lady said – your secret about Daddy.'

'But my secret's about Aunt . . .' interrupted Hannah. She bit her lip hard. 'Go on, Rosie.'

'Daddy's still alive. He ran away from us. He's not dead after all.'

Hannah turned away, so that Rosie could not hear her gasp or see the look of horror on her face. After a moment she turned around again to hold the whimpering Rosie in her arms, and comforted her until she fell asleep. But Hannah couldn't sleep. Images flashed before her eyes as she tried to remember everything she could from the past years. Somewhere, somehow, there was a clue to all this, and she thought that Aunt Nancy knew more than she was ever going to say. Far more, she suspected, than her own mother.

The new electric lights on Wakefield Road turned off one by one as if by magic when the late summer sun began to pale the sky the next morning. Yet Hannah was still wide awake, not daring to sleep, lest she missed some flicker of memory or thought that might give her the smallest clue to this mystery.

Chapter Twenty-One

Caleb offered his pipe to Walter, who politely declined. He returned it to his mouth, leant back against the side of the boat and drew in for a second, then released two or three small clouds of smoke into the early morning air. 'What's botherin' yout? You been more miserable these past few days than when you was in prison.'

Walter leaned over the side of the *Bluebell* and ran his fingers through the water. The only sound for a few seconds was Bessie taking a few clumps of grass from under the hedge along the towpath. He shook the drops from his fingers, looked up to the slowly lightening sky and said nothing.

'You should have gone back to 'er,' Caleb continued. 'She must have thought you'd abandoned her on that ship. She didn't know the truth, Walt. If she's back with her folks in Bradford you can stay on till we get there, and search her out. She'll come back to you if she knows the truth.' He rose and climbed on to the towpath, carrying the collar and tackle.

Walter took the towrope from its hook and followed him. 'I know. I found out she went back to Wallasey to look for me after she came back from America. Our so-called good neighbours were as vile to her as they were to me. They told me so to my face.' He patted the neck of the patient horse as Caleb slipped her collar on. 'No, it's not that. I still love her, but she'll have to make her own way in the world now. There's nothing I can do about that, or anything.'

Caleb turned to Walter in surprise. 'What do you mean? Givin' up ain't in your nature. You showed real guts those months in prison. I've seen

154

it break many a man. Why you talkin' like that? Them stars up there, they may be right pretty but they don't control your life. You do, my lad.'

'Exactly, Caleb! That's the problem.'

'You're talkin' in riddles.'

'When you got out of prison – well, the day after, I went to see the prison doctor about my stomach pains, thinking it was the prison food. Life is full of strange coincidences. He recognised me. We'd met before.'

'How come, Walt? You ain't lying to me. You hasn't been in prison before?'

'No. I met him six years ago in the Free Hospital when my cousin Albert died . . . of the pox. Pretty horrible it was.'

For a few moments Walter's eyes clouded as he recalled that terrible event. He remembered his cousin's pale deathly face, and the lesions and swellings that distorted his once handsome features. Then he brought to mind the happy memories: the tricks they'd played, the girls they'd loved, their rivalry and their deep friendship. A cock crowing brought him back to the present. 'That doctor . . . he didn't put it on the death certificate – not in as many words. I asked him not to, to save my cousin's family from the shame of it all.'

'What's that to do with you now?'

'The doctor recognised me. Wanted to know why I was in jail. I told him my story. He was ever so kind and understanding. He gave me a real good examination to see if he could find out what was wrong with me. It wasn't the prison food that was making me so sick.' Walter put a hand on Caleb's shoulder. 'He found it. It's a lump growing inside me. It's a canker – and I doubt I've got more than a few months to live.'

Caleb knocked out his pipe, and for several minutes he was lost in thought. He stroked the black head of his faithful dog, who had crept almost unnoticed to his side.

'So that's what made you so quiet,' he mumbled. 'I can see it now. I'm sorry, reyt sorry, lad.'

'No, it's not that which is making me so quiet. I've been thinking about Eliza and my children, and Annie too. Eliza's got to get on with her life without me. It's best for her. I can accept my fate. Can you see that?' Caleb nodded. 'It's what to do about the others, to try to put some things right.'

'Aye, Walt. Your family's important too. You can't forget them.'

'I'm going to live my last few months as a doorstep salesman, on my own – walking the streets, getting out in the country and seeing as much of this bit of the world as I can. I want to make a bit of money, which I can put aside for my wife and family. It's the least I can do for them after what I did. You'll look after that side, will you? Keep my bank book. See the money gets to them.'

'Course I will. You can count on me. You know that.'

'But I want to see my kids as well, one last time. But I don't want them to see me, not in this state. I don't want them to upset themselves on my account. I've already been responsible for too much heartache.'

'I understand.'

'There's a contact you can make for me if you're planning to stop off at Shipley.'

Caleb was silent. He had not told Walter about the last time he had stopped off at Shipley: his run-in with Lem, and Lem's subsequent death. He had heard of it a few days later, much to his regret.

'It's a letter to be delivered to a lady who works at a small church in the middle of Bradford. A place called Silsbridge Lane.'

'Aye, I've heard of that. A right hole it is. You meet some rough families and hard men out here on the water, but it's as bad there as you'll ever find. She must be a brave lass to work down there.'

'She is. She's a remarkable person. She's my wife's sister Nancy.'

'Aye, Walt. Of course I'll do it for thee.'

'Please don't breathe a word of this to a soul, will you?'

'I promise. You can count on me. Be sure of that.'

Caleb relit his pipe. Two herons flew low over the boat, their wings flapping slowly like heavy sheets on a washing line, caught in the sudden breeze that had sprung up over the North Lancashire plain.

* * *

The rope creaked against the wooden guides fixed to the corners of the bridge. Its surface was grooved in several places by the thousands of ropes that had slid along it as boats negotiated the long right-hand bend. In the early morning silence the noise echoed under the vaulted stonework. Walter held the tiller and watched as carefully as he could, despite the throbbing in his head and the ache in his body. He knew that one snag of the rope could send Bessie tumbling into the water ahead. Had he had too much to drink last night? Was it the effect of the home-made punch that had been served at the end of the night's celebrations, after they had all been thrown out of the Boatman's Arms and had moved to the lock side? He looked up. Caleb was forty yards ahead, leading Bessie along the towpath, which was wet with September dew. Thunder followed at his heels, darting left and right, chasing back to the boat to see if everything was all right, then rushing on again to his master's side. By noon his burst of energy would be gone and he would return to sleep on the cabin or watch from his perch on the prow.

Any pain Caleb felt that morning was not caused by Daniel Stone's potent home brew. His enormous capacity and iron constitution could bear even that. His discomfort stemmed from his blackened eye, swollen lip and numerous bruises. He had never liked or trusted Jack Thorn, or his wife for that matter. She had an evil tongue that had started many an altercation, and Jack had an equally sly, underhand disposition. A man who was as cruel to his horse as he had once been to his children was a man to be despised. Still, there had been some satisfaction in knocking him out cold, a just reward for the insults he and his wife had spread about Jenny and the friend who was temporarily sharing their home.

Jack Thorn's boat was not at the moorings at daybreak: he had obviously slunk off early with his cargo of coal, bound for the Leeds wharf. How he got what few contracts he did Caleb could hardly imagine. A man who had lost two horses through cruelty and neglect would normally be shunned by all, boat people and merchants alike. Whether it was through threats of violence Caleb was not sure; or perhaps it was bribery, from the proceeds of his many thefts and burglaries. Why Jenny had let the couple attend their wedding celebrations he couldn't understand: she despised them as much as he did. But blood was thicker than water, even when it was so tainted by her second cousin.

Caleb's thoughts turned to other things. What a way to spend your first night of married life, condemned to the stern of the boat under a blanket and tarpaulin, next to Walter – the price of a night of wild and drunken celebration.

'When's the Foulridge tunnel coming up?' Walter's voice rang through the still morning air.

'About another quarter mile. It'll be up to you and me to do the work this early of a morning. The steam tug won't be running yet, so you'll have to help me do a bit of legging.'

'Will it be hard work?'

'It will after a night like we've just had!'

Walter smiled. He could remember the service itself, but only a little of the celebration afterwards, through a haze of drinking, singing and dancing.

'Jenny, my love,' Caleb called, in as soft and sweet a tone as he could. 'Would you wake Leah in a minute. We'll need her for t'hoss.'

There was silence from below for a few seconds, then a head poked from the cabin door. 'Ah, I sees you're up and working. And now you wants us all to do your bidding, 'usband, lord and master.' There was a pause as if she were waiting for a reply. None came. Caleb didn't dare. 'You needn't worry about this part of the business. It's running as smooth as clockwork. Your daughter will be ready to tend the horse when the time comes, and your breakfast will be ready in thirty minutes, if you'se in a fit state to eat it. We'll all be waitin' as is necessary to do as you says.' Jenny smiled to herself and returned to stirring the porridge, with a little more violence than before. She had deliberately let the children sleep on in her bed after the night of excitement and mayhem. She was not smiling at the events in the inn, where chairs had been smashed to matchwood and the two boatmen had laid into each other like bull elephants; she was remembering the simple ceremony in the small stone chapel some fifty yards from the canal basin. It was a place she had visited many times before for prayer, solace and the company of other boatmen's wives. It was also a place where she had taken her children for lessons in reading and writing from the two Christian young ladies who gave their time so freely and their love so generously to the children of any boat people who accepted their invitation. Leah had come on so well, and with the help Walter had given her, she had finished the two books that had been lent to her. She knew this would surprise and delight her teachers when they passed that way again. Jenny smiled again. Her children need not be condemned to a life of squalor. They wouldn't need to ask an innkeeper or the pastor at the boatman's mission to read their letters to them. They would be free from the prison of ignorance, and could decide whether to stay on the water or make a better life for themselves. They would never have to mark a cross on their certificate of marriage, as she and Caleb had had to do at that chapel the day before.

Jenny was happy now, with a contentment that would last for the rest of her life. She was married in the sight of God to the man she loved, and their children had been baptised into His family. 'What right has Jack Thorn's wife to say anything about my children?' she muttered to herself, 'when they live such a wicked and sinful life, and let their daughters ply their trade so wantonly in the boarding houses around Leeds . . .'

'Tunnel ahead!' came a bellow from above. 'Where in God's name is our Leah?'

Jenny quickly roused the children from their slumber. 'Dad wants you to lead Bessie over Reedymoor Lane to the other end of Foulridge tunnel. You've got to wait for him by the Hole in the Wall.'

'I'm hungry. Can I have my breakfast first?' complained her daughter.

'No. Your dad needs you now. We've got a clear passage through. Nothing's waiting. Now come on, Leah. Your dad's ready. Make haste.'

The boat gently juddered against the small stone quay, and the plates and pans rattled on the wooden walls. Caleb took the rope end and pulled the boat to a stop with one arm, lifting Leah onto the bank with the other. She took hold of Bessie's bridle and proceeded to lead the horse up the steep track to the top of the tunnel entrance. They vanished from sight over the hill.

'Now, Walt,' Caleb shouted, ''tis our turn to do the work.' With his pole he manoeuvred the vessel into the entrance to the tunnel, then lay flat on his back on the cabin roof. Walter copied his movements. 'Don't push too hard.' Walter tried vainly to push on the wet slimy bricks with both his feet. 'No, lad, we walks it nice and slow to start with. Together, Walt, together!'

It didn't take Walter long to get it right. Being roughly the same height as his friend was useful, but he did not have the same force as Caleb did with his muscular calves and thighs. This proved a problem, as the boat veered into Walter's side of the tunnel and he had to bend his legs to the left to keep the *Bluebell* from scraping the wall. Caleb moved his body more to the centre and relaxed a little. Walter was able to extend his legs to a natural walking pace, and gradually the vessel glided into the darkness in a straight line. It was not complete darkness, since the tunnel was dead straight and the pinpoint of brightness nearly a mile away was clearly visible, while the air vents also cast pools of light every five hundred yards. Walter saw plants struggling from their vertical sides, reaching upwards to the sky far above. Water dripped on to his face but he didn't mind. The bricks on the roof were quite dry: only the ones towards the edge were covered with slime or small white stalactites. Even with Caleb taking most of the load, it was as hard a task as Walter had undertaken since his time in prison. He felt the pain in his stomach starting again as the muscles grew tired.

Gradually the tunnel became lighter and lighter, and after twenty minutes they shot out into the fresh, calm air, now being warmed by the gentle sun, which was dispersing the mist in steamy trails. The boat moved over to the bank, to the spot where Leah and Bessie waited for them. Caleb jumped off and tied up the barge, before heading to the tunnel-keeper's cottage to pay his ticket. Leah attached the horse to her rope with a resigned sigh. Bessie had proved an obstinate companion on their walk.

'Now,' said Caleb on his return, 'I could do with a nice bit of breakfast.' He looked down to the cabin. His enquiry was met with a sardonic smile.

* * *

A day later the boats rested up under Gargrave locks, waiting until the afternoon before continuing their journey. Green hills and distant grey moors and mountains surrounded the quiet rolling countryside. Sheets, lace curtains and garments of every size and shape were stretched out over the hedges to dry in the warm September sun. Three women had moved their stoves on to the bank, and their cauldrons were bubbling and frothing, the near-boiling water filled with yet more washing. They sat in a nearby circle, making cotton lace and examining each others' patterns. Jenny held sway. Hers were the most complicated and most admired designs. She was the queen of the tatting circle, and could make the most intricate decoration almost at will.

'Jack Thorn and his missus didn't stop. They've gone on without waiting,' Nelly said. She was a large woman with fair hair and a cherubic round face.

'Must have taken a hell of a beating from your Caleb,' observed Hilda, the smallest of the three. 'Deserved it, no doubt. What they said about you and Caleb! No nicer couple on the canal than you two. I know Jack's your cousin, but I'll say this: they're wicked, them two. Them pair deserve each other.'

'Let it be,' said Jenny, "Tis all done and dusted, and I don't suppose we'll come across 'em for a long time. By then it'll all be forgotten.'

'And what a filthy hole that boat of theirs is!' said Nelly. 'Coal and manure, it's all it's fit to carry.' Hilda nodded, but Jenny stayed silent. 'Hey, I like that fellow you've got on board,' Nelly continued, sensing Jenny's embarrassment and keen to change the subject. 'If he wants a change of scenery he can take a trip on my boat any day of the week.'

'And he's got such lovely things for sale in his case,' added Hilda, 'such pretty lace and ribbons and buttons. Made young Dorothy's dress right nice it did. Where is he, Jenny? He's not left you, has he?'

'No. He's gone into the village to sell some of his stuff.'

They stopped their chatter on seeing Walter walking towards them. His tall thin frame moved slowly and deliberately over the stones and dips of the steep path. His face was lined, but bronzed by the sun and wind. He set his case down in the stern and cheerfully approached Caleb, who was painting over the bluebell design on a part of the cabin that had weathered and faded. Walter stopped for a second to watch, and stood there amazed at his friend's artistry and dexterity. It was as if he were a different creature, filling in each leaf and petal with the delicacy of an artist.

'I've got the paper and envelope from the village,' Walter said.

'Good! Don't worry. I'll deliver that letter for you when we tie up at Shipley junction in a couple of days. I ain't going to take *Bluebell* on the Bradford arm: it's not worth the trouble. It only goes a couple of miles, and there aren't many winding holes along that stretch.'

'Thanks, Caleb.'

'Don't mention it.'

Oh, there's one more thing.'

'What's that?'

'Can you teach me to pick a lock?'

* * *

Eliza knocked and walked into the hall. Nancy was talking to Mrs Mullarkey. For once she seemed a little flustered and not her usual calm, confident self. Eliza could not help overhearing part of the conversation, for the cook's Irish brogue echoed throughout the hall. 'There's rumours Charlotte is up to her old tricks again. They say she met up with a fellow in a pub last night. She didn't come in to the hostel till past midnight. And she was as drunk as a lord. Gave me a right mouthful, she did, and was right nasty to poor Deborah.'

'Oh dear,' sighed Nancy. 'I always felt we might lose with that one.'

'You mark my words, Miss Nancy. I won't miss 'er when she goes. Bad influence she is on the other girls. We'd be better off without her.'

Nancy noticed her visitor. 'I'm so sorry, Miss Eliza. You've caught us at a difficult moment. One of the girls may be back to her old ways. Sometimes the temptation of easy money is too great.'

'I won't detain you too long.'

Nancy led her to the small office. They sat down on a couple of rough wooden chairs, typical of the furniture in the simple mission church.

'What I want to say, Miss Ackroyd,' said Eliza, her face pale and strained, 'is that even if Walter wants to come back I've decided not to resume our affair. It's not that I don't love him: I still do and perhaps always will. It's just that I realise our life together was based on deceit, as much from me as from Walter. I know now that you can't build a whole life together on that. And I can see the harm it's caused his wife and family . . . you've shown me that.'

'I'm glad I've helped you to come to your decision.'

'When you talked about Walter's family you made me realise that every child deserves the best we can give them, and that no child should suffer through the thoughtlessness of grown-ups who put their own desires first.' Nancy was silent, reddening slightly as if troubled by Eliza's words. 'If he wants to go back to his family I won't stand in his way. You can tell his wife that, if you would.'

'I'm afraid I haven't said anything at all to her yet,' admitted Nancy. 'It's been so difficult to find an opportunity.'

'It must be a terrible thing for you to decide. How do you shatter the illusion that he still loved her? How do you convince his children that he loved them, even though he ran away from home?'

Nancy rested her face on her hands. 'Telling Annie about this is the hardest thing I've ever faced.' She lowered her voice almost to a whisper. 'Apart from one other, many years ago.' She looked up. 'I just don't know what to say to her.'

'I can't help you with that,' Eliza said softly, 'but there's something I might be able to do for you. Don't think I'm trying to make amends, or ease my conscience: it's really nothing to do with what's happened.'

'What is it?'

'Well, it's of a practical nature. My mother told me of the wonderful work you do here, and I've seen for myself the selfless and caring way in which you look after these young girls, who so desperately need the shelter and love that you give them.'

'Yes?'

'I don't think I could do what you do. You're so brave and kind. But I can offer some help.'

'What kind of help?'

'If you need help with your accounts, or paperwork, or even raising funds to keep the hostel going, I'd be happy to be of assistance.'

Nancy sighed. 'We do. The bookkeeping and receipts all get too much for us every so often.' She smiled. 'Your help would be greatly appreciated.'

Eliza rose to go out, but Nancy caught her by the arm. 'Please don't go yet. There's something else . . .' Eliza sat down. 'You've been very honest with me. You've accepted my criticism and condemnation, listened to my point of view, and been as considerate and sensitive as possible in such a difficult matter. I feel I can trust you. Perhaps you can give me some advice on a dilemma I've got. Some of your words struck a chord in me.'

'Can't you confide with your pastor?'

'No, it's not to do with the church. It's something that for the present I'd not wish to be spoken about outside this room.'

Eliza looked puzzled. 'Can't you tell your sister?'

'Oh no, I can guess exactly what Annie would say.'

For the next half hour the two women remained deep in conversation. When they had finished Nancy escorted Eliza through the hall to the door, and shook her hand.

'Thank you. You've been of great help to me.'

As she spoke, the door opened and Deborah walked in. She smiled at the stranger. 'I've just come from Kirkgate Market, miss,' she said to Nancy. 'I've been helping Hannah on t'bookstall. Mrs Clough says she's a bit short on twopenny Bible stories. I set out a pile for her yesterday. Can I take them up back to t'market?'

'Of course you can, Deborah.'

Nancy smiled, and the girl trotted off to the back of the room, picked up the bundle of books and slipped out of the door again.

'Now that one is becoming a lovely girl,' said Nancy, 'the kind who makes this mission worthwhile. She causes me no trouble whatsoever.'

Chapter Twenty-Two

The early morning sun shone through the canyon between the high walls of Salt's Mill and the New Mill as Bessie plodded the last mile into Shipley. The traffic at the Bingley five lock staircase had put them behind schedule, and in the woods down in the Aire Valley it had become too dark for the horse's safety, so they had tied up the night before at Hurst Mill Lock, a mile out of town. It was a peaceful Sunday morning. The hundreds of looms in Salt's Mills were silent: any other day you could not hear yourself speak for their incessant clatter. The only sound was the cooing of some doves, sittiing on the edge of the mill roof.

Caleb shielded his eyes against the early morning light as they negotiated Jane's Hill Bridge. Walter was ahead, leading Bessie. Both men constantly checked the passage of the rope through the numerous bridges. Just past a narrow footbridge by the Bull Inn, Caleb called a halt, and the *Bluebell* glided into a stretch of empty bank. He tied the boat up to an iron cleat.

'Are you sure you don't want a bit of breakfast before you go?'

'No thanks,' replied Walter. 'I've got a lot to do and a fair distance to walk. I wouldn't mind a piece of bread to chew on, though.'

Caleb vanished below, returning with a thick chunk of bread and dripping. 'There, lad, that'll keep you going for a bit.'

Walter gave a grateful smile. He walked back to the footbridge, climbed the iron steps and began to cross. Half way over he stopped and leaned over the rail, not looking back at the boat but westward over the sleepy town. It had come as a shock to find himself looking again at the landscape he knew so well. The first thing that had struck him was the murky sandstone of the buildings, darkened by the soot from thousands of chimneys. There was hardly a red brick to be seen, quite unlike Liverpool and the mill towns of Lancashire he had left behind. He gazed over the rooftops towards the green fields beyond and his eyes lighted on Shipley Glen, which wound up from the Aire towards the moorland beyond. Ah, Shipley Glen! Where he had kissed Emily Lumb that Whitsuntide, for the last time. Poor beautiful Emily, who had been so cruelly blighted – as he himself now was. Walter's stomach ached again, but was this from anxiety rather than his condition? He had one chance and he had to take it, but he feared the consequences if everything went wrong. He walked on, his feet clattering on the iron bridge, then into Briggate and on to the Leeds Road. He would be in Bradford within the hour.

'What's he up to, Caleb?' Jenny asked. 'He's been acting strange, not like his normal self.'

'I don't know, my love. I suppose it's 'cos he's back 'ome, only it's not 'is 'ome, like.'

'What do you think's in that letter he's given you?'

'How should I know? And before you ask . . .'

'Oh no, I wouldn't do that.' She laughed. 'It wouldn't do us much good anyway: we'd have to ask someone to read it for us. I was wonderin' if that young lady at the church might let you know what he's thinking. After all, if we knew we might be able to help him.'

'That's up to her. My instructions were to deliver the letter and say who it's from. That's all.' Caleb picked up the letter and climbed on to the towpath without saying a word. Women! They were always trying to find things out. They always had to poke their noses into people's business. If a man wanted you to know he'd tell you, and that was that.

At Junction Bridge Caleb crossed over and walked up the Bradford Canal. He passed the railway bridge and the old lock-keeper's cottage, no longer used for this miserable stump of foul, stagnant water. After a mile the water came to an end, and he had to negotiate his way along a dried-up bed. It was overgrown and strewn with rubbish, but had not yet been blocked off. 'Such a bloody waste,' he mumbled to himself. 'Waste of a good canal.'

In forty minutes Caleb was in the heart of a quiet city, the only sound that of church bells. Even Silsbridge Lane was quiet. The revelry of Saturday night had laid most of its inhabitants low. A few children hung around the alleys, and some God-fearing souls wandered down the lane towards a small stone church. Its simplicity and apparent wholesomeness in the midst of this festering slum reminded him of the church where he had married Jenny some four days earlier. A young dark-haired woman was at the door, welcoming the congregation. She was just as Walter had described.

Nancy looked at the giant towering above her. He had kind blue eyes and the grasp of his hand, though strong, was gentle. 'God bless you, sir. You are most welcome to join us and rejoice, and be saved by His almighty grace and love.'

'Good morning, miss. No, I've not come to pray. I've a letter for you.' He handed her a white envelope. The words 'To Nancy' were on the outside.

'Thank you. May I ask who it's from?'

Caleb stuttered and stumbled for a few seconds. Finally he managed to blurt out, 'It's from Walter.' He turned and was quickly gone, down the steps and back up the lane. Nancy stared after him, open mouthed.

'Oh, yes, good morning,' she said to a couple whose greeting had caught her unawares. 'Welcome to our service.'

Nancy's mind was not on or anything that happened in the next hour. Her reading was hesitant and she forgot some responses. She mouthed some of the hymns instead of singing. Having tucked the letter into her prayer book, she held it tightly. She could not wait for the service to end.

* * *

It did not surprise Walter that his family no longer lived in the house on Bowling Park Road. He saw the family who now lived there emerge, dressed in their Sunday best. From the direction in which they were walking, he guessed they were going to the Weslyan or Free chapel further down Wakefield Road, rather than to St John's Church. He realised that Annie and the children would have moved back into the family home, and would be even now getting ready to go along Wakefield Road to the church on Dudley Hill. If he cut through the park and followed the old track down to the Cross Keys he could get to the main road in less than ten minutes.

Walter reached the inn in just over ten minutes, but he had to run. His breathlessness brought back the pain for a few minutes. He skirted the Albion Mill and found a perfect spot by the mill ponds behind the railings. Between the bushes he had a clear view of the road, across to the Cricketers' Arms. It was a peaceful morning. A few birds were singing in the bushes, and ducks were paddling up and down the pond in tight formation. A few carriages rumbled down the road, carrying worshippers up the hill to church or the other way to the chapels, but most people were walking, and the church bells were busy summoning them to worship.

And then there they were. Annie led the party, her mother on her right arm and leading the restless Agnes with her other hand. Rosie held Thomas's hand. Though three years younger, he was now as tall as his sister, as fair as she was dark. They chatted as they walked along, just behind their grandmother. Hannah lagged behind, dragging her feet. She seemed pre-occupied, and looked worried.

'Hannah, come along. Hurry up or we'll be late for church.'

Her mother's rebuke brought her back to her senses, and Hannah stepped out more firmly.

'Aye, get a move on, lass.' Her grandmother did not miss the opportunity to join in with a reprimand. 'By this rate they'll be half-way through the sermon before we get there.'

Walter smiled to himself. Mary Ackroyd was still the miserable old woman she had always been. The leopard had not changed her spots, even in her daughter's present circumstances. Words of kindness from her had always been few and far between. He and his mother-in-law were always at daggers drawn, particularly after the discovery of Nancy's affair with Albert. She had always blamed him as much as his wayward cousin for her daughter's misfortune. Walter gripped the railings in frustration. He would have loved to rush out and hug his family, even to kiss Annie's sad and careworn face. He drew the line at Mary, though.

Annie, her mother and the children disappeared from view. Walter walked back round the mill and turned left down Wakefield Road. He pulled his hat down, not wanting others to see the tears in his eyes, and not wanting a chance meeting, a sudden recognition, to spoil his plans – not that he would be recognised in the rough boatman's clothes.

After a quarter of a mile he turned down a side street and slipped inconspicuously through a wooden door set in a high garden wall. He knew it was always unlocked. He dodged behind some bushes and observed the house for over a minute. Was it empty? Would Susan, the Ackroyds' servant, still be in the house on a Sunday morning? It seemed empty, confirming Walter's memory that it was the custom of the Ackroyd family not to have a cooked meal at Sunday lunchtime but take cold meats instead. This meant that Susan could go off to the morning service at the Wesleyan chapel round the corner, and then take the rest of the day off.

He crept round to the back door and inserted the thin-bladed knife that Caleb had lent him into the lock, feeling for the tumblers as he had been taught. His friend had made it look easy, but it wasn't. He heard the click of one metal lever through the keyhole, but nothing else moved. Beads of sweat ran down his brow. Minute after minute passed, and still the lock wouldn't budge. Walter glanced round to the gate and the neighbouring houses, praying that he wouldn't be seen. Eventually he put the knife away and wandered round to the back of the house, looking for another way to get in.

It was a few minutes before he spied his opportunity: the sash window lock in the parlour had not been fully turned. He tried to lift the window with his fingers, but there wasn't room to get any purchase between the window sill and the groove in which the frame sat, and the weight of the window might snap his blade. Looking for something more substantial, Walter wandered over to the shed in the garden and began to root around. Yes, it was still there after all those years. No one had bothered to clear the rubbish out, and there at the back, behind the tiles, pots and bits of wood, was the old spade, the one he had broken trying to dig a potato patch. He picked it up by its filthy, splintered shaft, took it back to the window and began to lever up the bottom sash. With a jump the closer sprang free, and the window finally moved. Walter was inside in a second, and carefully pushed the frame down again.

He wondered where he might first start looking for it. After twenty minutes he discovered it in the wardrobe in what he guessed was Annie's bedroom. A feeling of guilt, mixed with a sense of excitement, came over him while he searched, just as it had done all those years ago. It was when he was eleven and had found the tin box in his parents' wardrobe – with the guilty secret of his birth on that yellowed certificate. The guilt and shame had stayed with him all his life, and with it the mystery. Whose name should have filled that space, instead of that perfunctory dash? His mother would never say, and despite his yearning he would never know.

Walter cleared his mind. He had to think straight. Someone might return early or discover that the house had been searched. Like that careful and precise little boy rummaging through his parents' wardrobe, he was deliberate in his actions. He lifted the photograph album on to the bed, noting what papers were on top and in which order, and then he opened the treasure of memories. That photograph they had taken on their last family holiday was there. He looked at the faces staring into the camera. There he was, full faced and handsome, not gaunt and hollow-eyed as he was now. Annie sat looking serious, with Agnes in her arms. Their daughter was blurred: she could not keep still, even for three seconds. Rosie and Thomas stared ahead with faces that had not twitched a muscle, just as the photographer had ordered. But Hannah, ah yes Hannah, the rebel, the individualist, was smiling into the camera as if she was about to burst out laughing at the ridiculousness of it all. It was her usual confident smile, etched on to the photographic plate for all eternity. And there at the back of the album, in the pocket that held the spare photos, was the extra one they had had printed. One was for the album, one for the frame, one for his mother, one for Mary Ackroyd, and here was the spare one. Annie was so precise, so organised, so prepared for all eventualities that there was always something to cover emergencies, even lost or damaged photographs. He lifted it from the pocket to discover that it was in pristine condition.

The words 'J. Brooksbank Photographic Studios, Regent Road, Morecambe' were impressed in the corner.

Walter cast a glance through the window. 'Must be quick,' he said to himself as he saw the first people wandering back from morning worship. He put everything back, carefully closed the wardrobe door and sneaked down the stairs. As he walked to the downstairs window he noticed a small pile of pictures on a chair. He recognised them in an instant: they were Hannah's sketches and paintings. Browsing through them, Walter came across one he had never seen before. She had tried to copy the picture that hung over his mother's mantelpiece, the one she, for some reason, treasured above all. Though not possessing the fine hand and background detail of the original, Hannah's copy was a remarkable effort for a child aged only twelve. Without further thought he folded it and put it in his pocket, before climbing back through the window. Closing it behind him, he slung the spade back in the shed, and was on his way down Wakefield Road in a couple of minutes.

Walter arrived back in Shipley early in the afternoon. Jenny had kept a pan of stew warm for him. He finished it off quickly, too quickly. He felt tired and the pain had returned, so he tried to sleep. Caleb returned at four, having been drinking round the corner at the Black Bull. 'I delivered the letter as you asked,' he told Walter.

'Thanks.'

'We'll be stopping off at Dobson Locks tonight, where Jenny's brother-in-law is the lock-keeper, We won't make Leeds till Monday evening. There's stabling for Bessie and I can fill up with fodder from the canal warehouse.'

'Oh. I told Nancy in the letter to meet me here on Tuesday afternoon.'

'That's not a problem. I've just got to unload a bit in Leeds and there's nothing to pick up till we get back to Burnley. We'll make it back here for Tuesday easy.'

Walter nodded his thanks and lay back down. The day's adventure had drained him of what little energy he had. He slept, sometimes roused by the pain from within him, but falling asleep again through the overwhelming need to rest his aching body.

Chapter Twenty-Three

The last sinners had left the church, renewed in their faith and absolved of their sin, though frequently reminded of it from the small wooden pulpit. They had sung hymns and shouted blessings, and went back to their miserable homes rejoicing in their simple faith and the promise of salvation.

'I'll lock up for you, if you wish,' Nancy said to the elderly pastor.

'Thank you. Prudence and I will be on our way home. I've got to get ready to preach at the Gospel Hall in Bradford tonight. I don't know what we'd do without you, my dear. You're a treasure. The call you had to help us here was God's work, of that I'm sure.'

Pastor Robinson and his shy, equally elderly, companion embraced her briefly and made their way to the door. Nancy turned away, almost running into the small room at the back of the hall. She slammed the door and quickly tore open the envelope, placing the letter on the table. The building was empty and silent. The girls, as was their custom on a Sunday morning after church, had gone back for dinner to the homes of those kind people who helped the Mission with its work. Nancy began to read.

> Dear Nancy,
>
> I know this may come as a terrible shock to you, but as you now must realise I am alive. The man who gave you this letter, my friend Caleb, is a boatman on the Leeds to Liverpool Canal and I am at present living on his boat, the *Bluebell*. We will be moving on to Leeds today,

but we will be back at Shipley Wharf by the
Bull Inn by mid-afternoon on Tuesday. For the
sake of Annie and the children please meet me
there. I love them, more than anything in the
world. Do not tell Annie about me yet. There
will come a time when it will be right to do so,
but not for now. I know what you may think of
me. I have done many wrong and foolish things.
Now is the time to make amends with your
help.
     Walter

Nancy stared at the note for a minute. It did not tell her much more than she already knew.

'Oh, Miss Nancy, come quick, come quick.' Mrs Mullarkey's voice was raised in the hall. Nancy left the letter on the table and rushed out. 'Oh, Miss Nancy – Charlotte's gone. Met that man after church and he's taken her to Leeds. At least that's what Rebecca says. Gone back to the life she had before.' Mrs Mullarkey sat down on one of the chairs. Her face was red and her breath came in short gasps.

'Calm yourself. No blame can be laid at your door for this. You've always done your best for her, and neither of us can watch over the girls for every hour of the day.' The news did not come as a shock for Nancy, and she guessed that the spare bed would soon be filled. There were many desperate girls on the streets of Bradford, lured into that vile trade by false promises of employment in domestic service or of a bed for the night in so-called 'boarding houses'. Nothing had changed in the ten years since she had started this work.

'What shall we do, Miss Nancy?' Mrs Mullarkey's words brought her back from her thoughts.

'I'll come back with you, and we can question Rebecca and anyone else who knows anything, but I fear we'll be too late. She'll be far away, and the police will take little action – though we can but try.'

'I think you're right,' replied the old Irishwoman, who had regained her composure. 'Heaven knows, there'll be other young girls to save, and the next one may be more appreciative of that bed and the chance of salvation.'

'Well spoken, Mrs Mullarkey. If she has left the district I'm sure we'll find someone else quickly enough.'

'Excuse me, miss, but please may I get some paper and an envelope from the cupboard?'

Nancy had not noticed Deborah standing by the door. 'Why haven't you gone with a family for dinner?'

'I'm going up to your house to see Hannah, miss. And I'm going to meet Rosie, Thomas, little Agnes and their mother. Oh, and their grandma, Mrs Ackroyd. I've got to be polite and quiet and pay special attention not to upset her nerves.'

Nancy laughed. 'My mother doesn't always appreciate having lots of children in the house, and I think that's very considerate of you. But why do you want some paper?'

'Well . . . Hannah and I are going to write another letter to my friend May in the orphanage. Oh, don't worry, miss,' she said as Nancy's face clouded. 'We'll show it to her mother first. There'll be no secret letters.' She hesitated for a second. 'Though it is all right if we ask May to send our best wishes to Gideon, and that we hope he's happier now?'

Nancy turned away to hide her face for a second. She looked through the frosted glass of the plain, square window at the blurred shapes of the houses and chimneys across the street. She gripped the window sill tightly. 'Yes I'm sure it is. He would welcome that. Be quick and get the paper. Mrs Mullarkey and I are going out but we'll be back in ten minutes.' She turned and briskly left the hall, with Mrs Mullarkey in her wake.

Deborah walked into the back room and went straight to the cupboard, taking out two sheets of paper and an envelope. She only noticed the letter lying on the table when she was on her way out. She didn't know why she even glanced at it, and at first she did not realise its significance: it was only as she closed the door that the name at the bottom of the sheet sprang back into her mind. She slipped back inside the room and read the letter properly, poring over each word and trying to make sure she understood it all. After a few minutes she closed the door behind her again, and walked thoughtfully across the hall. The small clock on the side wall was showing eleven o'clock.

'Oh, God,' she said to herself, 'I'll be late. That'll never do!' She hurried out, down the steps and up the lane, all her thoughts turning on the visit to Hannah's. A pony and trap was waiting for her on Westgate, and there was Hannah's uncle, Mr James, sitting patiently, reins resting on his lap. She gave him a big smile and announced herself. 'I'm Deborah. Pleased to meet you, Mr James.'

'And you, young lady. I'm glad to be of service. Please step inside. Your carriage awaits you.'

Deborah felt like a real lady, dressed in her Sunday best, sitting in a carriage and being whisked off to an important social event. She held her head high as the small trap hurried through the quiet streets. She imagined she was a duchess, or even Cinderella, being whisked away to the ball. James amused her throughout their drive up Wakefield Road. He was funny and charming, just as an uncle should be. They drew up before a large house that seemed like a palace in comparison with the mean terraces she had once lived in. Hannah was waiting to welcome her by the front door. Deborah was so excited that she forgot about the letter, at least for the present.

Hannah was relieved to have such a hectic day in front of her, to take her mind away from the worries that beset her. She threw herself into everything – welcoming Deborah, assisting her mother in setting out the lunch, and afterwards helping Uncle James to lay out some of the props for his magic tricks and acting as magician's assistant. She was pleased that Deborah was as enthralled as the others, even with the vanishing egg trick: 'It's there, still in the bag!' they all called out. The other tricks went better, particularly those that involved sleight of hand. Uncle James had practised hard, and surprised them all by bringing the vanishing coin back from Rosie's ear. Even little Agnes was amazed, and begged him to take one from her ear as well. All too soon the performance came to its finale, with their uncle retrieving a rabbit from his magician's top hat It was not a real rabbit but the much-loved dog-eared one from Rosie's toy box. This made the audience laugh more than ever.

After the show they moved through to the back parlour, to read or play. 'Mummy, I was going to show Deborah my pictures,' Hannah said, 'and one of them's gone.'

'I've not touched them. Are you sure it's not in your bedroom?'

'I'll have a look, but I'm sure it's not. Did Susan move it while she was dusting?'

'What would she want with your picture?'

The two girls ran upstairs, which provoked a shout from Mary, who had retired to her bedroom to sleep after lunch, away from the mayhem of the magic show, the noise and the children. Deborah looked worried and paused half-way up the stairs. Hannah smiled and beckoned her on, and they giggled as they closed the door behind them. Scarcely had they sat down on the bed when the door opened again, and Rosie's head appeared.

'No, Rosie. Deborah and I want to talk on our own.'

'But it's my bedroom too.'

'Yes, but Mummy hasn't given you permission to leave the parlour. She said I can come up to look for a picture.'

'That's not fair, Hannah! I want to be Deborah's friend too.'

'Leave us alone, Rosie. Ask Uncle James to do some more magic tricks, or draw some of his funny animals for you.'

Deborah smiled at the sad figure in the doorway. 'We've only just met, Miss Rosie, but I'm sure we'll be good friends. When I come again you can show me all your books and toys.'

Rosie gave a polite but resigned smile and turned back down the stairs. Hannah opened her drawer and from beneath some petticoats brought out Gideon's letter.

'It were, was, such a pity,' Deborah said, 'that he was sent back. I had another letter from May. She didn't tell them how Gideon got his letters, so I can still write to her and they don't suspect anything. But he can't get any letters without they see them first, and they've been worse than ever since he were taken back.'

'I told my mother I burnt them all in the parlour fire but I hid this one. Whatever happens we mustn't forget him, and this'll remind me of what he's having to suffer.'

'Them's terrible places,' her friend replied. 'Not all of them, but them like ours.'

'Will you ask May to say we're still thinking of him?' Deborah nodded. 'Now, if you sit very still while you're writing, I've got a surprise for you.'

'What surprise? What are you up to?' Hannah smiled but said nothing.

Deborah began to write. For a short while she kept still, but then craned round to see what was happening. To her surprise Hannah was sketching her. From time to time Deborah stopped, took a peek and smiled. It was the first time anyone had tried to capture her likeness, and she was excited, wanting to see the finished portrait.

When Hannah finished the sketch Deborah took a long look and sighed. 'Oh, that's wonderful. Just like the new me, with a happy face and little wrinkles round my eyes. You've even got my nose right. I know it's a bit pointed, like, a bit like my old dad's, but . . . oh deary me . . .'

'What's the matter?'

'With all this happening today and all this fun and things to do – I forgot.'

'Forgot what?'

'The letter.'

'What letter?'

'Oh, Hannah, I've been so selfish, thinking just of myself and all the fun I've been having. And there's you not knowing about your father and . . . well, I just forgot.'

'Don't blame yourself, Deborah. But what do you mean? What did you forget to tell me?'

'It was a strange letter. To Miss Nancy it was. She left it on the table in the church.'

She turned to look Hannah straight in the face. 'It were from a man called Walter.' Hannah drew in her breath, almost shrieking. 'That was what your dad was called, wasn't it?'

'Yes it was. Tell me! Tell me, what was in the letter?'

'Well, first of all he said he weren't dead as everyone supposed. Then he asked Miss Nancy and everyone to forgive him. Then he said he still loved his family and wanted to make am . . . amends, whatever that means.'

'Did it say where he was?'

'It weren't posted. It were hand delivered. It said he were on a barge called the *Bluebell*. Nice name that is, very pretty. It said that Miss Nancy were to meet him on Tuesday afternoon at Shipley, on the canal somewhere by an inn. I can't remember its name.'

'It's at Shipley, then, this canal boat.'

'Yes. No. It isn't now. Let's see . . . It were going on to Leeds to unload. Should be there tomorrow morning. Then it comes back to Shipley on Tuesday.'

'He said he loved his family?'

'Yes, he definitely said that.'

'Did he say he was coming back to us?'

'No. He didn't say that exactly. He said he'd done foolish things. Then he said about making amends. What does that mean, Hannah?'

'It means he wants to make everything all right. It must mean he's coming back.'

'It didn't say that,' Deborah insisted.

Hannah jumped up and ran to the window, gazing down the road towards the city. 'But he must come back, no matter what he's done,' she cried. 'He's no more than five miles away. Why doesn't he come back now?'

'Oh, Hannah, I can't say what he didn't say in that letter. I just don't know.' Deborah held the weeping girl in her arms. 'There, there. It looks like it's going to turn out all right. Miss Nancy will help sort it all out. You've got to trust people, that's all.'

'Hannah, Deborah, how long are you two staying up there? Haven't you found that picture yet?' Annie's voice rang up the stairs. 'It's nearly time for Deborah to go. I think it's high time you came down and joined the rest of us.'

The two girls trooped down the stairs. Deborah said her goodbyes and left with Hannah's uncle, carrying Hannah's sketch firmly in her hand. Her friend kept a brave face and waved goodbye.'

'Are you all right, Hannah?' her mother asked.

'Yes, Mummy.'

'Did you find your painting?'

'What painting? Oh no, Mum, I didn't. It wasn't important.'

'What's the matter, Hannah? Something's not right. You look as if you've been crying. Have you two girls had an argument?'

'No, Mum, not at all.'

'I think you've had too much excitement for one day. Either that or you're sickening for something, my girl.'

The door banged as Nancy arrived home. Sunday was always a

busy day for her, what with the Mission service, the Sunday School, visiting and often preaching. She made a cup of tea, took a plate of cold meats and preserves out of the larder and ate quietly by herself in the parlour.

'Has it been busy today, Nancy?' her sister asked.

Oh, Annie, it's been a day to forget. One girl's run away. There was such a commotion, and it seems as if the police will do nothing about it. I don't think we'll see her back again.' Nancy resumed her meal, wrapped up in her thoughts.

'That Deborah seems a nice girl, the one Hannah's made friends with. Though I do worry about it, Nancy. With a background like that you never really know what they're like. And it was through her that Hannah got into such trouble over . . . Well, you know.'

Nancy nodded but paid little attention to her sister's chatter. Normally she would have jumped to the defence of one of her fledglings, Deborah in particular, but she seemed preoccupied.

'The afternoon went well,' continued Annie, 'and James did his magic tricks to keep the children happy, not that I really approve of it on a Sunday. At least he didn't do any card tricks: that would have upset Mama. You know what she calls them – 'fifty-two soldiers in the devil's army'. And then with all the noise she had one of her turns and went upstairs to rest . . .' Her voice trailed off. Nancy was not listening at all. For once Annie lost her temper with her sister. 'You've not heard a word I said. What with Hannah looking like she's lost sixpence and found a penny, Mama in her usual mood just because of the children and you all but ignoring me when you get back home, what's the matter with this family today? Is there something going on I don't know about?'

Hannah did not sleep. She lay awake from the moment her head touched the pillow and her mother kissed her goodnight. She heard the gentle wheezing of her sister lying beside her, and she didn't move an inch. As she stared at the patterned ceiling and the shadows cast by the chandelier above, her mind was tortured with questions, with half-truths and uncertainties.

What had the letter meant? Had Deborah forgotten some parts or read them wrongly? What if he came back? Would her mother accept him and forgive him, or would she make it worse? What if he didn't come back? How could she go on living if that happened? And yet he loved them more than anything, of that she was sure. The letter had said so: Deborah was insistent. He was so near, almost within her grasp. She felt she could almost reach out and touch him.

The streets outside had lost their inky blackness. The dark curtains greyed slightly as the first rays of the morning light crept through the dark velour. Now was the time to make her move.

Chapter Twenty-Four

Molly Fitch sat puffing her clay pipe and watching the world go by. It was a dirty, grimy, smoky, unforgiving world, but it was the only one she knew. The docks were crowded with barges of every kind and colour, mostly blackened by their daily toil. The water beneath them was a thick, black, swirling mixture of chemicals, sewage, ashes, dyes and mud, churned from its banks and washed into the mix, but it did not stink as badly as it did in midsummer, when mills and offices around the basin closed their windows to keep out the unbearable stench.

Her son William led the piebald horse down the paved towpath and on to a wharf. In half an hour the canal side would be heaving with stevedores and wagoners, winching up the cargo of slate. The load had made its tortuous way down from the mountains of Wales by train, from the tiny harbour of Porthmadoc by ship and from the docks of Liverpool by Molly's barge, along miles of canal to its final destination in Leeds.

This part of the basin was dominated by the six-storey warehouses on the northern side of the canal. Their crab winches and wall cranes were already busy hauling sacks and bales out of the barges, which lay three abreast and almost filled half the waterway's free passage. William Fitch tied up the *Mallard* and went off into the sheds, no doubt to check in his load with the wharf manager. He returned ten minutes later. 'I'll be off for a drink or two, Mother, down Bridge End.'

'I'll have your dinner ready by two,' Molly shouted back. 'Don't you be late or all you'll get is cold leftovers.

William waved, and was soon up on to the sturdy iron bridge that spanned the murky water. He passed a girl leaning over the parapet, staring down at the dock, observing the boats, and looking beyond towards St Peter's church, its tower brooding over the crowded skyline and its clock already showing ten. Molly watched her cross in the opposite direction to her son, and look back towards the broad confluence of river and canal, with mills and wharfs to the west. Bowler-hatted men hurried across the bridge, while a few boatmen leaned on the rail and chatted. A gentleman wearing a top hat was pointing out the canal's various features to his son.

The girl looked down at the kindly grey-haired woman, then came down the iron steps. As she drew level with the boat she called out, 'Excuse me, I'm looking for a boat called the *Bluebell.*'

She was a well-spoken girl, Molly observed, no boatman's child or ragged, foul-mouthed street urchin who would lob stones, mud and manure from the bridges above. What was she doing here? 'You mean Caleb Stone's boat, do you, miss?'

'I don't know. I only know my father's on it, and it should be coming into Leeds today to unload.'

'It ain't no use us shouting to each other, miss. Come aboard and tell me about it.'

Hannah hesitated, then gingerly stepped from the quay on to the stern of the boat. She noticed that it was clean and well painted.

'I knows Caleb and his missus and their kids. Nice kids they is. Don't cheek or shout at you just 'cos you're old.' Molly looked at the girl. She was tall, nigh on twelve or thirteen years old, with thin bony shoulders and smooth white hands. Obviously she worked on no barge nor in any mill. Her hair, damp and bedraggled by the misty rain, looked mousy brown, but Molly guessed that dried and combed it was a striking golden colour. And she was quite well dressed, not the kind of girl you normally saw at the canal basin. 'Why you down here of a mornin' lookin' for a boat and your father? Where you from, girl?'

'I'm from Bradford.'

'Bradford, are you? We used to go there in the old days with bales of raw wool for the mills. You could get a boat right down into t'city, when I was a girl. That was before they closed most of it down. A right mess it is now. Railways have taken away the wool, and all we got now is coal, slate, stone and chemicals.'

She puffed on her pipe for a second. 'How you got from Bradford, then?'

'I came on the early train into Wellington station. The ticket man pointed me down Swinegate to the canal. But it's so big. How am I going to find him?'

'Well, you're best staying here on t'bridge and watching for it. Nice craft the *Bluebell* is. Right pretty she's painted. You can't miss her. You wouldn't believe it if you saw Caleb. Big, strong fellow he is with long black hair and enormous hands. But he's an artist, sure enough, and so is she. Taught Jenny some lace I did when she were a girl, but she's better than me now. She's best tatter on this canal by far.'

'Who's Jenny?'

'She's Caleb's wife, and mother to his four kids.'

'What happens if the boat doesn't come in?'

'Well, if you haven't seen it by afternoon, you'll have to walk along the wharfs, to see if it's already berthed. It could have come in this morning and be laid up somewhere, waiting for unloading. You'll have to search west for half a mile then another mile to the east beyond Bowman Lane. Or he could have a load of coal on board for one of the mills. You'll have to look in the small side basins and factory wharves as well.'

'Thank you for your help, ma'am,' said Hannah, turning to climb out on to the wharf.

'My, you are a polite young lady, and I don't even know your name.'

'It's Hannah.'

'Well, Hannah, mine is Molly. I'll tell you what, before you go searchin' the docks stay and have a bit of dinner with us. I've got some stew on the stove and can make some drop scones on the hot plate. You'll like 'em, you will. My grandchilder don't half like 'em when they comes to see me.' Hannah smiled. 'You've got a nice smile, young Hannah. But I wants to know if your family knows you're hereabouts, lookin' for your father.'

Hannah reddened, and shook her head.

'I thought not. Now you be careful, young lady. It's not too safe round here, especially when it starts gettin' dark. There are some round here that wouldn't think twice of doin' you harm. So don't speak to strangers and keep a lookout for trouble, street gangs and the like.'

* * *

'Where in heaven's name has she gone?' Annie cried. 'Her bed's been slept in, but her night clothes have been hidden under the bed and her day clothes and coat are missing.'

'I'll ask Rosie first,' Nancy said. 'She must have seen her get up.'

When a sleepy-eyed Rosie was led into the drawing room by her aunt, she rubbed her eyes and looked around at her three inquisitors.

'Where's Hannah?' her mother asked. 'She's gone, and we don't know why or where.'

'Tell the truth, child. Your sister's been up to something and we've got to find out,' barked her grandmother.

Rosie's face reddened, and she looked as if she was about to cry.

'Mother, we won't get anything from her if you shout and frighten her. I think you'd better leave this to Nancy and me.'

Mary Ackroyd looked from one daughter to the other. 'I might as well shut up, if my own daughters don't want the benefit of my experience,' she complained.

'I don't think you're helping, Mama,' said Nancy. 'Rosie is as upset and worried as we are.' She turned to her niece and whispered, 'Don't worry. It's not you who's in trouble.'

Mary rose from her chair and stormed out of the room. 'It's a bad day,' she shouted, 'when you're not even mistress in your own house.'

They waited till her footsteps had faded.

'She wasn't there when I woke up,' answered Rosie. 'I think she must have got dressed early, and very quietly.'

'So you didn't see or hear her get up at all?'

'No, Mummy. When I saw she wasn't there I thought she was poorly and had gone to your room, or that you'd got her up early to do something for you.'

Annie and Nancy looked at each other. Rosie caught the anxiety that passed between them. Fear crept into her large, dark eyes. 'She's not run away, Mummy? Like Daddy did?'

The room was silent. Rosie suddenly realised what she had said. Nancy's expression suddenly turned from fear to acute embarrassment. Her face went from white to red, then back to white again.

'What do you mean, Rosie? Saying something like that about your father?' Annie's voice was shrill with anger and shock.

Rosie turned to look at her aunt. She didn't know what to do or say. She felt as if the world was tumbling on top of her, and she was trapped.

'You knew,' gasped Nancy.

Rosie's eyes filled with tears and she nodded.

'And did Hannah know as well?'

'Yes, yes, Auntie. She saw me crying after that lady came to see you, and she got it out of me.'

Annie had sunk down into her chair in utter shock. She stared into the blazing hearth, not moving a muscle.

'Oh, Annie, I didn't want you to learn about it like this,' Nancy sighed. 'I was going to tell you that Walter's alive, but I wanted to break it to you gently, when the moment was right.'

'I think Hannah and Deborah were talking about it yesterday,' whispered Rosie between her sobs. 'They wouldn't let me into the bedroom, and that's why they were up there so long.'

Nancy buried her head in her hands. The only words that they could make out amid her gasps of shock were, 'Oh no, the letter! Deborah must have seen the letter!'

* * *

Dobson's Lock was as tranquil a spot as you would find on the Leeds to Liverpool Canal, situated in the Aire valley between Shipley and Leeds, a short distance from Apperley Bridge. The canal slid its way through meadows and woods, neat stone buildings housing the lock-keeper's house, the canal company warehouse and a few stables. Walter was helping Caleb load bags of fodder, the children were playing in nearby woods and Jenny had settled in the front room of the cottage with her sister-in-law, where they were exchanging gossip and drinking copious amounts of tea from flowered china cups.

'I suppose you wants to get back to Shipley, then, after our call in Leeds,' said Caleb.

'I'm sorry if it's an inconvenience to you, but it is important.'

'I knows that, Walt. We'll get going by one o'clock, after Jenny has had her fill of tea, cakes and gossip, and we should make it by six. We'll unload first thing in the morning and we'll be back at Shipley junction by mid-afternoon. You can see that Nancy and sort out your business with her.'

'Thank you so much. You've been a real friend to me these past few months. It's you who's made everything bearable for me.'

They sat together for an hour in the autumn sunshine. The water rattled and gurgled down the race past the locks, but apart from this gentle sound and that of a soft breeze shaking off the first leaves of autumn there was nothing to disturb them, deep in their own thoughts.

* * *

Leeds Basin was at its busiest. It echoed to the shouts of men, the rattling of chains from cranes and hoists, and the hammering and grinding from a hundred workshops scattered around the wharves. Hannah was oblivious to the turmoil. She had watched and waited from the bridge for a full four hours, but *Bluebell* had not made its appearance.

As her son had not returned from the public houses on Bridge End, Molly shouted up from the barge and offered her some dinner. Though not feeling hungry, Hannah felt it impolite to refuse and picked her way fastidiously through a dish of stew. The drop scones had been nice, though, freshly cooked on the iron plate above the stove. Hannah had eaten two when Molly said, 'There's more for you, love, if you want. If that lazy beggar can't drag himself away from the Lion or the King's Arms and get himself a decent dinner, then it's his fault. And I'm not cooking for him again when he gets back. You can be sure of that.'

'Thank you for the meal. Can I pay you for your trouble?' She reached into her pocket for one of the two sixpences she kept there.

'Certainly not, my dear, I'd be offended if you tried. We boat people is hospitable folks, despite what outsiders may say. And as your dad's a friend of Caleb's, then there's an end of it.'

Hannah smiled. It was a sad smile but a grateful one.

'God bless you, little un. You're a well-meaning lass, to be sure. Now if you're still looking for your pa you'd best get up on the bridge and keep looking around. If he hasn't come by four then have a look around t'wharves. Then you'd best come back to me. You can stay here for t'night, and don't even think of payin' me owt. You keep that money in your pocket for the train back to Bradford.'

Hannah resumed her watch. Boats were still coming in: large boats, small boats, fly boats, colliers, sail barges from down the river and even a small steam tug, which puffed its way back and forth assisting boats that could not use their horses on the crowded quays. But no *Bluebell* – and as the afternoon wore on the traffic decreased. Eventually she decided to take Molly's advice and started to walk down the towpath, checking all the wharves and mill basins. As she wandered along she saw that the basin was gradually transformed into a slow-moving river, as the canal almost imperceptibly joined the Aire navigation. She was damp and cold but still determined; she had to find him, and persuade him to come back home. Nothing else mattered.

Hannah passed the tall church. Here the wharves were fewer and the waterway wider. Its murky waters were less obnoxious, still brown and muddy but without the vile stench of industry and sewage that she had smelled upstream. A sail barge wound its way slowly up the river, nearing the end of its journey from one of the coastal ports. Turning back, Hannah made her way towards the canal basin again.

'What's a young lass doing in t'docks so late in the day?' a woman's voice asked.

Hannah turned to look. The barge was an extremely scruffy coal boat. No charming lace curtains hung from the small cabin windows. The name on the boat was unreadable. The paintwork had blistered and faded long ago.

'I'm looking for my father,' Hannah replied. 'He's coming in on a boat today sometime.'

'He won't be coming in this late in the day. He'll be mooring up beyond Armley for the night. You'll find him docked up tomorrow morning, no doubt.' The large, brassy woman smiled as sweetly as she could. 'What are you going to do for the night then, my love?'

Hannah did not catch the interest or meaning in her voice. 'A woman's offered me a place on her boat for the night,' she answered readily.

'I wouldn't do that if I were you, my dear. T'canal side's a dangerous place a night for a young girl. All kinds of things go on at all hours. Drunkenness, fights, thieving and attacks, especially on women. You knows her? Is she family?'

'No, not really.'

'Well then. Best place for you is a boarding house, a safe room behind locked doors.'

'But I've only got two sixpences left, and I have to use them for the train fare home if I can't find him.'

'Oh dear! That does put you in a plight. I wonder . . . I wonder if my sister might put you up for t'night. She runs a boarding house off Kendall Street. It's only a quarter of a mile away. She's got a few, er, young ladies and girls who stay at her . . . establishment. If I asked her I'm sure she'd do it for free, just for one night. You might have to share with another girl, but you'd be safe and secure. I can promise you.'

Hannah was unsure, but the thought of a safe bed for the night seemed preferable to one by the dark and stinking canal. 'That's very kind of you, ma'am. Thank you.'

The woman vanished into the cabin and came up on deck a few seconds later with a fair-haired man. He was broad and muscular, and the features of his face were somewhat obscured by bruising, a black eye and a swollen lip. 'Me and my husband will take you round, if you don't mind. Introduce you, like.'

The woman took her hand. It was a rough, dirty hand but the grip was gentle, and she looked down and smiled at Hannah as if to reassure her. It gripped a little more tightly as they walked round a large youth who ambled along the towpath with an unsteady gait. If the two parties knew each other they didn't acknowledge it; in fact they studiously avoided each other's gaze. The young man swayed round them, then staggered along another two hundred yards until he tumbled unceremoniously into the back of a boat tied up alongside the slate wharf.

'Where's you been all day, William?' his mother shouted.

'Sorry, Mum. I've been doin' some business up Briggate.'

'No you hasn't. Don't lie to me. You never got as far as Briggate. Spent your time drinkin' in t'pubs around Bridge End, more like. Anyway, there's no dinner for you. Gave it to a girl who was down here lookin' for her father.'

'She wasn't that tall, thin girl that was hangin' about this morning?'

'Yes, that's the one.'

'I've just seen her going off with Jack Thorn and his missus in the direction of town.'

Molly turned to look at her son, with a worried expression on her face that made it even more wrinkled. 'Oh Lord above, protect the poor mite!' she whispered.

Chapter Twenty-Five

The knock at the front door was loud and the two occupants of the front room were startled for a second. Then Annie rose and walked down the hall to the front door, where Susan was standing with a tall man dressed in a blue serge uniform. The sight of a policeman at the front door gave her sudden hope – but it was quickly dashed.

'This lady was sent down to the station by the mistress of the house,' he explained. 'Something about a missing girl, I believe.'

'Oh, yes, do come in, Constable,' whispered Annie.

'It's Sergeant, ma'am, Sergeant Fearnside.' He took off his helmet, put it under his arm and stepped into the hall. Susan made her way back to the kitchen and Annie showed the visitor into the front room.

'Mama sent for the police,' she informed her sister.

'I suppose in the circumstances it was the most sensible thing to do,' replied Nancy. 'She's the one person who's thinking straight.' She turned her attention to the visitor. 'Please take a seat. Would you like a cup of tea, perhaps?'

'No thank you, ma'am. That's very kind of you, but I've a lot of cases to attend to this morning. I understand this is about a missing girl who has run away from home.'

There was an embarrassed silence. 'It's my daughter,' said Annie.

'Only she hasn't run away from home,' interrupted Nancy. 'It's more that she's run off in search . . .' She hesitated. 'She's run off in search of her father.'

'Oh, he's missing too? Is that another person to note, then?'

'No, no, not really,' whispered Nancy. 'We know roughly where he is.'

184

'Do we?' asked a startled Annie.

'I'm afraid we do. He's on a barge on the Leeds to Liverpool Canal and he's due in Leeds some time today. My brother-in-law disappeared some eighteen months ago and Hannah, Mrs Clough's daughter, may have found out where he was from a letter he sent to me. We think she may have gone to Leeds to meet him.'

Annie sat in the armchair, her mouth wide open.

'Is that right, madam?' the policeman asked. He was slow and deliberate in his questioning, and leant towards her with his eyes screwed up a little and with a quizzical expression.

'Er, yes. I think what my sister has told you is about right. Do you need a picture of her, Sergeant?'

'That would be helpful, if you can find one.'

Annie hurried out of the room, her expression a mixture of anguish and bewilderment.

'How long before you can organise a search?' asked Nancy.

'I'm not sure whether we can. It's up to Leeds police, and with so many girls and boys going missing we can't keep tabs on them all. If you could give us a description together with a photograph, it would help. We'll phone Leeds today: we've got a direct line to them now. Photography, telephones, fingerprints: with all these modern scientific devices, policing isn't what it used to be, you know. In a few years criminals won't stand a chance!'

Annie returned with the album under her arm, a little more composed. 'I can show you a photograph, but it's over two years old. She's a lot taller now. Oh dear. We had a copy of this, but it seems to have gone.'

'I've written a description for you,' said Nancy. She handed the policeman a piece of paper.

'Age twelve – long, darkish blonde hair– thin face – about five foot four inches tall – wearing a dark green dress and a black coat. Yes, I think that will be very useful. I'll take it with me, and the photograph if you don't mind. I'll return it as soon as we've printed it. I'll get it all sorted straight away.'

'Thank you, Sergeant,' said Annie, almost in tears. 'We appreciate it.'

'A pleasure, ma'am – and don't you worry. As she's from such a good home I'm sure she'll turn up soon enough, particularly if she comes back with her father.'

Annie burst into tears. The policeman looked embarrassed as Nancy showed him into the hall and out through the front door. When she returned she sat down facing her sister.

'I suppose you want an explanation, Annie.'

'Indeed I do.' Annie had dried her tears and was staring at Nancy with hostility.

'Oh, how can you forgive me? I must take the blame for this and yet . . . and yet I did it all with the best of intentions. You must believe me, Annie.' Her sister's face remained impassive. 'I thought I could deal with it all myself, to save you from the shock of suddenly finding out what had happened – and the children too. I was just waiting for the right time to tell you, please believe me. God puts vanity in our way, Annie, making us believe we can act as gods ourselves, instead of trusting in Him and being honest and open with each other.' Nancy put her head down on the arm of the sofa, tears streaming down her pale cheeks.

Annie came over to comfort her. 'I know you did it for the best,' she sighed. 'I don't blame you.' Her next words brought her sister up with a jolt. 'I suppose there's another woman involved?'

'How did you guess?'

'I think I always knew. When you've been married for a while you always know when there's something else in the way. I often wondered – but in Walter's case, it might have been the love of his job, the yearning for a better, more unfettered life, even his regard for Albert. I reckon at times *he* blighted both our lives.'

Nancy dried her tears and faced her sister.

'Was it that woman who came to see you when we were out?' asked Annie. 'The one who Rosie saw, and must have overheard?'

'Yes, it was her.'

'Why did she come to see you?'

'She came to tell me that Walter was still alive. We met again at the church.'

'Is it over between them?'

'I believe so.'

'That's why he's living on a canal boat, of all places?'

'I don't know. All he said in his letter was that he still has some feelings for you and he adores his family.'

'Then why doesn't he come back? I'd have him back. You know that.'

'Oh, Annie, why ask me? I don't know. Perhaps when I meet . . .'

'Meet him where?'

'He asked me to meet him at Shipley Wharf tomorrow.'

'Why?'

'He said to make amends to you and the family.'

'To come back?'

'I just don't know. He didn't say that.'

'Should I come as well?'

'I don't think so. Surely he would have asked me to arrange that if he wanted you to. I sense there's something else that he wants to say, but I've no idea what it is.'

Annie sat silent for a minute. 'Then it's better we leave it to you. At least we know he's alive. I must use all my energies to find Hannah and get her back safely. Don't you see, Nancy, it's because people put their trust in you that they want to use you as their helper or go-between. They have faith in you. They know you'll always act unselfishly and wisely; that you'll always give good advice. I'm too hot-headed, too sharp-tongued for my own good.'

'I try. I do try. But don't think I always get things right. Just look at how this has turned out.'

'I don't blame you for this. I'll leave everything in your hands and to your wisdom.'

Nancy was still tearful. 'Oh, Annie, be steadfast for yourself and for me. I don't always do the right thing. And if we get over these troubles there's something else I've got to do, to change things, to amend a great wrong. And for once it's something I've got to do for myself.'

* * *

They turned a corner into a mean-looking side street, the buildings towering above on them on each side. It was an old part of the city, with houses of every shape and size thrown up rather than built, crowding in higgledy-piggledy, leaning at all angles. They all had the same ugly hue of smoke-darkened brick, blackened sash windows and peeling or rotting woodwork. Rain dripped on to the pavement from broken gutters. Some were mean shops, some three- or four-storey houses, others just tiny hovels. Shopkeepers were bringing in their meagre wares for the night, while two men leaned on each other outside the dimly lit entrance of an ale house.

The street was a dead end. As they went further along it, it seemed to be closing in on Hannah. When they reached a dark and narrow ginnel at the end, panic started to grip her. 'No, I don't want to go in here,' she shouted, tearing her arm free from Florrie Thorn's grasp.

'You'll be all right, my dear,' coaxed Florrie. 'It may be a run-down part of town, but my sister's boarding house will be welcoming and safe, a lot better than the canal. Just wait and see.'

'No, no, I'm going back!' Hannah screamed, and turned to make her escape. Scarcely had she taken a step than she felt her right arm gripped in a vice. Jack Thorn had got hold of her, and no matter how much she struggled she couldn't break free. The two drunks turned to gaze at the commotion.

'You ungrateful girl,' shouted Florrie. 'Trying to run away from your dear mother. What a wicked soul you are, to be sure.'

The two men seemed to be taken in by this charade and turned to face the shop window, engrossed in their conversation. This was a normal occurrence, and it wasn't their business anyway. Hannah was propelled into the dark alleyway, and though she still struggled she instinctively knew that she would never break the man's iron grasp. Florrie hammered on a large wooden door, and when it opened Hannah was pushed inside. Jack did not loosen his grip.

'Well, if it isn't our Florrie!' a fat, dark-haired woman said in surprise. Although more bloated than her sister, she had the same facial features.

'Got a new one for you, Queenie: a runaway, an orphan.'

'Here? Are you sure? She looks well dressed to me.'

'I found her roaming around the wharves. Says she were looking for her father. Don't worry, she won't be missed for the present. Not from hereabouts. Says she's from Bradford. And if her folks do realise they won't know where she's gone. Hardly anyone saw us, and she thought we was finding a nice boarding house. Came along like a mouse. She only struggled when we got to your front door.'

'All right then. Take her upstairs, Jack, second door on the left.'

'Make sure you lock the door,' added Florrie. We don't want her trying to run off.'

Hannah's sobs and screams disappeared up the narrow staircase.

'Best send one of the girls to keep an eye on her,' said Queenie. She turned to face her sister. 'Is she . . . ?'

'Must be, so young and coming from a decent home. I'll want a good fee.'

'Bridget!' Queenie shouted. 'Come here, you lazy cow.' A thin-faced, red-haired girl with missing teeth appeared from the back room.

Queenie took a sheet of paper and envelope from a wooden cupboard and wrote a note, resting the paper on the top of the cupboard. Even her sister was surprised at the speed with which she wrote. She folded the note and stuffed it in the envelope.

'There'll be a reply. Don't go off without it. Note the address: Victory Street. It's one of those large houses up in Chapeltown. An important gentleman lives there. Now get going!'

As the girl closed the front door, Queenie turned and winked at her sister. 'A gentleman with particular tastes,' she whispered. 'She should suit him fine. He pays very well, so I suppose you wants your share?' Florrie nodded and smiled. Queenie took out her purse and delivered the sovereigns into her sister's hand.

'How's my girls getting on, Queenie?'

'Oh, very well. Making some good money, and they helps me round the place. They keeps the other girls in check. I gets no thieving or cheating when they're around.'

'No trouble with the coppers?' asked Jack, who had come back down the stairs.

'No, not at all, especially when we've got customers like that gentleman coming tonight. He's chairman of the Watch Committee, and there's a few other clients who's important people in this town. The coppers knows their place, and when to look the other way if it's for their own good.'

'We'll see you then,' said Florrie. 'We'll have a reyt good time tonight, won't we, Jack?'

Her husband looked at her and smiled. It would have been an ugly, evil smile at the best of times, but the blackened eye, the scars, the bruises and the broken teeth made it more hideous than ever.

'Here, what's happened to you, Jack?' Queenie asked. You looks as if you've had a run in with an army of coppers.'

'It was another boatman, married to one of my cousins. Couldn't take a little joke and caught me unawares. But next time – and there'll be a next time – I'll be ready for 'im. You mark my words.' The grin became more wicked than ever. Jack clenched his fist, but not as if he was about to deliver a punch. It was as if he had something grasped inside it.

Hannah lay sobbing on the bed, which was covered by a rough, stained blanket. She heard the door close downstairs, the voices fade and for a minute the house was still. Raising her head, she looked around the bare, filthy room. A ragged brown curtain was half pulled across the one window. There was no rug on the floor, just uneven boards. Apart from the bed the only furniture was a small brown cupboard with a handle missing. Hannah looked around again to check if there was another door. There wasn't. She crept to the window and pulled back the tattered curtain. It was hard to see through the filthy glass, but a broken pane gave a view of the drop straight down to the alley. She tried to open the sash, ready to risk injury or death to get out, and heaved at the frame. It was no use. The sash was nailed shut.

Footsteps tapped down the landing towards the room. The key ground in the lock, and Hannah turned to see who it might be. She had an idea. If she rushed the door she might squeeze past the surprised newcomer. The door slowly opened. The young woman was older and much bigger than her, and Hannah's hopes disappeared. The woman had positioned her powerful body squarely in the narrow doorway, making any attempt to get out impossible. Her round face was caked in thick make-up and her blonde hair was crimped in ringlets down to her shoulders. She wore a low-cut dress that hardly contained her full young breasts. No longer did she have to wear the dark and modest dress that Hannah had once seen her in.

'Well, if it isn't little Miss Bookstall herself!' she said with a broad grin.

Chapter Twenty-Six

The blue-painted barge pulled into the remaining space on the towpath. Caleb spotted some men still hanging round the wharves for work and went over to them. After a brief discussion he returned. 'I got a couple of men to stay on and unload tonight,' he shouted to Walter. 'Then we can be on our way first thing in the morning. Mind you, I had to promise them an extra shilling each.'

Walter smiled and reached into his pocket. 'Look, the least I can do is to pay their bonus after all you've done for me.' Caleb reluctantly agreed, and Walter handed over the two shillings before settling himself in the stern. The pain had increased over the last couple of days. He tried to make himself comfortable and to sleep for a while, assisted by a potion concocted by Jenny and a swig or two of whisky.

Caleb began to untether Bessie. Thunder lay on top of the cabin, to all intents asleep but keeping one eye on the stevedores, who had clambered aboard and with a chain hoist were beginning to unload the timber that *Bluebell* had carried from Liverpool.

'Caleb, Caleb Stone, is you there?' The voice along the towpath was shrill and urgent.

'Molly Fitch! Bless you, love! What you doing here?' asked Caleb. 'And in such a hurry too.'

'Caleb, has you got a passenger with you?' she gasped. 'A tall young feller called Walter?' On hearing his name, Walter turned round. 'You Walter then?'

'Yes, I am.'

'A girl was here today lookin' for you. Tall, thin girl, she was. Called herself Hannah. That right?'

Walter nodded. He was stunned. How had his daughter known where to search for him, or that he was even still alive?

'You'd best take him to her,' said Caleb.

'I can't. I can't. I told her to come back to me if she didn't find your boat, but she didn't. It were only when William got back from the pubs on Bridge End he told me he'd seen her. She were going in t'direction of the city in the company of Jack Thorn and his missus. Oh, I hope no harm 'as come to her. I know he's your wife's cousin, Caleb, but they're evil, them pair, and you knows it as well as me.

* * *

'Well, isn't it nice to 'ave you here, back among friends?' Charlotte's mocking voice rang out across the room.

Hannah began to panic. She could not understand why she was being kept prisoner in this awful room. 'Will you please let me out?' she begged.

'What? Me let you out? No, I couldn't do that. Miss Queenie wouldn't like that at all, especially as she 'as such a treat lined up for you.'

'A treat? What do you mean?'

'You're having a visitor this evening, a very special visitor. A very rich gentleman, he is; one of the most important gentlemen in Leeds.'

'Will he help me to get back to my family?'

Charlotte laughed. It was a cruel laugh that knew no remorse or pity. 'God bless you, Miss Bookstall, he ain't come to do that. He wants to be your friend, though. He likes young girls like you, young and fresh girls. And you've got to entertain him. Not with tea and crumpets though!' She laughed again at her joke. 'And if you're nice to him he'll be very kind and generous, and maybe he'll come calling again.'

A slow realisation was dawning. Hannah had feared imprisonment, dreaded starvation and beating, but this was far worse. She had guessed at this kind of unmentionable horror from her conversations with Deborah, and the things that she had hinted happened to her at the hands of her evil stepfather, the man whose name she would never mention. But Hannah had always put such things to the back of her mind, refused to imagine or contemplate such goings-on. But now she dreaded that whatever it was might happen to her. She felt a sick revulsion spreading through her whole body.

'Mind you,' her tormentor continued, 'you won't get any of his generosity, not to start with at least. You'll have to hand it over to Miss Queenie to pay for board and lodging. We can't keep you and feed you and give you a comfortable bed to sleep on and you not pay a brass farthing for it, can we?'

Hannah dashed to the door, trying to push past Charlotte, but it was no use. The older girl was too strong for her. 'My father's here in Leeds,' Hannah shouted as she struggled, 'and he'll find me. And my family will have informed the police, and they'll be looking for me as well. You'll all be arrested and put in jail for this.'

Charlotte gripped both her wrists in a strong hand and with the other grasped her throat, holding Hannah's face to the dim light from the window. 'Bless you, little Miss Bookstall, you're so innocent in the ways of the world, aren't you? You believe that everyone's so good, so pure. Well they're not, and you won't be for too long either. Coppers, they turns a blind eye to all that goes on here. Miss Queenie does business with some very important people in this city, she does, and they won't lift a finger to help you. You best enjoy tonight and what's coming to you. You'll learn a lot about the ways of the world, you will. You'll be a different girl by tomorrow morning.'

She laughed and let go of Hannah, then walked over to the door and unlocked it. She stood half in the doorway, as if tempting her to make another futile dash to escape. 'It ain't no use trying to keep your 'and on your ha'penny. That won't help you at all.' She laughed again, and locked the door behind her.

Hannah sank on to the foul-smelling bed. She was too terrified, too desolate even to cry.

* * *

Caleb had got to Jack Thorn's boat in a minute. His boot went straight through the faded, rotten wood of the cabin, splintering it with a deafening crack that echoed around the empty warehouses of the canal basin. The boat rocked back and forth, banging against the stone quay. 'Jack Thorn, what have you done with that young girl, you evil bastard?' he yelled.

Jack, who had been sent tumbling inside by the jolt, was soon on his feet. Out of the cabin in a moment, he leapt on to the towpath. Facing his adversary, his right hand was hidden behind his back. 'None of your bleedin' business, Caleb Stone,' he shouted.

'It is if she's the daughter of my friend Walter, best man at my wedding. You remember him, do you, Jack? I'd say this is very much my business.'

Caleb had not seen the stiletto knife hidden behind Jack's back, but he was always wary of the tricks Jack might use. He was able to dodge the first lunge, and looked round for some kind of weapon for himself – but there was nothing to hand. He knew he could beat Jack in a fist fight, but he had not expected him to come out armed. He realised he would have to stay on the defensive and seize any chance that arose. For once there was fear in Caleb's eyes. He knew that if Jack got a blow in with the knife there would be no mercy.

Jack Thorn was not going to miss the opportunity to get his revenge. Wild with hate and fury, he lunged and slashed at Caleb, but from a distance. He knew he could not match Caleb's strength, and if his opponent managed to grab his right arm then the advantage of the stiletto would be gone. Both knew that this would be a fight to the end, so they circled each other warily, Jack lashing out then retreating, and Caleb dodging with a nimbleness that belied his size, his eyes intent on Jack's right arm. But as Caleb leapt back, he slipped on a mossy patch of stone, and Jack saw his chance. Caleb rolled away from the thrust at his shoulder, but he was not quick enough as he rose to his feet – nor did he expect the downward lunge into his leg. He punched the side of Jack's head, which floored him at the exact moment his knife pierced Caleb's right thigh. The big man let out a roar of pain as he tumbled down on to the greasy coping sets at the edge of the towpath. He tried to struggle to his feet, but the dark stain spreading across his thick serge trousers confirmed the stab from Jack's knife. He tried to rise but his leg collapsed beneath him, and he sank back down on to the towpath.

Jack rose to his feet, stunned but still conscious and fully aware of the advantage he had over his sworn enemy. He gripped the knife and stood above him, his weapon poised.

'No, no, don't murder him!' screamed Florrie, who had emerged from the cabin. 'Let him be, Jack, let him be.'

But he wasn't listening. He hated the man too much. Jack towered above his helpless victim. A couple of blows and he would be king of the water, the man who killed Caleb Stone, the most feared man on the whole of the Leeds to Liverpool Canal. Everyone would submit to his will.

Walter and William Fitch were running along the wharf as fast as they could: Walter's intense pain and William's drunken state had left them trailing in Caleb's wake. Even from fifty yards away Walter could see the helpless Caleb struggling on the ground, and Jack Thorn standing above him ready to strike again. They were both too slow to help him – but Thunder was not. He passed them in a flash, and reached the prone figure of his master as Jack's arm came down. His fangs were at Jack's throat as the knife pierced his black, shiny fur. The impact of five stones of flying lurcher sent them both tumbling into the water, but Thunder did not release his grip even as the blows rained down upon his back. For twenty seconds or so they churned the dark water, before both bodies rose to the surface, lay still, then floated slowly away into the middle of the canal, gradually drifting out of view.

William ripped the shirt from his back and pulled off Caleb's blood-soaked trousers, holding the shirt as tightly as he could around his friend's leg.

Walter had eyes for one person only. Before Florrie Thorn could cast the boat adrift he jumped on to the stern and grabbed her round the neck, by her shawl, choking her as tightly as he dared. He wouldn't have cared if he had squeezed tighter and choked the life from her, but he needed her. He pulled the shawl tighter, bringing her face close to his so that he looked straight into her eyes. 'Where's my daughter? What have you done with her?'

Slow realisation spread across her face. 'Your daughter?' she gasped. 'Your daughter? 'Oh God, no!'

'Yes, my daughter. She was round here looking for me. Tell me what you've done to her or I'll choke you to death. I don't care about the consequences, you can be sure of that.'

'Up Dock Street,' she gasped. 'It's called Sheepfold, an alleyway off Kendall Street, first door on the right.' She fainted in his grasp and he let her slide to the floor.

By now Jenny and Molly had arrived, and the noise of the fight had attracted the attention of other boat people from the barges around. They crowded around Caleb, and Jenny had to push her way through to get to her husband. She removed the bloodstained shirt and took off her apron, tearing it into strips to make a bandage for the wounded leg.

William put his shirt back on and joined Walter. 'I know where Kendall Street is,' he said.

'Then let's get there as fast as we can. There isn't any time to lose.' Walter's deeply sunken eyes glowered with grim determination. All pain had vanished from his wracked body. The blood throbbed through his veins and adrenalin coursed through him. He had no difficulty in keeping up with William as they ran along towpaths, over bridges and down darkening streets.

* * *

The door downstairs banged shut. There was the murmur of voices and she heard heavy footsteps climbing the stairs. Hannah was petrified, not able to move her smallest finger, let alone get off the bed or hide behind the door. She heard lighter footsteps following a man on the landing; then a key turned in the lock and the door slowly opened. Sitting up, Hannah summoned every ounce of courage. She turned to face the door.

'There, sir, she's nearly ready for you,' came the shrill voice of the fat woman she had met when she was first dragged into this abominable place.

All Hannah could hear of the man's reply was the word 'good'.

'I'll lock the door on the outside, for safety's sake,' Queenie continued. 'We don't want her running off. You give me a knock when you've finished with her.' She closed the door, and the key turned again.

Hannah heard breathing, soft but quick. She smelt the pungent aroma of a sweet and powerful perfume, rather like the eau-de-cologne her mother used. She looked up. Greying hair, a lined face. It was a confident face, but with a hint of deep cruelty that was obscured by a slight grin. The eyes were pale and staring. They were not sympathetic: they were narrow and piercing, the kind of eyes that always got their own way. They watched her every movement as if they were looking for a sign of weakness. They even watched while the man took off his coat and laid it, with his top hat and silver-topped cane, on top of the rough wooden cupboard.

Eventually Hannah dropped her eyes. 'Oh please, sir, don't, please don't hurt me. Let me free to go back to my family,' she begged.

The eyes sharpened and brightened. The breathing quickened. 'There, there,' said a shrill voice. 'You've been a wicked girl. You must accept your punishment.'

Hannah realised that any entreaties would be useless. She slumped back on to the bed, her face against the stinking mattress, and tried to block out all sensations and feelings: the filthy room, the cloying scent, the quickening breathing, the hands that were now moving over her, the chatter of voices from another room, and the banging and shouting from below. She closed her eyes and then her mind, trying to see nothing, hear nothing and feel nothing. The noise and shouts below were growing louder, the breathing in the room became more intense and the hand on her back felt heavier . . .

Hannah lay stunned. She had heard the door bang open, followed by a sharp thud. She had heard a cry of pain, then felt a tremor run through her body. Was it the blow to the back of her head that had clouded her mind? She still felt the weight of the man's body pressing on hers. It was crushing her and making it hard for her to breathe. But then she realised he was not moving: he was squeezing every drop of breath from her, so that she could not scream or call. Then she felt him move again, as if trying to raise himself up, but there came another thud and another tremor, which sent him crashing back on top of her. She felt a slight trickle of warm liquid down her neck, then became aware of another presence in the room. She heard someone else breathing heavily and rapidly. She closed her eyes again and wished she were dead. For a few seconds nothing happened, and the rapid breathing subsided.

Then, as if from far away, she heard a voice. 'Hannah? Hannah, my darling, you're safe now.' It was the voice she wanted to hear more than any other in the whole world.

Chapter Twenty-Seven

Hannah opened her eyes, but trapped beneath the body she could see nothing.

'William, come and give me a hand,' she heard the voice call, and she felt the weight crushing her suddenly lighten. She raised herself on to her elbows and looked around. Was she in a dream now, or had it all been a dream? She couldn't tell. The face above her gradually came into focus. She stared at it in total disbelief.

Below an old bowler hat, which was somewhat askew, a smiling, unshaven face looked down on her. The figure was thinner than she had remembered, and the workman's clothes he wore were dirty and torn. But it was the eyes that drew him to her. They were wrinkled and tired, sunk deep into the sockets of a pale and gaunt face, but they were still the bright, blue, intelligent eyes she had always known.

'Daddy, is it really you?' It was a stupid thing to say but she had to be certain. It was like pinching herself to make sure she was awake.

'Yes, my darling Hannah, of course it is,' came the familiar voice.

She was aware of another person helping him lift the limp body away from her – a large young man with long fair hair, his grey shirt stained red on the front. He was helping her father dump the lifeless form in the corner behind the cupboard, followed by the walking cane, its peculiar silver-topped handle now deep red with blood-matted hair.

Hannah flung herself around her father as soon as she was free, and he held her close, wrapping his long slender arms around her shoulders. The large youth turned away and stepped back on to the landing.

At last Walter detached himself from her grasp. 'Hannah, we've got to go now. If the police don't get me the ruffians around here would make mincemeat of us, if they ever find out what happened.'

'Oh, Daddy, I'm cold and they've taken my coat.'

He took off his jacket and wrapped it round her. 'Go with William here. He'll take you to safety.'

She would not take the stranger's hand but clung to her father.

'Hannah, no!' Walter ordered. 'He'll take you back to the *Bluebell*, and you'll be safe with my friends. I'll be with you in just a few minutes, but I've got a few things to finish.'

At last she seemed to understand, and took hold of William's hand. He led her down the stairs and out into the street.

Walter surveyed the carnage: the bloodstained body and equally bloodstained bed, the smashed lock and the prone figure of Florrie's sister at the bottom of the stairs, lying under the broken front door. He raced down the stairs and wrenched a spar from the broken woodwork. The door to the front room had been locked, and behind it he could hear cries and weeping. He leant back against the wall and with his foot sent the flimsy door flying open. This raised a further chorus of screams from half a dozen girls who were huddled round the stove for warmth and mutual protection. Walter swung the spar around his head and they scattered in all directions, some out into the street, others to the back door and a couple back up the stairs. He put his foot to the stove and sent it crashing to the floor, scattering the lighted coals around the room. He prised out the rest with his piece of wood, and soon there were fires spitting and roaring in every corner of the room. He ran out, throwing the burning spar at a couple of men who had come to see what the commotion was about.

After five minutes of hard running Walter had made the towpath. He was completely spent: his body ached and his stomach burned. He almost collapsed into the stern of the *Bluebell*.

The first rays of the sun peeked over the church, and lit the drab canal basin in a weak morning sunlight. The water reflected a murky orange and the bright reds, greens and blues of the boats stood out in the silvery-grey drabness. There was a tapping on the cabin roof of the *Bluebell*. Caleb hobbled past the sleeping forms of Walter and his daughter and opened the door. William's face peered in. 'Best be on your way. There's a few coppers further down the docks. They've found Jack's body, and with the trouble we caused at that place it looks as if they've put two and two together. One of the boatmen laid up at Bridge End says they're lookin' for a tall man and a girl.'

'Thanks, William. You've been a friend in need. We won't forget it.. Little un's still asleep, but I knows that she and Walt can't thank you enough. What are you going to do? You don't want to get the blame for all this.'

'Nah. They didn't see much of me. I smashed down the door, then kept out of sight. They all thought it was Walt's work. My mother will swear I was fast asleep drunk through last evening. We'll meet sometime on the water soon, eh? We'll have a drink and a natter about all this.'

'And the drinks are on me, lad. Remember that. Bye for now, and the best of luck.'

With great difficulty Caleb climbed up on to the towpath and shook William's hand. William waved goodbye and returned back to his boat.

Untying Bessie, Caleb attached her to the prow with the short rope. With his pole he manoeuvred the vessel past two colliers, then steered the boat out of the basin. In half an hour they had left the dark, silent warehouses behind, and he woke the sleeping Leah. She climbed out and hitched the long rope to Bessie's collar, leading her into the outskirts of Armley.

Leah walked silently on, the morning dew coldly caressing her bare feet. After an hour Caleb called a halt, unhitched Bessie and woke them all up. Jenny lit the stove for breakfast.

Walter took Hannah for a walk along the canal side. His thin body was shivering as she was still wearing his jacket.

'When are you coming back to us, Daddy?'

'I can't, Hannah. You've got to know that right now.'

'But why? They won't ever catch you for killing that man. You had to kill him, didn't you?' Walter was silent. 'They'll think we were boat people. You'd be perfectly safe at home with us.' She pulled him back and looked into his face. 'And I wouldn't ever tell a soul. It would be our secret for ever.'

'For ever might not be a long time,' he replied.

She looked at him, puzzled. The October morning sun cast his face in a sickly pallor, making his eyes appear even deeper set and highlighting his projecting cheekbones and the transparent skin that stretched tightly over them.

'Are you ill, Daddy? Is it from living by all this dirty water? I know Mummy's always warning us not to play by ponds or drains. You'd get better soon, especially if you came back to us. You'd be well again in no time.'

Walter slowly shook his head. 'No I won't, my darling. I can't get better. You must understand, as young as you are, there's no way back. I'm a very, very sick man.' He held her close.

Tears filled her eyes as she slowly realised the awful truth. 'Oh, Daddy! No, no, you can't!' She clung to his thin frame: if she held on he would always be there; he would not succumb.

'You must be brave, Hannah. I'm going to die. I doubt if I have another month in me, two at the most.' He could not stop her tears, which soon soaked his shirt. They stood on the edge of the bank like carved figures locked in a rigid embrace.

After some minutes she lifted her head and stared into his skeletal face.

'Hannah,' he whispered, 'I would not want your mother or your brother or sisters to see me in such a state. Can you understand that?'

She nodded. Her tears rolled down her cheeks and dropped on to her dress

He laughed for a moment as a thought came to him. 'I assume Mummy's already claimed on the insurances I left. If I died again the companies might get a bit suspicious, and you might have the police knocking on the door.'

She tried to laugh, if only for his sake. He was still the dearest daddy he always was, trying to make her laugh whatever the occasion. But her giggles were mixed with sobs, even though the tears had almost dried.

'Come on, Hannah, we've got to get back to the others. You've got to show a brave face. You mustn't let Caleb's children see you've been crying.'

She turned towards the barge and drew a deep breath. He saw her lift her sleeve and wipe her eyes, and she turned back to him, her face drawn and pale but rock steady.

They resumed their walk. Jenny was stirring the porridge which was bubbling away on the stove. Bessie chomped the grass under a hedge. The children chased around. Caleb was settled on the back of the boat, smoking his pipe, his foot propped up on the edge of the boat. But there was a melancholy air about him. Walter, who had seen this scene so often, knew it would never be the same. He sighed.

Hannah and Walter accepted Jenny's invitation to breakfast, but he had little appetite for the steaming bowl of delicious porridge.

By half past nine they had resumed their journey. Hannah walked for a time with Leah, who led the patient Bessie along the grassy bank. The villages passed by: Kirkstall, Rodley, Calverley. It was a repeating pattern of woods, fields, bridges, mills and stone cottages. The faint sound of people and industry was interspersed with the silence of tranquil countryside. Occasionally a train passed by, crossing canal, then river, then road, then canal again.

Walter took his turn at steering and Hannah walked back to sit beside him. He showed her how to use the tiller, and she carefully followed his instructions. It seemed like times long past when he had taught her to fish, ride a bicycle, play a new game of cards or hold a cricket bat. It seemed as if time had stood still, as if nothing of the past two years had ever happened and that things would go on just as they always had.

He left her steering the boat for a minute and vanished into the cabin. When he returned he was holding two pieces of paper, face down. 'You see, I'll remember you all,' he said, showing her the family photograph.

'How did you get that? Did you take it with you when you left?'

'Not exactly,' he replied, and turned over her painting.

Hannah looked at it for a moment, then smiled. 'I don't want to leave you . . . ever,' she whispered.

'But there comes a time when we all must,' he replied, 'and these will help me to remember.'

'And I must have something to remind me of you, Daddy,' she said, tears welling up again. 'But not just for me, for everyone.' She went into the cabin, and after a minute returned with a piece of paper and a pencil, and a board on which to rest the paper.

Walter sat in the stern, his hand on the tiller, while his daughter sat sketching him. It was not a pretty drawing. It showed every line, every shadow, every stark feature. But it was her best work ever. It had to be.

Hannah had just finished when Caleb hobbled out of the cabin to join them. 'My, you's a real artist, missy,' he remarked. 'I reckon I might show you how to paint pots and pans with flowers and country scenes.' He winked. 'My speciality's bluebells. You might have guessed that.'

'Thank you. I'd love to do that.'

'You'll find it's very good for your peace of mind, like. When you're concentratin' on getting all those petals and leaves just right, you forgets other things: the hard times, the terrible things that may 'ave 'appened to you, the foolish and wicked things you've done.' He stopped for a second and gazed out at the canal bank and the fields beyond. 'Your dad said it was *therapeutic*. Now ain't that a clever word?'

Caleb dived back into the cabin, returning with his paint pots and an old battered jug which he had scoured back to bare metal. Hannah needed only a little instruction from her tutor before she set to work capturing a rural canal scene with all the precision she could muster. Caleb was right. She was so engrossed in her work that her cares and sadness seemed to vanish for a time. In deference to her tutor and his boat, she endeavoured to include some bluebells in the landscape.

'Yon's a real talent,' Caleb observed to Walter. 'I suppose you was artistic like.'

'I could sketch a bit,' replied Walter, 'but not with any artistry.'

'Must be in the blood,' continued Caleb. 'There must have been a painter in the family fer genius like that to show. That's summat special, I'm telling you, Walt.'

Walter was lost in thought. He looked at his daughter's sketch, then back at the watercolour she had copied at Harriet's, then back again. He leaned against the rail and smiled. It was as if he at last understood.

Just after three o'clock that afternoon *Bluebell* pulled in just past the Shipley Junction Bridge. A dark-haired lady watched the boat as it glided underneath her, and gave a surprised smile when she spied Hannah in the stern, steering the boat as it pulled gently into the bank. She waved, but her niece did not see her as she was too intent on her task to perfection. But when the boat was safely tied up she spotted her aunt, and waved back.

Walter immediately climbed off, and Hannah made to do the same. He turned to her. 'No, wait there, Hannah. Please.'

The old Hannah would have argued, pulled a face, thrown a tantrum or disobeyed, but this time she sat obediently in the stern and watched her father walk slowly to the bridge, with difficulty mounting the iron steps. Nancy had to reach down and help him.

Hannah could see her father and aunt clearly as they talked. Her father had been carrying a large envelope, which he handed over to Nancy – who seemed upset. Hannah could guess why. For a minute her aunt leaned over the bridge, put her head in her hands and cried. Walter comforted her for a few moments, then looked directly at her. She lifted her head, then returned his gaze, listening to everything he said and nodding in agreement. It seemed like an age before they shook hands and shared a brief embrace. He turned and walked away in the direction of the town.

'Hannah, Hannah, come here,' called Nancy.

Clutching her precious drawing, Hannah met her aunt on the middle of the bridge, both shedding tears of sadness and relief.

'Where's my father gone?'

'He's gone. We won't see him again. It's all for the best.' She waited with her arms half open, expecting her niece to fall into them in a flood of tears.

Instead Hannah looked out over the canal and beyond the rooftops. 'I see,' she said calmly. 'It's the way he wanted it.' If there was the trace of a tear in the corner of her eye, she dashed it away, gripping the rail of the bridge and staring at the purple hills of Baildon Moor in the distance.

'There's a lot to say to your mother,' said Nancy. 'I suppose Rosie will have to know something, but I think Thomas and Agnes should be older before we tell them anything. Don't you agree?'

'I think that's best,' Hannah replied.

'In the meantime I've a lot of things to think about myself.'

Nancy took her niece's hand, and they walked off the bridge in the direction of Shipley railway station.

Chapter Twenty-Eight

Walter made a slow and tortuous progress through the back streets of Skipton.

The boat had docked in the basin and he had made his way along Coach Street and up to Belmont Street. He stopped on the bridge to rest his aching limbs and to look back for a last time at *Bluebell*, which had been his home for the last two months. He leaned heavily on the walking stick that Caleb had made for him: a stout, straight piece of ash, the top carved into a head. It was not a pretty head, but the form of an old, wizened creature. Below the head was a collar of flowers and plants cut deep into the surface, and among them, carved with immaculate precision, was a bluebell. Walter turned right and dragged himself down a straight road in the direction of the railway station, between a pair of imposing new spinning mills, their new stonework golden in the morning sun.

He reached the station at twenty past nine, bought his ticket and made his way across to platform two. Waiting patiently for his train, his frail body slumped into the corner of a wooden seat for support. His pale eyes stared out across the lines to the station entrance, with the houses and mills of the town beyond, and to the distant mountains and rolling hills of the Yorkshire Dales. He would have loved to wander round Skipton's narrow streets and yards, to inspect its formidable castle and roam out into the delightful countryside, just as he had done when he visited the prosperous town as a travelling salesman all those years ago. But his condition forbade it. He had to content himself with his single view and his memories.

Walter carried no suitcase. He couldn't have managed it anyway. He had left it with its remaining contents in the cabin of *Bluebell*, and Jenny would sell the last items of haberdashery at gatherings of boat women or at canalside inns. The money would be hers, scant reward for the kindness she and Caleb had shown him during these difficult weeks. They had nursed him through excruciating pain. She had provided herbal potions and Caleb had managed to acquire some laudanum to ease his suffering; Walter hadn't asked where or how. Last Monday they had helped him up to Skipton Market, where he had sold his wares from his case. It was a fine, warm, October day, the street was bustling with farmers and their wives and he had sold most of his stock. He had deposited the last of his takings in the bank, and on his return had handed over the bank books to Caleb for safe keeping.

'I'll be in Shipley next week, and I'll give them to Miss Nancy at the mission.'

Walter had put a letter inside, witnessed by Jenny in front of a local solicitor. She had even managed to sign her name instead of her usual cross. That was Walter's doing. In the last few weeks he had been teaching her and her children to read and write, and Jenny had proved to be a quick learner. Sitting there, waiting for his train, Walter smiled. Everything had been put in place. The smile wrinkled his eyes and the corner of his lips, making him look even more hideous, but he was alone on the platform. There was no-one to see him.

Walter was the only person boarding the ten o'clock train to Morecambe. This late in the year there were no crowds of holidaymakers from Bradford and Keighley. He hauled himself up into an empty compartment and propped himself up in the right-hand corner. A whistle blew and the train chugged out of the station, to break free from the town in just a couple of minutes. It was a slow journey, the train stopping at every village along the line, all with their curious, comical names: Gargrave, Bell Busk, Hellifield, Giggleswick. Walter didn't mind: the sedate pace gave him time to watch the hills as the autumn sun and clouds traced distant patterns on them. When the pain got bad he took a swig from the small bottle in his pocket. It made him drowsy, but it took away the agony inside.

Walter's eyes half closed, and he imagined he was that small boy, nose pressed against the window, on his first visit to the seaside. The dream faded but he was still there on that train, on his honeymoon, with his beautiful bride dressed in her lilac trousseau.

'Oh, Annie, you look gorgeous,' he whispered. 'Could any man have such a beautiful young bride? Come over here and let me kiss you, lass. No one can see us apart from the sheep in the fields.'

Sometimes in his dreams Annie became Eliza, and once she turned into a tall, gipsy-like, fifteen-year-old girl with jet-black hair, sparkling brown eyes and the thin sensual lips that were always so inviting, yet unobtainable. It was ever so with Emily Lumb, his very first love.

The bleak Pennine peaks of Ingleborough and Pen-y-Ghent changed into the wide Lune valley. There were lush, green fields and trees in their last thinning coats of autumn edging the river and partly hiding the distant villages. He seemed to become that little boy again, his excitement mounting as they approached the coast. He remembered his first glimpse of the magnificent keep of Lancaster Castle, set above the wharves of the river port, then the flat estuary of the winding river and, at last, his first ever glimpse of the sea. He dreamed of that wonderful holiday, of his beautiful blue sailing boat and the trip on the waters of the bay.

The train was slowing down again, but this time it was Morecambe. He pulled the window down and a rush of cool, sea air fanned his face. It succeeded in waking him, but brought back the pain.

No one noticed the tall thin man in the dark suit as he stopped inside the station to look around. The glass roof let in low shafts of autumn light that played on the patterned brick walls. It was as light and airy as he remembered, despite the steam and smoke drifting in from the platforms. With his last coins he bought a paper from the news stand and sat down to read it while he took a rest. There was no need to buy anything to eat. His body would not accept it now.

Walter found little in the *Morecambe Visitor* to interest him. The new cycle railway was still open for the entertainment and exercise of any visitors who still might be around . . . A shoemaker from Bare had punched a man who had accidentally kicked a stone at his son . . . Walter folded up the paper, tucked it under his arm and hobbled across the promenade. The many empty seats made convenient resting places every thirty yards or so. Whenever he sat down he took a swig from the small bottle in his side pocket, but never too much: it had to last him until the afternoon, and he did not want to pass out on the promenade. Someone might call the police or have him taken to hospital, and that would never do.

The Midland Hotel stood at the base of the stone jetty. As he passed he remembered Enos's argument with his mother twenty-six years before, when his stepfather planned to spend the last day of the holiday there, in the bar with his drinking pals. How Harriet had flown into a temper! Eventually Enos had returned for the boat trip as drunk as could be, and had been as sick as a dog in the waters of Morecambe Bay.

'Served the old fool right!' Walter chuckled to himself.

He found a seat on the jetty that offered a good view of the sea and the West End and opened the paper again. It would occupy him for the time being and offer some cover from the eyes of curious strangers. It worked for nearly an hour.

'Good afternoon to you. A fine afternoon it is, to be sure.' A man plonked himself on the other end of the seat with his bottle. He drained it to the last drop, then took another from his pocket. 'And where are you staying in Morecambe?'

'I don't really know for the present,' answered Walter. 'I might decide not to stay.'

'I don't recommend the Klondyke Hotel,' interrupted his new companion, 'especially the fourpenny huts. You see all this?' He stood up, swayed for a couple of seconds, then indicated to Walter and the world at large the stone jetty and its buildings. 'In a few years all this will be useless, because of the harbour we Irish are building for you.'

Walter could see the construction work over towards Heysham. He had also heard of the Klondyke and Dawson's Creek, temporary villages built to accommodate the hundreds of workers, well away from the genteel reaches of the town but, as he wryly observed, not far enough away. A couple on an afternoon walk deliberately gave their bench a wide berth.

'That's right, ignore us!' his companion shouted after them. 'Some of you English don't appreciate what we're doing for you, building you the finest harbour in all England for your packet boats and ferries. You don't care a damn. And my friend James O'Halloran won't see any of it. Blown up by the dynamite he was. Wicked stuff it is, indeed. The drunken Irishman stood up and faced the unfinished breakwater in the far distance. He removed his bowler hat and placed it across his chest. Walter felt it prudent to do the same. The steam shovels were silent and no wagons moved along the distant mole. His companion was not the only one taking the day off to celebrate O'Halloran's wake.

'Would you like a sip of mine before I go?' the Irishman offered. 'It's Irish whiskey, the real stuff, not like this Scottish piss you drink around here.'

Walter took a small swig. It burned inside him for a second, then began to ease his pain. He had paid his tribute to the hero of the harbour gang. The reveller clapped him on the shoulder, gave him an extravagant wave and was on his way back towards the town.

Walter sat for over half an hour looking out to sea and occasionally taking a sip from his bottle. At half past four he judged the time was right. He got up and made his way slowly and painfully down the slipway and on to the sands. He did not walk out towards the sea at first, but along the shore in a north-easterly direction. He found it difficult, ploughing his way through the softer sand, so he turned seaward. The wide line of pebbles scrunched under his feet. Once he had passed them he was on to the firm sand of the bay itself. The calm October day had descended at dusk into a misty grey emptiness that rendered him invisible to anyone on the promenade. The sand's ribbed pattern, inlaid by the tide, hurt his feet but he staggered on. The memory of his walk on this very stretch some eighteen months before brought images flooding back. So much had happened in that short time. He remembered the hazards he had met, the cocklers and fishermen who had crossed his path and his brush with disaster, all in the search for a new life, the goal of adventure, love and fulfilment. That was all behind him now. He was alone and invisible. Everything around him had disappeared into an empty nothingness.

Walter bent down to pick a young mussel from the side of a rocky outcrop just poking above the sand. He hadn't the strength to do it. The mollusc was determined to cling on to its home, its very existence. If dislodged, it would be washed away by the incoming tide, and so it clung on to life. Walter had no such need. The effort sent him tumbling on to the sand, where he lay, unable to raise himself.

For a few minutes there was silence, then the distant sound of rippling water. It was ahead of him, then to his left and right, and even behind him. It became a gentle roar, then a lapping sound, as it washed over the small rocky outcrops. He looked around and realised where he must be. He was out on Priest Skear, and for a short while, with water all around him, he was king, king of his own island. But it was a vanishing island, which grew smaller and smaller until at last the ripples lapped around his feet and began to cover his legs. The waves were not cold and hostile but felt strangely warm and comforting. The water played little games with him, dashing in and out of his legs and round his back so that he could not guess where the next wave was coming from.

All Walter's pain, the burning inside his belly, the ache in his bones, had vanished. He lay back and let the salty waters cover him. The Crooked Sea was welcoming him back.

Epilogue

And will I have a room to myself again?' The young boy's question took the old man by surprise.

'No. You will have to share a room with another boy who lives in the house. He's eight years old.'

'You've talked about my mother. Will I have a father too? Like when I was adopted last time?'

The kind grey eyes of the elderly clergyman looked over his spectacles. 'I'm afraid not. There will be no father for you this time. But there are some uncles and me. I'm a close friend of the family. You won't lack a father's guidance if you need it.'

The boy stood and tugged down the window of the compartment. He stuck his head out into the rushing air. As the train dived under a bridge it became a stream of rushing smoke. He stepped back quickly and sat down again, wiping his eyes. 'Will I have to go to church?'

'Yes. It's a good Christian family. They hold God's love dear, and you'll be expected to attend church and observe the Sabbath properly.'

The boy's face sank down on his chest, and he was silent.

The train was slowing down. Folding his newspaper, the clergyman stood up and lifted a bundle of clothes from the luggage rack, handing it to the boy. They alighted, and walked the length of the platform, stopping as the boy admired the green and black engine that had brought them to Bradford. Outside the station the clergyman hailed a cab.

Gideon had never travelled in such luxury before. His excitement was tinged with apprehension as he leaned out to watch the crowds and shops that flashed by. The cab turned up a long busy road, weaving past the trams and lumbering carts. Soon factories and warehouses gave way to houses, chapels and small shops, and he even glimpsed a park. Then the horse drew up in front of a row of large houses. Even though their sandstone had been darkened by years of smoke and soot from the city below them, their grandeur was not diminished.

The boy climbed down on to the pavement and waited for his elderly companion to pay the driver. It was a larger house than he had expected, with bow windows and steps that led up to a front door with panes of patterned glass. At the front gate he hesitated. This was far too grand. Had some mistake been made? Was he being tricked, perhaps being employed as a servant instead of being adopted? Gideon's hands froze on the gate latch.

The front door opened, and immediately his fears vanished. A sea of smiling faces welcomed him, among them that of a girl with blonde curls. She was the one who had written to him, who had met him in the market, who had promised to make his life better and be his friend for ever. But his eyes were not drawn to her, nor to any of the other children, but to a tall, dark-haired lady who stood at the front. She was looking at him with an expression he had not seen for a long time. Her dark, intense eyes were filled with tears and love – and a joy rose up from deep within Gideon's soul.

About the author

Trevor Raistrick was born in 1944 in Pudsey, West Yorkshire. He spent over thirty-five years as a teacher and headteacher in Staffordshire, where he now lives.

His first novel, The Crooked Sea, was published in 2009 by Bank House Books. It was inspired by a strange incident he discovered in his family's history.

Besides two novels, he has written numerous articles for local and family history magazines, and has given many talks on this and his writing.

See www.thecrooked sea.com

Lightning Source UK Ltd.
Milton Keynes UK
28 September 2010

160516UK00001B/25/P